Fallen Graces

Fr. Tom Book 5

A Novel by

Jim Sano

Full Quiver Publishing
Pakenham, ON

This book is a work of fiction.
The characters and incidents are products of the author's imagination.

Fallen Graces
copyright 2023
by James G. Sano

Published by Full Quiver Publishing
PO Box 244
Pakenham, Ontario K0A 2X0

ISBN: 978-1-987970-63-0

Printed and bound in the USA

Cover design: James Hrkach and Jim Sano

NATIONAL LIBRARY OF CANADA
CATALOGUING IN PUBLICATION
ALL RIGHTS RESERVED

No part of this publication may be reproduced, stored in a retrieval system or transmitted, in any form or by any means — electronic, mechanical, photocopying, recording or otherwise — without prior written permission from the author.

Copyright 2023 James G. Sano
Published by FQ Publishing
A Division of Innate Productions

Dedication

I was fortunate to meet Wayne Spiro more than twenty years ago. Some would call him "old school" in that he cared for his parents with love and devotion, was always there for his extended family, nurtured his friendships, and always took the time to be there for people regardless of the return to himself. He has also been an enthusiastic supporter of the mission of the Father Tom books. You can call it "old school," but I'll call it knowing the point of life is love and relationships. I dedicate this book to a good friend.

Books by Jim Sano

The Father's Son

Gus Busbi

Stolen Blessing

Van Horn

Self-Portrait

Fallen Graces

Chapter 1

Boston, January 12, 2009

The biting cold wind nipped at Mary Quill's cheeks as she pulled her tattered coat closer to her face and reached down to rummage through the trash can outside the Park Street subway station. Boston Common was normally dark and quiet at two in the morning, but hearing a group of tipsy young women approaching the station doors, Mary drew herself into the shadows. The young women found the doors locked. The last subway train had departed an hour earlier, so they shrugged and danced off into the night, singing Beyoncé's "Single Ladies." Mary squinted at the retreating figures, guessing it was a bachelorette party when they all pointed to one of the girls, shouting, "Put a ring on it! Put a ring on it!"

For a moment, she half-smiled at the fading laughter, trying to remember when she was that young and energetic, but the harshness of the late-night wind made her shiver, and the quiet stillness returned. There'd be no warm bed tonight nor even a bite for supper if she couldn't find any scraps of food tossed into the trash. Her teeth chattered as the cold seeped through her coat and ragged knitted gloves, numbing her fingers.

She rummaged through the next can. Nothing. Sighing, she gazed up at the lighted white steeple of the Park Street Church and shook her head.

The sound of water trickling behind her caught her attention, and she turned toward the large fountain cast in bronze, surprised to see the water flowing, considering how cold it had been for so many nights. Nevertheless, there it stood, with the gold dome of the Massachusetts State House in the background. She could only wish for summer when this square would be full of vendors and visitors, flowers blooming, and the fountain gurgling in the warmth of the sunshine.

Mary cocked an eyebrow and tilted her head to solve the puzzling scene. Maybe the rawness of the night and the emptiness of her belly were playing tricks on her, but as she reached out into the dark shadow, she felt the water dribbling from the fountain bowl above. Her eyes became acclimated to the darkness of the area around the fountain as she gazed at the prominent bronze figures at the fountain's base. Someone had once told her that one of the figures was a god of the sea. She dragged her clubfoot behind the other, circling the fountain to study each of the four figures, the last two looking like Greek lovers. As she gazed at them, one figure appeared to become darker, and then the water discolored.

She glanced farther up and let out a shriek in panic.

Mary's eyes bulged from their sockets. Blood dripped from a hand hanging downward from the upper-tier fountain bowl. Her eyes followed the drops of blood downward, and she screamed again, sheltering her eyes from the gruesome sight.

As she jumped from her crouching position, she felt the weight of someone's hand on her shoulder and slid her body sideways to see the large, looming shadow of a man.

"It's okay, ma'am. It's okay," said the man in a calming voice.

"Are you all right?" questioned a second voice. "We heard screams as we passed."

The strobing blue lights from Tremont Street lit up the policeman's uniform, but she continued to shiver and sob as she reached out and pointed her crooked finger back toward the fountain.

Chapter 2

While the officers called in the situation and taped off the area, another policeman crouched next to Mary on a nearby park bench. "Mary, I'm Officer Flaherty. Do you remember me?" He handed her a hot cup of coffee, which she gratefully clasped close to her chest with both hands. "Mary, you're gonna be okay. Can you tell me if you saw anyone in this part of the Common before Officers Spiro and Touhey arrived?"

Mary sniffed up her sobs and glanced upward; her eyes felt bloodshot, her skin worn from years on the streets. She shook her head and answered in a raspy voice, "No one."

"Are you sure? Not anyone? Think."

"No, ah, just some young girls trying to get on the trolley, but they left. They didn't come this way."

"Okay. If you remember anything, do you promise to let me know?"

She bobbed her head.

"Now, what are you doin' out on a night like this? I thought you were staying at Rosie's?"

Mary winced and squeezed her coffee. "My three weeks were up."

"But they always try to find guests a place. What about Pine Street for the night?"

Pulling back, Mary shot a glare at Flaherty. "I had trouble there last time, and I don't want to be hemmed in."

By that time, two detectives had arrived at the scene, and Officer Flaherty slipped Mary a ten-dollar bill before standing to greet them with a nod. "Detective Brooks. Detective Mullen."

Jan Mullen, maybe a few years older than the thirty-year-old Officer Flaherty, smiled broadly, her cheeks flushed almost as rosy as Flahery's naturally were when it got cold. "Officer Flaherty."

Detective Brooks, five-foot-ten with short dark hair and olive-colored skin, held the top of his old trench coat closed tight around his neck in a vain attempt to keep the cold out as he cleared his throat. "Okay, maybe you two can catch up when you're off-duty. What are we looking at here?"

Flaherty pointed toward the fountain. "Spiro and Touhey responded first. They've been checking out the scene while I've been attending to our important witness, Mary Quill, here." He stepped aside so that Brooks could get a better look at her.

Mary appeared to be in no shape for questioning as Spiro and Touhey waved the detectives over to the scene. Lifting the yellow police tape, Brooks moved forward and squinted at the hand extended over the edge of the upper fountain bowl. The water, dyed red with blood, continued to drip from the end of the fingertip.

Brooks let out a long breath. "Have you seen the rest of the body?"

Without a word, Touhey pointed to a bloodied bronze figure in the lower basin.

Mary quickly turned her head into Flaherty's chest.

Jan Mullen grimaced. "Geez! Oh my God."

Spiro aimed his flashlight, and there in the lap of the bronze-cast figure lay the ghastly sight of a cut-out, bloodied heart. Mary turned away and screamed again, but the sound of her voice was muffled as she buried her face into Flaherty's police coat. Flaherty wrapped an arm around her.

Officer Spiro lowered the police radio from his ear. "The crime lab folks should be here in a few, and we'll have some floodlights set up."

Brooks pulled a cigarette from his coat pocket and placed it in his mouth as he gazed upward toward the hand in the upper basin. "Tell them to bring a ladder."

Flaherty whispered to Brooks, "I'm going to take Mary over to St. Francis Convent. They'll have a safe home and extra bed to keep her from freezing tonight."

Chapter 3

The athletically built Father Tom Fitzpatrick, dressed in black with the white collar visible through his open coat, entered the Boston Police station on Harrison Avenue.

Peering over the wire-rimmed glasses that crookedly rested on the end of his nose, the desk sergeant raised his eyebrows. "It's been a while since our favorite detective has come to visit. How have you been, Father?"

Tom half-grinned at the sergeant. "As good as can be, Sergeant. How have you and Mrs. Doherty been these days?"

Doherty leaned in over the wooden desk and whispered as Officer Brian Flaherty entered the open area of the old police station. "Oh, as good as can be. I'll be retirin' at the end of the year, and I think the missus is getting a bit nervous at the idea of havin' me around all the time."

"Father Tom!" Flaherty said with a broad smile. "What brings you here?"

Tom gave Flaherty a firm handshake. "Well, unless I've missed you at Mass, it may be the only time I get to see you and Sergeant Doherty."

Doherty quickly lowered his head as if he was attending to some paperwork, and Flaherty simply nodded. "Did you hear about the body found in the Common last night? Pretty gruesome stuff."

"Sister Helen told me she had a visitor last night, Mary Quill. She had a bit of a fright and couldn't sleep all night. By the way, thanks for bringing her in out of the frigid cold last night, Brian."

Flaherty ran his hands through his thick black hair. "No problem. Mary can take care of herself, but I can understand her being upset by the sight of that poor old bugger. I was just getting off my patrol of the pubs on Washington, saw the commotion in the park, and there was Mary in a panic."

Tom leaned in, quietly asking, "Do we know who the victim was? Are there any witnesses?"

Flaherty smirked. "I heard you were retired, Mr. Holmes. But since you ask, we have no I.D. and no witnesses so far. I'm always curious about what drives people to do something like this."

Tom gave a slight shrug. "You always loved psychology. Have you finished that degree at BU yet?"

Flaherty tilted his head. "Two more classes, and look who's talkin'. I'm only going for my master's, and you've got a doctorate. I like the idea of helping and counseling people like you do. It's fascinating figuring out what drives a man or woman to do what they do."

"It is. I don't believe it's really in man's nature to be violent. I think we are more wired to have empathy, but something triggers a particular response to our experiences."

"Huh. I don't know how empathetic this guy was."

Brooks approached the entrance desk. "I hate to break up this Irish reunion, but—"

Tom extended his hand. "Detective Brooks. It's been a while. Thanks for inviting me to drop by."

Eyebrows raised, Brooks replied, "Look, you know how much it pains me to ask you here. I usually make sure the doors are locked when you pass by, but I need to ask for your help with something, if you don't mind?"

A broad smile made its way across Tom's face. "Deep down, I knew you missed me. I should've brought Angelo."

Waving his hand, Brooks quickly replied, "No, no, no. If I need a bank robbed or a house broken into, I'll ask for Salvato. Let's take a quick ride."

***

Five minutes later, Tom, Brooks, and Mullen stood in front of the Brewer Fountain, where the body had been found. The area was still taped off, with an officer on duty to keep the public away from the crime scene.

Mullen pointed to the blood-stained area where the hand had protruded from the upper basin. "We found the body immersed in a pool of water in the upper basin."

Tom peered up at the twenty-two-foot fountain, lips pursed. "Such a shame. What did you want to ask me about?"

Brooks gestured his open hand to the bloody spot above. "The victim's hand was positioned to point down to the figure below, where a human heart had been placed on the lap. The lab is checking, but we're assuming it had been cut while he was alive or shortly after he was killed."

Tom stepped closer to inspect the bronze figure. "Do you think this particular fountain has any significance to the death?"

Rubbing his chin, Brooks replied, "I don't know. There's more, but tell me if you see anything that stands out."

Tom squinted, pausing for a few seconds. "Well, I read that this bronze fountain was cast in Paris and has been in Boston since the late 1800s. I think the original won an award at the World's Fair in Paris. Water does seem to be a theme with the fountain and the figures." Tom pointed to each figure as he circled the large basin. "This is Neptune and his wife, Amphitrite. On the other side are the two Greek lovers, Acis and Galatea. From what I remember, the Sicilian cyclops, Polyphemus, was jealous of Acis and killed him. Galatea was a sea nymph who turned Acis's blood into the Sicilian river, named after him. The myth is that the river becomes his spirit, but I'm not sure if that has anything to do with this murder."

Brooks squinted. "Anything else? Anything at all."

Tom exhaled as he stepped back to gaze at the entire fountain. "Not really. The basin above where the body was found has four young cherub figures. You said the body was immersed in water, right?"

Mullen nodded.

"Seems odd. It's been really cold this month, and you'd think the basin would either be empty or full of ice. Why would the basin be full of water?"

Mullen glanced at Brooks and back again at Tom. "That's a good question. The lab is still doing their autopsy, but it appears the basin was filled at the time of the murder, and the water had traces of chlorine."

"Hmm. Chlorine kills impurities. It looks like we have an interesting case to solve," replied Tom.

Brooks feigned a laugh. "*We?*"

"Okay, *you* have an interesting case." Tom peered directly into Brooks' eyes. "I'm guessing you asked me here for more than an amateur guided tour of this old fountain?"

Brooks smirked and gave a slight nod as he pulled out what appeared to be a photocopy of a pieced-together note. He handed the sheet to Tom. "It's a copy of a soaking wet note we found in the victim's pocket. Someone said this chicken scrawl might be in Latin, and who else do I know that still knows his Latin?"

Tom studied the photocopy of the mangled bits of paper, trying to make out the letters: *Ecce him qui tollit innocentia m—*

"Let's see, um. It's hard to make some of this out—*Here him who takes away the innocence*—something. The grammar is poor, and that last word isn't legible. I don't know. It's very cryptic. Maybe there were more words we're missing?"

Brooks pulled the photocopy back, folding it up and shoving it into his coat pocket. "I don't think so. It was just a hunch, and I was hoping something might pop out at you."

Tom glanced around the area. "Nothing yet, but someone sure went to a lot of trouble putting the body up there. Ironically, this spot is the start of the Freedom Trail."

Squinting as he glanced upward at the three-tiered fountain, Brooks grumbled, "There's nothing free about being dead. Sorry to bother you with this, Padre. I owe you one."

Putting his hand on Brooks' shoulder, Tom replied, "Drop by St. Francis sometime, and we'll call it even."

Chapter 4

Dr. Franks opened the door, stepped aside, and let his patient head down the back steps.

"Angela, I'll see you next week, and think about what we discussed today. I'm feeling as if you might be making some important discoveries."

"Thank you, Dr. Franks. I promise I will."

He watched his patient descend the dimly lit wooden stairs that creaked on the way down, wondering how long she would need to see him to overcome her anxieties and struggle with self-worth. Shaking those concerns away, he decided to use the bathroom before his next patient arrived.

Standing in front of the sink, he rubbed his face with cool water and straightened his tie. He studied his face with its trim mustache, graying eyebrows, and horn-rimmed glasses pushed up on the bridge of his nose. There were days when he felt he made a real difference in people's lives and others when he wondered if he was doing more harm than good with his probing and suggestions.

His moment of introspection was broken by the sound of the front waiting room door opening and closing.

He opened the door to his office, brightened only by the sunlight coming in through the window and onto his antique desk with papers scattered on it and the brown leather chair and matching leather couch he had had since he started his practice. He swallowed a sigh. "I trust you had no trouble finding my office. I'm Dr. Franks." He motioned toward the couch. "Please, make yourself comfortable. I never got your first name, Mr. Murphy."

The new client smiled and sat on the edge of the couch. "You can call me Daniel. I want to thank you for doing this. I think it will be very helpful."

"That's the goal. Daniel. It would be great to know what you are hoping to get out of these sessions," responded Dr.

Franks as he lowered himself into his chair and rested a notebook on his crossed leg.

"I don't really know. What do you talk about if someone you see has no issues?"

Dr. Franks raised his brow. "You might be surprised. I think we all have areas worth exploring: childhood hurts, distorted self-perception, or habits that impact us in one way or the other. We can just talk about you and see where things go."

The young man nodded. "Okay. That sounds fair. I guess you're right that we probably all have something in our past."

"I like your openness. Our minds are pretty sophisticated at keeping us from digging in. Unfortunately, it has countless ways of avoiding addressing the real issues, even suppressing memories to keep us from finding the truth and healing ourselves. The mind can unlock the secrets to knowing our true selves and becoming our healthier selves, or it can be our own worst enemy, working against us, which is what we try to sort out here in a safe place."

Daniel sat back on the couch. "That sounds hopeful and scary at the same time."

"It is," responded Dr. Franks as he reached down for his pipe and breathed in the aroma.

Chapter 5

Angelo stirred his homemade Italian soup on the old stove while Tom sat at the rectory kitchen table, writing out the cryptic message Detective Brooks had shown him.

Ecce him qui tollit innocentia m—

Angelo Salvato had been an all-around maintenance man, gardener, and good friend to Tom since he arrived at St. Francis years ago after having spent the previous thirty years behind bars. He was short, bald, wiry, and in his late seventies, but you'd never know it. Tom enjoyed his company, his good cooking, and their chess games on the occasions Tom was allowed to win. "What's that you're writing down, Father Tom?" he asked as he ladled the hot soup into their bowls.

"You heard about that poor soul they found dead in the fountain next to the Park Street station?"

Angelo carried the bowls to the table. "I heard a little about it." He reached for the paper Tom had written on. "If I could read that scratch of yours, I still don't think I'd know what that means."

"Well, the English translation can be different depending on the situation. *Ecce* means *here*. And *him*—wait a minute!"

"*Him* means *wait a minute*?" asked Angelo with a smirk.

"No, no. I wasn't thinking when I translated this with Detective Brooks. I'm sure the note said, *Ecce him qui tollit innocentia m—* Whoever wrote this note doesn't know their Latin, or there's something I don't understand."

Angelo glanced at the scribble on the paper again. "I'm not following."

"I told Brooks it said, *Here him who takes away the innocence—* but there's no word spelled *h-i-m* in Latin, and I don't know what the last word beginning with the letter *m* is to put it in context," replied Tom as he let out a deep breath. "I know even less than when I sat down."

"Have your soup and tell me what you know so far."

Tom could tell the wheels were turning in Angelo's head. "I actually know very little. The body was found in the upper basin of the Brewer Fountain in the Common. Brooks said the victim's hand was positioned to point down to the bronze figure of Acis, and, here's the gruesome part, there was a human heart on Acis's lap. They don't know the dead man's identity or if the heart was his. The original note they found was soaked and in pieces in his pocket."

Angelo sipped his soup, his eyes distant in thought. "It seems as if the killer went to a lot of trouble and risk to place the body there. It's been well below freezing every night last week, so he had to bring the water with him."

"That's for sure. The water had some chlorine in it as well." Tom dipped a piece of bread into the soup but hesitated before bringing it to his mouth. "I'm still wondering if the word *him* was put in the note carelessly or on purpose. We don't even know if it was the victim or the killer who wrote it."

There was a faint tapping at the kitchen door. Tom got up, opened the door, and peered down to see a twelve-year-old student, who returned his eye contact without a word. Adding a slight Irish accent, Tom asked, "Now, what can I be doing for you on a fine day such as this, Michael?"

With a slight stammer, Michael replied, "F-Father Fitzpatrick, Sister Helen wanted to remind you that you agreed to give a talk to the boys in an hour. She wanted to know if you'd be on time *this* time."

Tom gave Michael a broad smile. "Michael, you can report back to Sister Helen that I won't be letting the lads down. I will be on time this time, and thanks for the reminder."

Michael didn't respond or move from his spot.

"Was there anything else you wanted to tell me?"

Michael hesitated for several seconds, shook his head, and dashed off.

Tom sat back down, but before he could take a sip from his spoon, there was another tapping at the door. "Somehow, I knew he'd be back," said Tom, but instead, he opened the door to Officer Brian Flaherty, rosy cheeks and all.

"Father Tom, I hope I'm not interrupting anything."

Tom opened the door and waved Flaherty in. "Not a'tall Brian. I was just letting my soup cool down."

Flaherty furrowed his brow, appearing perplexed as he entered the kitchen. "Angelo, how is Father treating you these days? Does he let you sleep in the house on a cold night?"

Angelo raised a bowl to see if Flaherty wanted some.

"I don't get much home cooking, so I'll take you up on that."

Tom stared at the steam coming from Flaherty's soup with raised eyebrows.

Angelo quipped with a smirk as he added more hot soup to Tom's bowl. "What did we say about letting your soup get cold?"

"This is good," remarked Flaherty, blowing on each spoonful before sipping the homemade broth.

Tom nodded as he did the same. "So, I'm guessing you didn't just drop by for a free lunch."

Flaherty tilted his head, beaming. "No, but my timing was perfect. I just wanted to tell you that they I.D.'d the victim from the Common. His name is—*was* Harry Simon. He was sixty-seven, had a wife and no kids. I can't imagine going out that way."

"Harry Simon? He's a parishioner here. His wife isn't Catholic, and I don't know her well. He kept mostly to himself, as far as I know. I think he used to volunteer his time to teach the kids at the Y, and he seemed like a good guy."

"Someone must have thought he wasn't. There was no sign of robbery."

Angelo interjected, "It's one thing to rush someone to eternity, but doing it like this raises lots of questions. No other clues or witnesses?"

Setting his spoon into the bowl, Flaherty paused. "Mary Quill was the only one we found in that part of the Common, and I haven't heard of anything else—except the dead bird under his body. He must have crushed it when he was placed in the fountain. I don't know." Flaherty rose from his chair. "Well, thanks for warming me up. I should get going. Father Tom, I did want to ask you if we could talk sometime. Like I said, I'm finishing up my degree and doing some counseling work, but I could use a little mentoring if you're up for it."

Tom stood. "I'd be very happy to talk anytime—Thursday is good for me if you're open. I think you'll be a great help to many people because of your strength, which will be your challenge as well."

Flaherty tightened his brow. "What strength would that be?"

"Empathy. Ever since you were young, you've been a protector by nature, and you have the gift of empathy that will help you care about the people you counsel because you will see their pain from their perspective. You will sometimes find it both a blessing and a burden."

Flaherty paused outside the door. "I'll have to remember that, and thanks for your confidence. I just want to be of some help, like you. Don't laugh, but I thought about being a priest when I was a teenager."

Tom chuckled. "That's funny. I never did, and now I'm a priest, and you're a cop. You never know, do you?"

Flaherty waved as he headed down the driveway. "I guess you never do."

Chapter 6

Tom was quiet as he and Angelo finished washing the bowls from lunch. Angelo chuckled, and Tom asked, "What? What are you laughing about now?"

"You."

"Me? What did I do?"

"I can tell. You're thinking about the case, aren't you?"

Tom raised his hands. "Aren't *you*? Huh. This was one of our parishioners, and I hardly knew him. I saw him at Mass, but I don't know if he ever even came up for Communion. I just can't imagine why someone would do something like that to him."

"There's always some kind of reason. Not usually a good one, but we're only seeing what's above water," replied Angelo as he dried the last bowl.

"Water. The killer had to fill that basin up with fresh water, and Brooks said the water had chlorine in it. Why chlorine? It doesn't change the freezing point."

"Maybe they didn't know that, or maybe it was a clue as to why they did it?"

Tom turned to Angelo. "Do you want to go over to that fountain with me just to see if I missed anything?"

Motioning his head toward the school, Angelo replied, "Maybe after your talk with the lads. We don't want Sister Helen blaming either one of us for missing that."

Tom laughed. "No, we don't."

Tom always enjoyed teaching, and that afternoon was no exception. It was part of a series of talks to the boys in the school on the characteristics of becoming a real man of God compared to what the culture was selling. Sister Helen gave him an approving nod after the talk was over, and then Tom made his exit to head to the Boston Common with Angelo, discussing the questions that needed to be answered.

As they stood in front of the fountain, now open to the public and without the crime scene tape or police detail, Tom pointed to the spot where Harry's hand had been positioned. He motioned down toward the bronze figure of Acis. "Detective Mullen said a bloody human heart sat on the lap of Acis."

Angelo scanned the area. He gazed up and then down toward the figure. "The killer had to have been really tall or brought a ladder with him. How do you get into the park with a body, enough water to fill that basin, and an eleven-foot ladder without being seen? Could more than one person be involved with this?" Angelo scratched his chin. "So, Professor, who is this figure, Acis?"

Tom took a second to study the young Greek figure who the beautiful Galatea to his left was obviously taken with. "There are several ancient myths about these Greek lovers—the mortal, Acis, and the immortal sea nymph, Galatea. According to the myth and Ovid's poem, the Sicilian cyclops, Polyphemus, was jealous of Acis's affection for Galatea and killed him with a boulder. Galatea transformed her lover's blood into the River Acis, which became his immortal spirit."

As Tom recounted the story, Angelo circled the fountain, studying each figure until he stopped at the figure with his back to Acis. "Who is this?"

"Neptune, the god of the sea. Why?"

"I don't know if it means anything, but this god's back is turned to Acis, or Acis has his back turned to Neptune. The note you were translating doesn't mention blood or a river, right?"

Tom shook his head. "Nope, just about *taking away the innocence* of something. Interestingly, the victim, Harry, is submerged in water, and these figures are all connected to water. Neptune, the god of the sea; Amphitrite, his wife, the sea goddess; Galatea, a sea nymph; and Acis, who was turned into a river. And why was his heart cut out and laid upon Acis's lap with the hand pointing to it?"

"Out for a sight-seeing tour?" came a voice from behind.

Tom's face turned red as he twisted to see Brooks standing behind them. "Yes. I told you about this being the first stop on the Freedom Trail, and it occurred to me that I'd never walked the trail with Angelo before."

"Father Fitzpatrick is an excellent tour guide. You might learn something if you join us," quipped Angelo.

Brooks rolled his eyes upward. "I forgot how much I missed you two. Well, you might be interested to know that we identified the victim."

"It was Harry Simon," interjected Tom.

Brooks sighed. "What else do you know?"

"Nothing to report yet."

"Well, you might be interested that we found another note. We also confirmed that the heart was the victim's, and it was cut out before the killer placed him in the water. This note was underneath, stuck to the organ, and covered with blood, so it took a bit to decipher." Brooks unfolded a piece of paper and handed it to Tom.

Tom held it out for Angelo to read with him.

Flumina de ventre eius fluent aquae ex mortis.

"What does it say?" queried Angelo.

"Hmm. Latin, again. Let's see, um. *Out of his heart shall flow rivers of dead water.* Huh."

Brooks retrieved the notepaper with his pointer finger and thumb. "*Huh?* That's all you have to say? What's so interesting?"

Tom peered down at the figure of Acis, envisioning the bloody human heart in his lap. "It's partly based on a line from Scripture—"

Brooks rolled his eyes. "Really? I have a feeling this will lead us nowhere, but let's get out of the cold. There's a coffee shop across the street, and you can teach Sunday school over a cup."

As they sat in the booth of the small café, Brooks held up three fingers for the waitress to bring them coffee. "I hope this is going to have some relevance to the case. What do you have?"

The waitress set down three cups of piping hot coffee and stared out the window toward the fountain. "Did you hear about the body they found last night? It spooks me just to look at that fountain now. I hope they catch whoever did it soon."

Tom raised his brow. "I'm sure Boston's finest are on it right now."

Her shoulders shivered as she returned to the counter.

Tom inhaled the aroma of his hot coffee. "I have no idea if there's any relevance, but I'm trying to find a connection between the notes you showed me. I was talking with Angelo and couldn't figure out why the writer of the first note put the English word *him* in the middle of a sentence in Latin. I translated it, *Here him who takes away the innocence*, but I think I might have a better translation now that you showed me the second note. I think the word *mundi* was cut off from the end of the first note. *Behold him who takes away the innocence of the world.* The actual scriptural writing says, *Behold him who takes away the sins of the world*."

Brooks squinted as he sipped his coffee. "You mean 'him' as in Jesus? This guy was no Jesus."

"I don't think the killer thought so either. He or she thought the victim was taking away the innocence, not the *sins,* of the world. I think it's from Scripture because the second note references the same thing and does a similar twist. The scriptural verse says, *Out of his heart shall flow the rivers of living water*. The killer substituted in *mortis* or *dead water*. See the pattern?"

Brooks tapped his spoon on the table. "So, what does this have to do with anything?"

Angelo leaned in. "Baptism. Do I have that right, Father?"

With raised eyebrows, Tom replied, "The killer went through all the risk and trouble of immersing poor old Harry in a running body of water and leaves notes related to the Baptism of Christ. I think Angelo might have something."

"I'm not following, and how does this help solve the case?" grunted Brooks.

Tom said, "I'm not either, but there might be something there."

"What kind of bird was under the body?" asked Angelo.

Brooks snapped his head toward Angelo. "How did you know about that?"

Angelo waited without a response.

Tom conjectured, "A dove."

Brooks darted a glance toward Tom. "And how did *you* know that?"

Tom held his cup with two hands. "Just a hunch."

"Yes, it was a little white dove, if you have to know. What does that have to do with anything—no, don't tell me—Baptism."

Tom replied, "Maybe. The murder occurred on January twelfth, correct?"

"And?"

"That was the feast day for the Baptism of our Lord. Jesus went to the Jordan to be baptized by John the Baptist and begin his ministry. It was there that He revealed his identity and his mission."

Brooks sighed. "So, you think the killer is revealing his identity and mission?"

Angelo said, "Or the victim's."

"Hmm." Tom stared into his coffee a moment before speaking. "Let's see. In the Gospel, John the Baptist doesn't think he's worthy to baptize Jesus, who doesn't actually need Baptism. Jesus doesn't need to repent or be cleansed of His sins, but He submits to it, descending into the river to sanctify its waters and beget God's sons. You see, Baptism wasn't new, but here Jesus confers upon the water the power of true Baptism, which would remove all sins of the world."

Brooks ran his hand across his forehead. "Okay. I see water. I see a river. And I see Jesus, but I see no connection to this case."

"I'm just seeing if anything pops out. When Jesus symbolically rises from the dead out of the water, the Holy Spirit descends upon him. The symbol of the Holy Spirit is—"

"Don't tell me—a white dove?"

Tom raised his brow with a smile. "Ding, ding. Exactly. This is when a voice proclaims Jesus as the Beloved Son of the Father, and everyone hears, 'Behold the Lamb of God, behold Him who takes away the sins of the world.'"

Brooks nods. "Okay, the note on Mr. Simon's body."

"Yep. Jesus gives the waters of Baptism the power to forgive sins, open up the heavens to us, and make us adopted sons and daughters of God. We receive the Holy Spirit and the power of God to avoid sin. We are a new creation with a new heart."

Brooks wrinkled his brow as if deep in thought. "So, are you saying that everything about this Harry Simon is the opposite of Jesus?"

Tom glanced at Angelo, who shrugged his shoulders. "Maybe. Taking away innocence is the opposite of taking away sin. He doesn't get a new heart; he has his heart removed completely. Out of his heart flows rivers of *dead* water instead of *living* water. There is a theme here, but I don't know if it helps solve the case. Baptism is supposed to be the door or the gateway to the spiritual life, sharing in God's life. We don't deserve this love, but He chooses us, loves us unconditionally. Jesus poured out His entire self for us to be part of His family."

Brooks finished the last of his coffee. "I don't know. All I do know is that Mr. Simon had his blood poured out from him, and we have a killer on the loose but no hard clues."

Angelo stood up with Brooks and Tom. "I think he's trying to leave us clues. I think he wants you to know why he's doing this and maybe who he is."

Brooks squinted. "Leave *us* clues? Who put you on the case, Salvato?"

Tom tilted his head. "Thanks for the coffee, Detective. Let us know if you find any more white doves."

As they stood outside to part ways, Angelo added, "Father Fitzpatrick said that the heart was left on the figure, Acis, who was killed by the cyclops. I would think there was a reason the killer went to all that trouble to hoist the body into that upper basin of that particular fountain. My guess is there might be a double layer of connections here."

Tom glanced at Brooks. "Angelo's instincts are always good."

Brooks grunted something and waved as he headed back to the station.

Tom put his hand on Angelo's back. "Thanks for coming over with me."

Angelo turned to see Brooks disappear into the crowd. "He's going to need some help, isn't he?"

Chapter 7

Tom attended to some administrative duties for the school before sitting in the church to quietly pray for Harry's soul and guidance as to what his role should be. There was something about this sacred space, the high arching ceilings, the hint of incense, the old wooden pews, and the beautiful altar area that helped him feel peaceful and present with God. The feeling didn't last long. A sound from the entrance caught his attention. He looked up. A woman stood by the baptismal font, glancing about.

It was Harry's wife. Tom stood, genuflected toward the tabernacle, and made his way to her.

"Mrs. Simon, I'm so sorry for your loss. It was such a horrible shock. I was just praying for Harry when you came in."

"Well, thank you. You can call me Esther. They said I could find you here."

Tom had only met Esther once. He guessed she was in her late sixties, but her straight posture and conservative clothes made her appear reserved yet still attractive. "I suppose you know that I am not a religious woman. No offense to you, but I think Harry would like to be buried by the Church."

Tom waved to offer her a seat, but she shook her head, fiddling with her handbag. "Of course. We can have a Mass for him if you wish."

Esther exhaled. "I didn't know if that would be possible. His first wife left him, and we married. He didn't take Communion or whatever you call it because he said you people considered him to be still married to her. I don't know all the rules and regulations. I just wanted to honor his wishes."

Tom gazed into her eyes without judgment. "Esther, none of us are perfect. I would be honored to offer Mass for Harry and pray for his soul."

Esther adjusted her hat. "Thank you, Father. Just tell me what I need to do. He was a troubled man, but I never knew what haunted him so. He often told me how much he loved teaching those kids how to swim for all those years and that he was never the same after he stopped."

"Huh. He taught swimming. Now, I never knew that. It would be great if you'd tell me more about him so that I can share it with the others attending the funeral."

Esther peered up at the high vaulted ceilings of St. Francis Church. "I wish I had a lot to share. He never had kids, and his wife disappeared some fifteen years back. We married about ten years ago. In all those years, I don't know if I ever really got to know him."

"We will do the best we can, and I am very sorry for your loss."

After his brief exchange with Esther, Tom ambled back to the rectory where Angelo was cooking pasta to go with the sauce and meatballs heating up in a separate pot. Angelo glanced up at Tom and then back down to the pot.

Tom squinted. "What?"

Angelo continued to stir the sauce as he curled his bottom lip. "Nothing I know of."

Tom lowered his head. "You have a good poker face, but I can tell when something is up."

Suddenly, a pair of arms appeared from behind and grabbed Tom's shoulders. "Why would anything be up, Tommy?" said a familiar voice with a laugh.

Tom quickly turned. "Luke!" He embraced his younger brother, who was now twenty-six years old, tall and slim, with longish dark hair and a scruff of a beard. He stepped back to gaze into Luke's eyes. "When did you get back to Boston? Why didn't you tell me you were coming?"

"It's a long story," Luke replied as he breathed in the sauce's pleasant aroma.

Angelo pulled out three bowls. "Let's feed this hungry young stranger."

Luke raised his eyebrows. "Not feeling so young anymore."

Tom and Angelo exchanged glances and laughed as they set the table to share some bread, red wine, and Italian pasta for dinner. They brought Luke up to speed about everything during dinner, including what they knew about the Harry Simon case.

At one point, Luke drifted off, saying, "Until last year, I would never have believed people could do such a thing." He shook it off. "Do they have any possible suspects?"

Tom replied, "Nothing yet. It's a complete mystery. No enemies that we know of. No clues left that were clear enough to lead to anyone in particular."

Luke said, "The murderer obviously had some strong emotions or reasons to make a statement like that. It's hard to tell if the emphasis was on the Greek theme or the Baptism references. What do you think?"

Tom scratched his head. "I wish I knew. Speaking of Baptism, I talked to Harry's wife—his second legal wife, anyway—in the church earlier today. She seemed to think he was haunted by something from his past. She also said that she never really felt as if she knew him. She seemed sadder about that than his death."

"Huh," said Angelo as he twirled the spaghetti on his fork. "Does she want you to have a funeral here?"

"She does, but she's not Catholic. She thinks he would've wanted it. She said that he really enjoyed teaching the kids swimming. I'm assuming that was at the Y, but he stopped doing it some fifteen years ago," replied Tom.

"There's a connection," muttered Angelo.

"I'm lost. What's the connection?" asked Luke as he lifted his head.

"Ahh. Chlorine!" exclaimed Tom as Angelo nodded in agreement.

"Chlorine? What chlorine?" queried Luke.

Angelo slurped the last string of spaghetti off of his fork. "The water in the fountain basin where they found him had traces of chlorine in it, and he was a swimming instructor."

"*Was*. But, Tommy, you said he stopped doing that a while ago, right?" inquired Luke.

"That's what she said," responded Tom as he took a sip of wine. "Possibly forced to quit."

After a round of chess, where Luke watched his brother lose in a close game, Angelo left them for the evening, heading back to his small quarters in a remodeled shed. Luke helped Tom finish the dishes, and without glancing over, Tom quietly asked, "How are you really doing, my brother?"

Luke rubbed the bristles on his chin but didn't respond, and appeared to be drifting off to another place.

Tossing the dishtowel over his shoulder, Tom turned to look Luke squarely in the eyes, only to see how vacant they appeared, which was not something he normally saw in his optimistic and spirited brother. He didn't want to push Luke too hard for a response, so he put his hand on Luke's shoulder to let him know he was there for him.

Tears began slowly and then poured down Luke's cheeks. His breaths became shallow, and Tom pulled him into a hug, feeling tears stream from his own eyes. He loved his brother more than anyone he knew, and seeing him in this pain made his heart ache for him. Tom could hear a muffled voice from the head buried in his chest.

Luke stepped back, tears still streaming. "I didn't know how much this could hurt. I loved her so much, and I can't bear to know I'll never see her again. I just didn't know."

Luke had traveled with Kathryn to Peru on a mission trip seven years ago when he was only nineteen. Luke had said that Kathryn was different. Fun, intelligent, loving, and committed to her faith. He had no problem honoring her commitment to waiting for marriage, and Tom could tell from the look in Luke's eyes that he was thoroughly smitten before venturing off. Luke wrote to Tom weekly to tell him about the school they were helping to set up and other projects they were working on in the small and impoverished town in the mountains. That summer mission trip had turned into six years of service while they still worked remotely on their degrees from Boston University. Tom had made the long flight and trekked down to South America twice, once to officiate at Luke and Kathryn's wedding after two years and then again last year for Kathryn's funeral.

Luke dropped down into the kitchen chair and stared at the table.

Tom sat, wanting to take away his brother's pain but knowing he could not.

After several moments, Luke raised his head, eyes red and still glimmering. "I never really knew how much pain you must have felt when you lost Corlie. I knew you still grieved her death even after all those years, but I never really understood."

Tom was taken by Luke's empathy for him when the visceral rawness of his own pain was still so present. "Luke, I can't tell you how sorry I've felt about Kathryn and you. My heart aches, and I've prayed for you every day."

Luke nodded. "I know. I've been struggling with God these past twelve months. When I left for Peru with her, I knew there was no one else like her. I knew she was the one. I can't believe how much I loved her. It made me grow up fast to begin thinking more about her than myself."

Tom's eyes softened. "I remember the day you introduced me to her. I could tell as soon as I saw her—her smile, selfless nature, and most of all, the way you gazed at her. I was so happy for you."

Luke returned a half-smile. "I couldn't believe how happy I was. Living in those poor conditions should have seemed rough, but I thanked God every day for her, the gift of her soul. She—" Another tear rolled down his cheek. "She showed me what real love was about. I felt so alive and so excited about taking our journey together. It was like I understood what you'd been trying to teach me all those years, but this was the real thing. How could God do this to her? To us? What possible good could come out of letting that happen to her?"

Tom pursed his lips for a moment. "Suffering and evil. Those are the two things that make people lose their faith and trust in God. I struggled with that same question."

"I blame myself. Those drug cartels warned us to leave, but Kathryn wanted to continue working for the families and the kids." Luke let out a quiet laugh. "She loved those kids. I should have been stronger for her. I should have protected her."

"Luke, you can't blame yourself. As horrible as what happened, I have to believe she is smiling down on you and in loving hands right now."

"They tried to rape her at the school, and she fought back. They slaughtered her to make an example. How could anything like that be allowed to happen to someone like Kathryn? I kept thinking she would come back and that it was just a bad dream. Now I only have bad dreams every night."

Tom placed his hand on Luke's shoulder to comfort him. "I know how it feels to blame yourself and to ache in grief, missing someone you love more than yourself. I had to keep asking what Corlie would want me to do. How could I honor her in how I lived? When you stayed there to carry on the mission, I worried about your safety, and I worried you wanted to avenge her death."

"More than you know," replied Luke in a hushed tone.

"You have always been a protector. When protectors can't be there to protect, they often want to seek justice for the ones they love. Sometimes we have to leave the justice part up to God."

Luke stood up and strode toward the door, glaring back at Tom. "I couldn't trust God to protect her from those animals, and now you want me to trust Him with justice?"

Chapter 8

Daily Mass was at seven a.m., and Tom was always surprised to see how many neighborhood people attended or stopped on their way to work. He was even more surprised during his homily when he peered out at the congregation to see Brian Flaherty sitting in a side pew. He couldn't remember Flaherty attending anything at the church since he was a teenager outside of a funeral for a close friend. After Mass, Tom said goodbye to everyone as they exited to the light snow falling outside the main entrance doors.

Flaherty, the last to reach the exit, raised his eyebrows at Tom. "What's that big smile all about?"

Tom continued to grin, shaking Flaherty's hand. "Oh, nothing. It's just good to see your face inside this house."

"Yeah. Yeah. Hey, you said that it would be okay to drop by today."

It took Tom a second to recall the conversation. "Oh, yeah. That's right. Just give me a minute to change. I'll meet you over at the rectory."

When Tom reached the rectory, Luke was just letting Flaherty into the kitchen. Inside, Tom motioned to Luke. "I don't think you two have met. Brian, this is my not-so-baby brother, Luke. Luke, this is Brian Flaherty, your not-so-typical Boston cop."

Flaherty shook hands with Luke. "I hope I'm not intruding on family time. Father Tom said it would be okay to drop by."

Luke turned. "No. It's fine. I can take my coffee to another room. Would you two like a cup?"

Flaherty nodded. "Feel free to sit with us. I just wanted to ask your brother a few questions about counseling."

In a few minutes, the three sat with their cups of hot coffee.

Tom squinted as he took a small sip from the piping hot cup. "Luke's been in Peru for the past seven years doing mission work for a small, poor community."

Raising his cup, Flaherty said, "I'm impressed. Helping others is what it's all about. I'd love to hear about your work."

Luke grinned. "Maybe when I'm fully awake. So, is my big brother in some sort of trouble with the law?"

Tom laughed out loud. "Not since the last case."

"No," Flaherty replied. "I've been studying psychology and doing some counseling and just wanted your brother's advice."

Tom raised his brow. "I didn't know you were already doing some actual work. Is this part of your school practicum?"

"Not officially. It's just a group of guys struggling with different situations. The counselor who started the group couldn't do it anymore, and they wanted to continue, so I've been struggling along to keep it going for the past few years. I don't want to bore Luke, but I was just wondering what key things you emphasize and pay attention to when you counsel people working through problems in their lives."

Luke leaned forward, turning to his brother. "I would love to hear about this. Since I was born, he's been working on me, but I've never looked at it through my brother's eyes. I'd love to know what he's been doing to me all these years."

Tom reached over and gave Luke a gentle push to his head. "You're my only success story." Tom turned to Flaherty. "Well, that's really a big question. It depends so much on the person, their history, how they've responded to the situation, and how much they really want to address their situation."

"I get that, but you must have some high-level guidance when working with men who have faced difficult situations," asked Flaherty, staring intently at Tom.

Tom scratched his head. "I hate to be so general. Some people face devastating traumas and come out stronger. Others never recover to live life fully, and a whole range in between. Take an abusive or absent parent. That can have an overwhelming impact on their children for their entire lives."

Brian paused. "Hmmm. My dad didn't leave us, but sometimes, I almost wished he had."

"Sorry to hear that."

"Yeah. Me too. He ignored me, almost as if I didn't exist. I craved his attention. Just an approving glance or a hug, but it never came. I almost felt as if he was disappointed or ashamed of me all the time. I used to think if he *had* left, I could at least imagine he missed me or loved me. I finally had to let him go and be stronger—better than him, you know."

Tom gazed at him. "Brian, you've certainly done that in so many ways. I think it's your focus on serving others that might be your key."

"Maybe. But I can use all the help I can get."

Luke tapped his brother on the top of his hand. "Tommy, you always have good advice. You once quoted me some psychologist. What is it he said?"

"Your mind is like an unsafe neighborhood; don't go there alone," replied Tom.

"Right. There must be some things you can say to help Brian out to go there with his patients?"

Tom took a deep breath. "Sure. Sure. Brian, as a counselor, you have the gift of empathy, which is hard to teach. You've always listened well and cared. You probably know that it's not the bad things that happen to people that lead to their problems but the strong desire to avoid dealing with them. People resist looking at their wounds because they are deathly afraid that what they fear most might be true. As children, we adapt to survive physically and mentally. A child might withdraw, numb themselves, create a false exterior self, or act out to protect, cope, and survive. When we maintain those adaptations as adults, they become maladaptations and keep us from fully being ourselves and living life. You might be surprised at how strong and deceptive our mind is in resisting and avoiding facing our problems."

Flaherty nodded. "Makes sense. I knew both of those things, but you put it in simpler terms to remember. What I can't figure out is why people would resist getting a better perspective and healthier thinking about something that wasn't their fault. You know, stop blaming themselves for what may have happened."

Tom took a sip of his coffee. "That may be one of your biggest challenges as a counselor. They have to be ready. There is a theory in psychology called self-verification."

"I've never heard of it," said Flaherty, sitting up with interest.

"In the simplest terms, people grow up needing a framework or perception of themselves to process the world coming at them each day and avoid feeling overwhelmed. Even if that framework is built on distorted and unhealthy thinking, they desperately need to hold onto it to process their world, or they feel they will be crushed or disappear. For example, take a girl who has been abused by her father for years and blames herself, thinks it was her fault."

"But, how can she think that?" asked Luke.

"Great question, but it's that unhealthy perception of herself that she will fight to hang onto. She will even seek out feedback to confirm that belief, often seeking out abusive relationships with men to validate that it was her fault."

Luke interrupted. "That's crazy. It wasn't her fault. Why wouldn't she be open to seeing she wasn't responsible and to know what she deserves? How can she be herself and live life with that distorted image?"

Leaning in, Flaherty said, "She can't, but I think your brother is saying she will resist hearing or believing she's worth more. She thinks her distorted image protects her and lets her process things, or else she'd vanish, be sucked into that black hole she fears. Is that close, Father Tom?"

Tom nodded. "At a high level, that's close, but you can see why the mind builds up so many layers of protection to avoid and resist even getting close to the truth—to a healthier perception of oneself. The sad thing is what Luke said. They will never be free to be themselves, to live the life intended for them, until they take the chance to dive into the waves instead of always running from them. To tolerate the uncomfortable and ugly feelings of facing the pain head-on. Some may even bury the memory that anything bad ever actually happened to them. Not to get too religious, but Satan's greatest tool is to get us to think less of ourselves and miss the amazing person God created us to be."

Flaherty appeared frozen for a second, staring at the empty cup in front of him.

"Brian, are you okay?" asked Tom.

He let out a long breath. "We lost one of the guys in the group, and I was just thinking about him. I've had a hard time trying to understand it."

Tom pursed his lips. "I'm so sorry to hear that. I really am."

Clearing his throat, Flaherty rose from his chair. "I think I'm going to go. Luke, it was great to meet you. Will you be staying with your brother for a while?"

Luke climbed to his feet, as did Tom. "I don't know yet. I've got a lot to sort out."

Flaherty half-smiled. "Well, luckily, you've got a great brother to help you through it. I never had that. Father Tom, thanks for your advice. It's all good stuff for me to think about."

Tom walked him to the door. "Don't ever hesitate to come over anytime. We can't get to everyone, but you can be a huge help to the people you see. And don't be too discouraged if most people won't want to cooperate or go very deep. It can feel like scary territory down there. Unfortunately, there are more bad therapists than good ones. I think you'll be one of the good ones."

Flaherty glanced up, his cheeks turning slightly red. "Thanks. That means a lot, especially coming from you."

Tom said, "Hey, any more progress on that Harry Simon murder? I didn't get a chance to know him myself. I talked to his wife yesterday, and she seemed to indicate that he was kind of aloof and was sad about leaving his job teaching the kids at the Y years ago."

"Interesting. I don't think there's been too much progress. More questions than answers, but that's not unusual at this point in the investigation. Were you able to help much?"

Tom shook his head. "I don't think so. It seems as if the killer was trying to make a strong statement, but it's hard to tell what it was."

Flaherty stepped out into the cold air, where a few flakes continued to fall. "That's for sure. Brooks is trying to locate all the people the guy knew or worked with over the years. We'll see. Thanks again."

Tom watched until Flaherty disappeared down the driveway, then Luke turned to him. "Is this Detective Brooks going to need Holmes and Angelo to come to the rescue again?"

Laughing, Tom replied, "What are you talking about?"

"Oh, I've heard things, brother."

Tom's smile turned to brotherly concern as he put his hand on Luke's shoulder. "How are you doing?"

"Hey, I'm sorry about snapping like that last night. Things still feel raw, but I shouldn't be taking it out on you."

"I love you, Luke. Don't ever apologize for sharing your feelings with me. That's what family is for."

Luke gave a tentative half-smile. "Well, I'm sure there's more to come, but it's good to have someone there for you—even if they can't fix it."

Chapter 9

Tom stood in full vestments at the back of St. Francis Church, waiting for the local funeral home to carry Harry Simon's casket through the entrance doors. Next to him stood Detective Brooks, scanning the larger-than-expected gathering for the funeral Mass.

Tom asked, "Do you think the killer would really attend Harry's funeral?"

"I don't know. Someone who went through all that trouble would be liable to do anything. We're not talking about someone who stole a stamp collection. Who knows what their frame of mind might be?"

Tom peered around the church. Angelo and Luke were standing in opposite wings to see if they noticed anything or anyone suspicious, while Detective Mullen and Officer Spiro were in another corner, taking notes. Brian Flaherty stopped a young man on his way to a back pew and exchanged a few words with him. The man with reddish hair appeared upset as Flaherty talked to him, but the sight of Harry's wife at the entrance grabbed Tom's attention.

He greeted Mrs. Simon as she entered with a man Tom was earlier introduced to as her brother, and behind them was the casket, which Tom then blessed with holy water.

"Mrs. Simon, I will proceed down the aisle, and you will follow. When we stop in front of the altar, would you and your brother like to place the white linen cloth over the casket? It's called the pall and symbolizes Harry's Baptism in Christ."

Esther Simon sighed. "If that is what you do here. I just hope this doesn't take too long."

Her comment saddened Tom, but he worked to focus on why he was there.

They proceeded down the aisle to the soothing voice of the cantor singing "Come to the Water." Tom tried to refrain from asking himself if each person he made eye contact with could've been the killer come to see Harry buried for good.

Esther had given Tom very few tidbits about Harry's life to share with those attending the funeral. She almost seemed more angry than sad about his death and their years together. He tried his best to say some generically positive things about Harry and then moved to talk to those in front of him. "They say, 'Life, in the end, has only one tragedy—not to have been a saint.' I think about that often, knowing I am so far away from that universal goal in life. When we lose someone in such a horrible way, we hope they are safely in God's loving embrace."

Tom glanced around at the blank expressions of those in the congregation. "So, why do we have a funeral Mass such as this? We certainly want the chance to say goodbye, have closure, and celebrate Harry's life and memories, but that is not the real reason for this sacred time. If you are a believer, we are here because of Jesus—to worship God. We are here to thank God for his mercy that fills us with hope. At this low moment in our lives, we are also here to renew our faith in the resurrection because Christ has conquered death for us. Finally, we are here to pray for Harry out of love. May his soul be on its way to heaven."

When Tom finished, he noticed that the man with curly red hair, who Brian Flaherty had been conversing with before Mass, abruptly stood up and exited by the side door Angelo guarded. Tom noticed Angelo motioning his head toward a side pew, and Tom scanned the darkened area for what Angelo was trying to call his attention to. The only thing that stood out was a large man with short white hair and a patch over one eye. Tom turned his attention to preparing the altar for the Liturgy of the Eucharist as Angelo quietly stepped out the side exit.

Brooks stood in the back, peering down at Mullen's notebook and then at the attendees. Tom was rarely distracted from his focus on the sacred nature of the sacrifice of the Mass, but he found himself conflicted today, especially when the large man with the eye patch stood to leave early during Communion.

After Mass, he realized no one seemed to have been there to celebrate or mourn Harry's death, including his wife. Some were reporters, and others were curious attendees because of the gruesome nature of Harry's death, but there were no tears or grief as one would expect.

Esther Simon insisted she didn't want any people, a service, or any prayers said at the gravesite, so there was no procession from Mass to the graveyard.

After everyone left, Tom found himself alone in the aisle of the quiet church with Luke. "That was the oddest service I've ever celebrated."

"It definitely wasn't an emotional funeral." Luke turned to Tom. "Thanks for reminding me to pray for Kathryn. It helps me to think she's still here in some way."

"In many ways, Luke. In many beautiful ways."

Back at the rectory, Tom took some plates from the kitchen cupboard. "Since we didn't get a chance to have breakfast, let me—"

The kitchen door opened, and Angelo entered, holding his hand out. "It might be safer if I make us up a lunch. I can heat up some meatball subs if that works for everyone."

Luke relaxed his brow with relief.

Tom chuckled. "I think you're right, but where did you slip off to during the funeral Mass? When that man with the red hair left, I saw you head out."

Angelo spooned some meatballs and sauce into a pan on the stove. "Luke and I scanned the people attending the funeral to see if anyone appeared suspicious. Did you notice that other man I motioned you toward?"

Tom sighed. "Yes, but I'm not supposed to be playing detective during Mass."

Stirring the sauce, Angelo queried, "What did you notice?"

Luke stepped toward Angelo. "You mean the big guy with the eye patch, right?"

Tom interjected, "I saw him. He was big, but what about him?"

Nodding, Luke replied, "I see where you're going, Angelo. Who killed Acis?"

Tom narrowed his eyes at them. "Polyphemus, the Sicilian cyclops. Okay, eye patch, one eye, and he showed up at Harry's funeral, leaving before it was over. But you left when the other man with the curly red hair scooted out?"

Angelo carried three toasted rolls full of piping-hot meatballs to the table and laughed as Luke's eyes widened. "I did. He seemed highly uncomfortable from the start. He sat in a dark corner and appeared agitated when he suddenly left during the service, so I thought I'd check him out." Angelo sat down and took a bite out of his sub without adding to his response.

Finally, Tom's impatience won out. "And? Did you talk to him? Do you know who he is?"

Angelo swallowed and grinned. "I told you he can't resist a mystery. Okay, like I said, he seemed upset, and he was walking pretty fast. I thought I was going to lose him, but he abruptly turned and stared me down, saying, 'Who are you, and why are you following me?'"

Tom glanced at Luke and leaned in. "What did you say?"

"Before I could respond, he said, 'Please, leave me alone.' I nodded, made eye contact, and replied, 'I'll respect your wishes. You just seemed to be upset in the church, and I wanted to make sure you were okay, that's all.' He looked down, shaking his head, saying, 'I'm okay. Don't worry about me.' Then, he turned and walked away."

Eyebrows raised, Tom said, "Angelo, that's it?"

Angelo finished another bite of his sandwich. "It could have been, but I called out, 'I'm sorry to have bothered you. It must have been hard for you to be there.' He slowed and turned, squinting his eyes; he stared at me for several seconds and said, 'Why did you say that?'"

Luke asked, "What did you do?"

"I stepped toward him and stared into his eyes. I could tell that he was very uncomfortable, if not angry. I said, 'It was just a feeling I had. Mr. Simon was not a perfect man.'

"He turned his head with a sarcastic laugh. 'Far from it, and he deserv—' he said, catching himself. I nodded to show some empathy and said, 'If you ever need anyone to talk things out with, I know a great person that could help.'"

Angelo glanced toward Tom, and Tom asked, "I like the way you approached him. Did he open up?"

"Nope. He turned, mumbling, 'I'm all set with *that*.' He quickly headed off down the street without another word."

Tom ran his hand across his forehead. "So, we don't know his name or relationship to Harry?"

Pulling a small piece of paper from his pocket, Angelo slid it across the table to Tom. "I followed him from a distance and got his address, so we can find out."

Chapter 10

After celebrating the Sunday Masses, Tom headed back to the rectory. Luke told him there was a phone call from Detective Brooks, and Tom laughed as he listened to the voice message. "Ah, this is Brooks. You don't know how much I hate to ask you this, but would you be able to drop by the station Monday morning?"

Monday dawned chilly and crisp, one week since the death of Harry Simon, and no clues as to who the killer was. Tom and Angelo trekked the mile from St. Francis to the Harrison Street Police Station they had visited so many times in the past.

Sergeant Doherty glanced up from the front desk with a grin. "Brooks only mentioned you, Father Tom. No offense, but I don't know if he's gonna be too happy."

Angelo smirked. "When is he ever happy?"

Doherty curled his lower lip and bobbed his head in agreement.

When Brooks peered out from the detective's room, Tom could see his head shaking before waving them in, saying, "I guess I should be more specific when I say, can *you* drop by?"

Tom patted Brooks on the back. "If you don't want the information Angelo has to share, I'm sure he won't mind heading home."

Brooks offered them some coffee and a seat as Detective Mullen joined them. "What've you got, Salvato?"

"Maybe nothing you don't already have."

Mullen opened up her notebook. "We took notes and photos of all those attending the funeral, but we'd still like to hear what you've got."

Angelo took the hot cup of coffee from Brooks. "You probably noticed the big guy with the eye patch. Father Tom said that he left before the Mass was over. He might be someone you want to check out."

Brooks sat on the edge of the desk, sipping his coffee. "I'm assuming you're trying to connect him to the Greek myth angle—the one-eyed cyclops?" asked Brooks, pointing to one of his own eyes. "Is that all you've got?"

Angelo's eyes narrowed. "It's worth checking out, especially if you're coming up dry so far," he quipped. "There was another man who left pretty abruptly during the service."

Mullen flipped through her notebook. "He left before I could get his photo or description."

Angelo handed Mullen the paper with the man's Tremont Street address. "He seemed pretty agitated and short when I talked with him."

"Keep goin'," said Brooks, motioning with his hand.

"Well, he stopped himself midsentence, but it sounded like he was about to say that Harry Simon got what he deserved. When I mentioned that Simon wasn't perfect, he didn't hesitate to agree. Then I said that I knew someone who would be good to talk to if he struggled with anything, and he snapped back, saying he had *that* covered. It sounded as if he might be seeing someone, but I don't know if it was related to Simon at all."

Brooks squinted. "Okay, if we have his address, we can find out who he is."

Angelo pointed to the notepaper. "I already checked around."

Brooks glanced up at the ceiling. "Should I be surprised?"

"His name is Sam Gately. He's around forty or so. Seems as if he's never been able to hold onto a job for very long. The last place he worked was at a restaurant around the corner. He never married and seemed to keep to himself. None of the neighbors really know him other than seeing him coming in or out of the building. I guess it was his mother's apartment, but she died a few years back, and he stayed on."

Brooks turned to Angelo. "Maybe he robs houses for a living?"

"It looks as if his father did. One of the older neighbors recalls him being abusive to the mother too and abandoning Sam when he was five or six."

"That's no father and no man in my book. Did this Gately guy look like someone who could have killed Simon? And why was he at the funeral?"

Angelo shrugged. "Those are great questions. I don't think he was there because he'll miss Harry Simon."

"All right, thanks. Well, we already checked up on our one-eyed giant. He goes by Jon, but his full name is Jonas Alpheus. He was a high school teacher for thirty years at Madison, teaching—you guessed it—Latin language and Greek mythology. He's also been a swimming director at the YMCA on Huntington for that same period after he moved to Boston. None of that means anything yet, but it's quite a coincidence."

"Huh," murmured Tom.

"What's that 'huh' for, Father Brown?"

"Probably nothing," replied Tom as he stared closely at the photo of the large man. He didn't appear like a killer to Tom, but then he wondered if he knew what a man willing to kill another man looked like. Tom pointed to the name on the file and said, "Alpheus is a Greek name of a river god. Remember the reference to the river on the note you found on Harry's body. *Out of his heart shall flow rivers of dead water*. It seems oddly coincidental with the water theme of the notes and the site where Harry's body was found."

Brooks glanced at Mullen with a slight shake of his head. "Baptism. Greek gods. Rivers. Give me something I can work with."

Tom replied, "This may not help, but Jonas has a meaning in Greek as well."

"And what's that?"

"It's a derivative of Johan's Hebrew name and means *dove* or *peaceful being sent by God*."

Angelo added, "And you found a dead dove under the body in the fountain. It's a lot of possible connections but even more confusing. If the murderer left the notes, why make such an obvious connection?"

Brooks turned to Mullen. "Let's get that warrant and see what our 'dove' might have for clues in his apartment."

Chapter 11

Dr. Franks spotted a single tear rolling down his client's cheek. "Remember, I might push you at times, but you should always feel safe to share or tell me you aren't comfortable going there yet."

Daniel wiped away a tear before taking a deep breath. There was a long hesitation before any words came out. "I guess I haven't let myself think about it too much. I never really knew my father well enough to figure it out. I guess I wanted the relationship with him so badly growing up that I denied that he might not have wanted it too."

Dr. Franks jotted down a note. "It's no small thing in our lives. We want to know we are loved, especially by those who created us, who saw us from the first moment when we couldn't be anything but our true selves. We had no protective armor or time to create a false public self, so they see our raw self, naked and unprotected. We need to know we were worth loving to feel as if we could love ourselves and that others would accept and love us."

"I'm confused. Are you saying that we wouldn't be worthy of love if one of our parents didn't love us?"

"Far from it. I'm talking about how our minds and hearts process things as a child that can impact our entire lives, hurts that can dramatically change how we see ourselves and impact our ability to have meaningful relationships with others. Remember, we don't get true validation for our self-worth from others, but we tend to look for it there. The gaze of a parent into their child's eyes lets them know they are worth loving, but it isn't the gaze that makes us worth loving. I don't normally share my life with clients, but—" Dr. Franks hesitated as he glanced upward for a second to regain his composure. "My own dad was a jerk. He was a drunk and never gave my mother what she deserved. He left us when I was quite little. It took me many years to realize that my value didn't go down just because he wasn't the father I deserved. I craved his attention and approval for so many years after he left, and then I realized it wouldn't have changed who I was, even if he gave it."

Complete silence filled the room for almost a full minute. Daniel stared at him, then looked off to the window. "I'd like to stop for today to think about what you said. Part of me feels very angry right now, and I need to sort it out."

Dr. Franks stood at the door as his client descended the stairs. "Remember one thing," he called out. "Uncomfortable feelings and anger can be clues and keys to unlocking the doors to those dark rooms that keep us from living."

There was no response as the back door to the street slammed shut.

Chapter 12

Tuesday morning, Tom peered out the kitchen window, feeling like a kid as he watched the snowflakes drifting down on top of the three-to-four inches that had already accumulated.

Luke sat at the table with his coffee.

Without turning, Tom asked, "Have you missed it? The snow falling outside?"

"Hmm," was the only sound Luke made as he stared into his cup for a full two minutes. "Tommy," he finally said. "I miss *her*. I don't even know the point of getting up anymore."

Tom took a few steps over and rubbed his brother's back, not saying anything. Not trying to fix or deny Luke's pain, Tom felt his own loss creep into his chest.

Luke continued to stare into his half-cup of coffee. "I'm not sleeping. I just keep thinking of her all night. Sometimes holding her or seeing us laughing together, then I see her mangled body and jump as if I could save her. I wasn't there for her."

Tom dropped down onto the chair next to Luke, letting his brother know he wasn't alone. He had no magic words to bring Kathryn back or stop Luke's pain.

Luke gave a throaty sigh, and his face tensed. "I, ah—I was thinking of that guy, Harry. Someone had to have been pretty angry to kill him that way, to make a statement like that."

"Are you thinking someone was angry with Kathryn?"

Luke shoved his chair back and paced. "No. I'm the one who's angry. I wanted to make the men who did that to her pay, to die like Harry did. I'm sorry; it's just this rage inside me to seek justice for her. I know it won't bring her back, but it feels so wrong that they are out there without any punishment. How is that right? Even if God eventually takes care of them, I can't stand for them to be living as if they did nothing wrong. She was so beautiful, and they were so brutal—so cruel."

Tom thought about how he blamed himself for his own loss, while Luke felt that there were actual killers who needed to pay.

Luke continued, "I scanned the church at Harry's funeral, and I wasn't looking for a killer but someone who might be seeking justice, righting a wrong. Why should good and innocent people suffer while the bad guys go free?"

Tom sighed. "I can't explain why things can be so unfair in this life. I can tell you that Kathryn is not suffering now, but I know you are. It breaks my heart to know how much you are hurting. I know there's no solace at the moment, but they won't get away with it on God's watch."

Luke's eyes were red as he turned to Tom. "Really? What if they just say they're sorry, and some priest forgives them? Aren't they forgiven? Don't they get away with it?"

"Luke, God is our Father. He wants all of us to find our way to Him, to His love and mercy. Yes, if you truly repent and ask for forgiveness, He promises us His mercy, but repentance must be real, not phony. Is there any part of you that would want them to wake up, know what they did was so wrong, and sincerely confess it?"

Shaking his head, Luke raised his voice. "I want them to pay for what they did, to feel the pain she felt. I don't think they deserve forgiveness. I know I'm disappointing you, but that's how I feel, and—sorry, I can't do this right now." He got up and went to the spare room, leaving Tom to himself.

Tom felt frustrated that he couldn't comfort his own brother, but Luke also needed to work through his emotions to get to a healthier place.

Deep in thought, the phone ringing on the kitchen wall startled him. He got up to answer it. "Hello, this is Father Tom."

"Padre. It's Brooks. We've brought Mr. Alpheus in for questioning."

"Great. Thanks for letting me know."

"Here's the thing, and I know this isn't normal, but nothing we do with you is normal. I was wondering if you were free to drop by the precinct to listen in on the interview just in case he brings up any connections to the clues left at the scene we might miss? You know, the Greek, Latin, and baptism stuff."

When Tom entered the station, the desk sergeant motioned toward the detective's room, where Brooks was waiting for him.

"I don't have to tell you that this is all confidential. You remember the viewing room you sat in for the Comghan case interrogations, right?"

Tom nodded. "I know. Two-way mirror, and he won't be able to hear me. Are you arresting Alpheus or just asking questions?"

Brooks fumbled with the unlit cigarette in his hand. "Let's just say we're closer to the former. Thanks for doing this."

Tom waited in the viewing room, watching through the two-way mirror for the detectives to enter with their suspect. While Alpheus was not a young man, he did seem larger and stronger than Tom had noticed during the funeral Mass. His hair was white, and his skin was tanned and coarse. Tom couldn't help but think of Anthony Quinn in *Zorba the Greek*. The man sat on the opposite side of the table from Brooks and Mullen, hands folded, a black patch on one eye as the other gazed downward.

Detective Mullen pushed a button on the recorder. "Mr. Alpheus, we will be recording this interview. For the record, could you state your full name?"

He lifted his head and gazed toward Mullen. "Why am I here?"

"Full name, please. We are just looking for information to help find Mr. Simon's killer."

"Jonas Christos Alpheus. Call me Jon."

Mullen opened the file folder in front of her. "Thank you. Mr. Alpheus, you've been acquainted with Harry Simon for quite some time. Can you tell us about your relationship with him?"

Alpheus replied, "He was one of my swimming instructors many years ago. I've had no relationship with him since he left the YMCA about fifteen years ago."

Brooks leaned forward. "That's very interesting. We have cameras outside of your apartment building showing him visiting you on the day he was murdered and a neighbor stating that there was a loud argument between the two of you that ended abruptly."

"Yes. He did show up at my home unexpectedly."

With a slight nod, Brooks said, "So, just a coincidence. What did you argue about?"

"Nothing important. Nothing relevant," replied Alpheus as he ran his hand across the old wooden table.

"Really? It must have seemed important to someone to get heated about. Just humor me and tell us what this loud argument about nothing relevant was about."

Alpheus turned his head and paused. "He wanted to come back to teach. He begged me to come back, and I said, 'No.'"

"Why is that?"

"I can't say."

Brooks squinted. "You can't say, or you won't say?"

His eye widened as his gaze turned back to Brooks. "I can't."

Mullen handed Brooks a sheet of paper from the file, and he stared at it for several seconds. "How long did he teach with you at the Y?"

"Fifteen years."

"And why did he leave if he seemed so anxious to return all these years later?"

"I can't say."

"Hmm. Well, he's dead, now, and we need to know. Let's see if we can help encourage you to cooperate. We found some interesting things in your apartment during yesterday's search. We found notepaper that matched the note found on Harry's body. The note was in Latin, which you taught for many years, and seems to match your handwriting based on other items in your apartment. We think the pen in your desk might match the ink used."

Alpheus remained motionless as Brooks continued.

"On your shelf, there was a book about Greek myths and Ovid's story of Acis and the sea nymph—what's her name? Gena or something?"

"Galatea!" snapped Alpheus.

"Ah, how the thundering giant now roars. I'm not into poetry, but I read the poem several times. Polyphemus loves this Galatea, but along comes Acis and woos her love away, and they mock Alpheus's songs of love for her. Do I have that right?" asked Brooks as he lowered his head.

"I am not Polyphemus. I lost my eye in an accident. I don't know what connection you are trying to make."

"Why were the character names, Acis and Galatea, underlined in that poem, with a notation, *H.I.M* on the margin. What did that refer to?"

Alpheus pressed his palms down upon the table. "I don't know what you're talking about."

"There was also a Bible on your shelf with pages folded to verses found on these notes in Latin." Brooks pushed photocopies of the two notes in front of Alpheus.

"I've never seen these before." He glanced from one to the other. "One of these doesn't even make sense, and neither are accurate quotes from Scripture. What are you accusing me of? The handwriting isn't even the same from one note to the other."

Mullen quickly turned the papers to check the handwriting as Brooks seemed unphased. "Mr. Alpheus, we found a black glove in your apartment that matches one from Mr. Simon's coat pocket and his DNA."

"He must have dropped it."

"We also found out that you have a job as a contractor maintaining historical city property such as monuments and fountains."

Alpheus's eye narrowed. "They are important history."

"And, behind your building, you park a large truck with ladders used for this job."

"I do."

"This truck with a ladder would make it easy to reach the upper basin of a fountain like the Brewer fountain, and it just so happens that you had worked on that same fountain just a few months earlier. Is that correct?"

"I may have."

"We have footage showing your truck between Park and Tremont Streets late that same night that Mr. Simon was found in the Brewer Fountain."

Alpheus pursed his lips. "There are plenty of trucks like that in town."

"Not with traces of Harry Simon's blood on the top of the cab."

Alpheus tilted his head back and rubbed his forehead with the palm of his hand. He turned his sight toward the mirror on the wall, almost as if he could tell Tom was watching from the other side, and said forcefully, "I did not kill Harry Simon!"

Chapter 13

Tom stepped outside the precinct to find Angelo waiting for him. "I'll never be lonely with you around, Angelo."

"So, you said they wanted you to listen in on a possible suspect?"

"Yes. Jonas Alpheus. I couldn't add much value," replied Tom as he filled Angelo in on the evidence during their walk back.

"Kind of careless, don't you think?" remarked Angelo as they maneuvered around a young couple embraced in a kiss on the sidewalk in front of them.

"Maybe, but it does explain a lot about a possible motive, the clues, and getting Harry's body into that basin."

Angelo peered up into the clouded sky. "You don't seem convinced. Do you know where this Alpheus lives?"

"It's on St. Botolph Street." He stopped and stared at Angelo. "Wait a minute. You aren't thinking of breaking into this apartment, are you? Then again, it's you, so of course, you are."

Angelo shifted direction and picked up his pace.

Tom hustled to catch up. "Angelo. We can't be doing this again."

"But you're questioning this Alpheus's guilt, right?"

"I don't know. He's definitely hiding something, almost as if he were protecting Harry."

"If this Alpheus is not guilty, would you be able to live with his conviction?"

Before he knew it, they were in front of the apartment building, and Angelo smartly held the door for an older woman making her way out. After making their way up three flights of stairs and down a short empty hallway, they were standing at Alpheus's apartment door.

Angelo's previous life as a professional thief came in handy. He reached into his pocket and pulled out a small sleeve holder for various-sized lock picks. When he found the one he wanted, he glanced up at Tom with a smirk. "You never know."

Angelo also sometimes put them in danger.

He quickly worked the lock and opened the door to the small dark apartment, then pulled a small flashlight from the pouch to help them navigate their way. He glanced at Tom, who whispered, "I know. You never know. This is crazy. If we get caught, I don't even know you."

From the look of the apartment, Tom decided Alpheus was an organized type of person, but it was obvious the police had been through every inch of the place.

Angelo methodically moved the light from corner to corner.

"What are we looking for?" asked Tom in a hushed voice.

"We won't know until we've found it," replied Angelo with a light chuckle.

The apartment was full of bookshelves. Tom scanned the books by Homer, Euripides, Sophocles, Aristotle, Petronius, Ovid—he stopped. There were several antique copies of Ovid's *Metamorphoses* and an opening on the shelf where the police must have taken some copies. Tom leaned over to Angelo. "No one that appreciates the classics like these could have been involved with a murder like Harry's."

Angelo was busy focusing his light on a locked file drawer of the wooden desk in front of him. He scanned the set of lockpicks from his pouch and chose one, turning the lock until it opened. He peered up at Tom. "They must not have bothered checking without the key." In the drawer were files that Angelo lifted onto the desktop. "These go back pretty far."

Tom whispered, "What are they? Mrs. Simon mentioned that Harry had to quit his teaching position at the Y about fifteen years ago, so around 1994."

Angelo handed Tom the 1994 file while he opened up 1993. "There's a bunch of different papers in here, but here are some records from the Y. One sheet with boys' names, ages, short descriptions, etcetera, and another with members of the staff—names, contact info, years on the staff, areas of responsibility, and things like that. Funny, I don't see anyone named Harry Simon on the list."

"I don't see his name in '94, either. What about further back?"

Angelo scanned the prior year's files. "Nope. I see a Harold Monnot as a swim instructor, but no Harry Simon."

"Huh. I saw that name in '94 as well. Right here," said Tom as he pointed to the name and the asterisk beside the name. "Monnot. Monnot. There's a note that says he was dismissed. See if his name is in '95."

"Nope. There is a new name, Arthur Wenkle, swim instructor. Seems like too much of a coincidence to have someone named Harold as an instructor, gone the same year Mrs. Simon says Harry left that position—and it sounded very reluctantly."

"How's your French?" asked Tom.

"Non-existent. Why do you ask?"

Tom stared at the name on the list. "I think the French name 'Monnot' translates into Simon." He shrugged. "I'm not one hundred percent sure, but it's a definite possibility."

Flipping through the rest of the files, Angelo replied, "So, the questions to ask are?"

"Why was he forced to leave his position and—"

"Why did he have to change his name? I think we need to locate Mrs. Simon, number one, or should I say, Mrs. Monnot?" Angelo carefully put the files back, locked the file drawer, and wiped down everything they had touched. Before standing up, he reopened the drawer and pulled the folders forward until he found the first file from 1979. There were few sheets on this file, but one had a photocopy of a much younger Jonas Alpheus. His eye had a bandage covering and not the black eye patch he wore these days.

Tom was beginning to get nervous that they were testing their luck. "Angelo, we'd better get going."

Angelo moved the light across the desk and onto the wall where a photo of Alpheus hung—without an eyepatch. There was also a photo of a strikingly handsome boy with fair skin and reddish hair, which may have been his son or grandson, but there was no evidence in the apartment that anyone besides a single man lived there.

Safely outside the apartment building, Angelo stood, appearing deep in thought as Tom peered up at the darkened window to what he believed was Alpheus's apartment. "We have got to stop doing this! Wait a minute."

Angelo turned to Tom, "Did you forget something in the apartment?"

"The name on the list—Harold Irving Monnot."

"I don't think I'd want it for a name."

"No, the initials would be H.I.M. Remember the translation of the note?"

Nodding, Angelo replied, *"Behold 'him' who takes away the innocence of the* something. You said the 'him' part was in English and the rest in Latin."

"Right. I couldn't tell if they were sloppy or did it intentionally. Maybe the killer meant, *Behold, Harold Irving Monnot, who takes away the innocence of the world*?"

"All the more reason to locate Mrs. Monnot to find out what happened."

Chapter 14

Wednesdays were Tom's "day off," but running a school, a church, and occasionally being suckered into a puzzling mystery rarely allowed for it. His old beat-up blue Honda hatchback started on the second try, which made him smile as he glanced toward Angelo in the passenger seat. "How do you find these things out?" asked Tom.

"I have friends in town who have special talents. Mrs. Monnot's address wasn't too hard to find. Let's see—it's Seymour Street in Roslindale."

"That's not too far from where I grew up in Hyde Park. Somehow, I don't feel good about this. I don't think she showed up at the funeral, so who knows what her reaction might be."

"Hmm. And everyone always tells me you're Mr. Positive," replied Angelo with a laugh.

In less than twenty minutes, Tom pulled down the quiet street lined on both sides with parked cars in front of three-decker homes; some maintained better than others.

Angelo kept an eye on the house numbers. "Why don't we pull over here to watch? Her house must be that red one, two doors down."

Tom didn't see much of anything other than a few people talking on the steps of one house and two teenagers wearing baggy jeans and their hats on backward, eyeing them as they passed by the car.

Angelo pointed to the second floor of the red house. "I think someone's home. I just saw a window shade go up."

Tom sighed, "All right. We might as well get whatever we're doing here over with."

Tom pressed the door buzzer for the second floor, and Angelo said, "By the way, her name is Alice Makin, now."

Tom gazed up and noticed the curtain moving in the window above. He could partially make out a woman's face peering down, hesitating to respond. Nonchalantly, Tom stepped back a bit and opened his coat so that she could see his collar.

Obviously, they weren't going to leave, and the door opened a crack. "I'm not buying anything, and we give to our own charities," quipped the woman.

"Mrs. Makin, we aren't selling anything or looking for money. We don't want to be a bother, but we would greatly appreciate it if you could help us out," offered Tom.

The door opened a bit wider, and Alice pulled her sweater upward toward her neck. Her shoulder-length hair was a mix of black-and-gray strands, and her eyes squinted with suspicion. "What kind of help?"

"Just a few questions. Would we be able to come in?"

Alice paused. "I don't know you. I don't even know if you are a real priest. What do you want to know?"

"Mrs. Makin, my name is Father Tom Fitzpatrick, and this is Angelo Salvato from St. Francis Church."

Her eyes narrowed. "So you *are* looking for money."

"No. No. We understand you were married to Harry Simon—"

The door began to shut but stopped short as Angelo had wisely slid his foot forward in anticipation. "Mrs. Makin, we only want to know if Harold Monnot was your husband and what happened to him fifteen years ago. Why the change in name? Why did he lose his position at the Y? And was that the reason your marriage broke up?"

Alice closed her eyes and put her hands over them, letting out a big sigh. After several moments, she finally glanced up into Tom's eyes and must have trusted something in them. She opened the door and waved them up a flight of stairs to her dimly lit kitchen. Hands shaking, she fumbled with her cup on the counter. "I just heated a kettle; if you'd like some tea?"

Tom replied, "That would be really nice, and I'm sure Angelo would like some as well."

They settled into the quiet of the tired-looking kitchen as they let their steaming tea sit. Alice broke the silence with her soft but strained voice. "What do you want to know, and why are you asking?"

Tom squinted and took a sip of the hot tea. "This is good. I'm assuming you heard about his passing."

She nodded.

"We had the funeral at St. Francis last week."

"I suppose he would have liked that," she murmured. "He went every week, rain or shine. I never knew why. Maybe he felt guilty?"

Angelo said, "Guilty?"

Tom tipped his hand to Angelo and glanced at Mrs. Makin.

"Mrs. Makin, can you tell us about Harry and anything that could help point to anyone who might have been angry enough to do this?"

Alice furrowed her brow. "I don't know. I've been thinking about it ever since the news came out." The slight bags under her eyes were dark as she stared into her tea cup. "He seemed like such a nice man when I met him at a dance. He was a little older but quiet and respectful. We got married in 1975, but it was difficult to get to really know him in any way. We never had children, and it was almost as if he was afraid to be a father. He didn't talk much about his childhood—I know it was hard. Difficult. Something happened to him, but he avoided talking about it no matter how hard I tried. Around our fifth anniversary, something must have happened that made him pull back more. We were like strangers living in the same house. He'd get physically angry when I brought up seeing a counselor but was fine when I just made believe everything was okay with being distant." Tears flowed down Alice's cheeks. "I couldn't deal with it anymore. I was so lonely in that house with him, but he didn't seem to care. I told him that I didn't hate him, but I needed something more. I needed a real relationship. I needed love, and he couldn't give it. I felt sorry for him, but

I couldn't take it a day longer." Alice took a deep breath and tightened her grip on her cup.

Tom leaned in. "Alice, you are doing well. I want to hear your story."

A forced smile made its way to Alice's face. "He couldn't be close, but he seemed deathly afraid of my leaving him. I didn't know what I should do, and I didn't know what he might do. He'd had an alcohol problem early in our marriage, but he was able to give it up for so many years. After I told him I had to leave, I could tell he started again. He wouldn't drink in the house, but he would stop on the way home from work or drink before heading to the YMCA to teach swimming." Alice paused. "Harold so loved teaching those boys swimming. He would talk about the ones who came in so afraid and timid and beamed when they couldn't wait to come back and swim. I don't know what happened, but one day, that director, Jon, told him to leave his position. He was heartbroken. I know he was not in a good place, but I had to start my own life."

Angelo reached over to her hand. "Mrs. Makin, I hope you've found that life. Do you have any idea at all why Mr. Alpheus discharged Harold?"

She sighed.

"Do you know why he changed his name?"

She shook her head. "I don't. Before I could move out of the apartment, he just disappeared. It took me a year before I could find him to get a divorce, and even then, he barely spoke to me. I know he married some woman, and they lived close to our old apartment, but I never spoke to him again. It wasn't until I saw the paper the morning after, that I knew he'd been killed. Such a sad life. I don't know if he ever had any peace in it."

Tom pursed his lips and paused. "Thank you for sharing a difficult story. I hope you've found some peace in your own life."

Alice shrugged. "I've had some days where I think I know what that might be like, but we all seem to go around in circles, making the same mistakes over and over."

Tom and Angelo thanked Alice again at the door and slowed their walk back to the car as they spotted Brooks and Mullen approaching them.

Brooks raised his head toward the sky. "Please don't tell me I'm seeing what I'm seeing."

Mullen nodded. "Okay. Do you want me to tell you what *I'm* seeing?"

Tom held his hand up to the side of his face, blocking his side view, as he and Angelo quickly passed them on the street.

"Hey, hold on, you two," chided Brooks.

They stopped in their tracks and backed up slowly, looking guilty as charged. "Angelo, look." Tom widened his eyes and tried to act surprised. "It's Detectives Mullen and Brooks."

"Should I even ask what you're doing here and how you found her?" asked Brooks.

"Probably not," quipped Angelo.

Brooks ran his hand across the top of his head. "I've got to call your bishop or boss to tell him you don't have enough to do. Can you two meet us at the station in an hour?"

"We'll be there."

Chapter 15

Angelo sat on the police station lobby bench as Tom approached the front desk. "So, are we looking forward to retirement after all these years?"

Sergeant Doherty grimaced. "I'm thinking of changing my mind. The missus keeps talking about taking trips."

"That should be fun. See the world. Have you ever been out of Boston?"

"I don't know. All I see are these buses loaded with old people waiting in line for a bathroom that's out of order and shuffling from one cheesy hotel to another. How can that be someone's idea of fun?"

Tom chuckled and then noticed Brooks and Mullen returning from their visit with Alice. Brooks waved them to the detective's room. Tom nodded to the sergeant. "Doherty, just take her to Rome and do your own thing. I guarantee you'll love it, and then you can visit the old sod on the next trip."

Doherty offered an uncertain smile toward Tom.

The detective's room was buzzing with activity as Brooks leaned on his old wooden desk, motioning for Tom and Angelo to sit.

Mullen handed Brooks a folder and peered over at Tom and Angelo. "I hope you guys got more out of Alice Makin than we did."

"Only that Harry had a troubled past that kept him distant from people, and something happened that no one wants to talk about," replied Tom.

"Well, Harry's troubles are over, and we've decided to book Jonas Alpheus for his murder. We just wanted to make sure we didn't miss anything from your unauthorized interrogation of Mrs. Makin. We have forensic evidence of blood found on top of Alpheus's utility truck—the same type of truck seen entering the Boston Common the night of the murder—a boning knife in his apartment with trace elements of Harry Simon's blood, and a witness who saw

Simon entering Alpheus's apartment and having a heated argument the night of the murder. You know all about the Latin and Greek connections to the clues left, the underlined phrases, and folded pages matching the written notes at the scene, and, on top of that, the suspect has no alibi. He is hiding something about the victim, and I'd say there's a pretty solid case for his guilt—" Brooks paused and looked up from the folder. "Unless you two detectives think we are missing something?"

Tom hesitated to comment, but Angelo chimed in. "I have my doubts. I do think he's hiding something from Harry's past, but some things don't click."

Brooks scowled. "Click? Is that an ex-con term or something?"

"Do you have the photocopy of the two notes left at the scene?"

Brooks flipped through the folder, pulled out the two copies, and set them in front of Angelo and Tom.

Angelo shook his head. "The writing style's different."

Mullen pointed to the first note. "We confirmed that this one is his handwriting."

Tom glanced up. "We think the *HIM* in English versus Latin might be for *Harold Irving Monnot*, Harry's real name."

"Monnot? So, you've been holding out on us," remarked Brooks as he pushed himself off the desk he was leaning on. "All the more reason to believe Alpheus had some grudge against *him*," said Brooks, making air quotes accompanied by a sarcastic smile. "His ex-wife told us that there was a lot of tension between the two of them when he was dismissed."

"Well, there's got to be a reason Harry changed his name after his dismissal by Alpheus," said Tom.

Brooks sighed. "And Mr. Alpheus doesn't seem to offer any help in that area, although I think he knows something. What is he protecting?"

"Or who?" added Angelo.

Tom and Angelo bumped into Brian Flaherty, who gave them a broad smile on their way out of the station. "Are you two thinking of joining the force? We could certainly use some of God's help these days. Hey, did you hear they may have their guy in the Simon case? That was pretty quick, so maybe we *are* getting some help from upstairs," said Flaherty.

Angelo grunted.

Flaherty asked, "You guys aren't convinced? I don't mean to use a bad pun, but he did sort of point the finger at himself if he's guilty. I'd love to interview him to see if he shows any psychological signs of a killer. Now that would be interesting."

Tom tilted his head. "Well, the truth usually comes out in the end. Now that he's being booked, it would be interesting to talk with him, though."

Flaherty laughed. "Maybe, I could use it as a case study for my final class. By the way, thanks again for talking with me the other day. Those tips were great, and I've tried to keep them in mind when listening to people. I'll have to buy you a beer sometime for another free lesson. You're a great observer of people and what makes them tick."

"I have a feeling that you might be describing yourself, Officer Flaherty," said Tom. "But since you are new at this, be careful. A counselor can do more harm than good if he doesn't know his audience and how they receive help."

Flaherty raised his brow. "I do worry about that. I can only know what they tell me, but what is really going on inside is a different story. I try to empower them to address their own issues, but I'll be careful. Safe home to you."

Tom patted Flaherty on his back before heading to St. Francis with Angelo.

Chapter 16

Standing at the lectern for the morning Mass Gospel reading, Tom looked across the church before beginning and was surprised to see Luke sitting towards the back. Luke rarely got out of bed so early, and Tom wasn't even sure if Luke had recently been attending Mass. He happily shrugged the thought aside and began with the verse from Matthew's Gospel. *"If you forgive men their transgressions, your heavenly Father will forgive you. But if you do not forgive men, neither will your Father forgive your transgressions."*

Tom glanced up, and his shoulders dropped as he realized that Luke had left during the reading. For several moments, he struggled to refocus on the homily he had prepared, part of his attention absorbed by his brother's reaction.

After Mass, he hustled back to the rectory to find Luke sitting at the kitchen table with a cup of coffee. "Hey, brother, how about some pancakes and bacon for breakfast?"

Luke stared into his cup without response.

"I'm sorry if anything at Mass upset you this morning. I was delighted you were there to—"

Luke's head shot up; eyes squinted as his face flushed. "What was that all about? What kind of God is He?"

Grabbing his cup of coffee, Tom pulled out a chair and sat with Luke, waiting several moments before he spoke. "I know."

"You know what?"

"I know how hard it is, except I don't."

"You are confusing me," said Luke with a shake of his head.

Tom's lips tightened. "I know about being angry with God, about being confused by this idea of a loving God and the suffering Corlie endured, the suffering I experienced. It made no sense, but I can't know all you feel because I only blamed God and myself. You have these men who committed evil to blame, to demand justice. I know you feel they need to 'pay' somehow, and it eats you up to know they are free and bear no responsibility. You feel no sense of peace or justice without their remorse. I know all that in my head, but I can't know it in my soul, heart, and bones the way you do."

Taking a deep sigh, Luke rubbed the tips of his fingers up and down on his forehead. "It can't be right for them to be free. No remorse, no price, or punishment for what they did! If God won't make them pay, someone has to!"

"Did the reading today feel wrong to you?"

Luke peered up toward the ceiling, appearing to be biting his tongue, but to no avail. "Yeah. It was wrong. Because I don't forgive these unrepentant bastards, God won't forgive me? What kind of loving, merciful, and just God is that? How is that fair?"

Tom reached out and put his arm around Luke. "I know it doesn't feel fair at all. And I know how much hurt you are still struggling with."

Luke buried his head in his hands for a moment before glaring at Tom. "Do you think I need to forgive these killers who have no remorse? Do you think that would bring real justice to Kathryn's memory?"

Tom gazed softly into his brother's reddened eyes. "I don't think you are looking for a religion lesson right now, are you?"

"I need to understand the right thing to do. I don't know how to process what you read this morning."

Taking a deep breath, Tom ran the palm of his hand across the table, thinking about what to say. "Loving our enemy, truly wanting the best for them, and forgiving people who have hurt the ones we love deeply is hard, confusing, and undesirable, to say the least. That's because we think like men instead of like Christ."

"What does that mean?"

"When we strive for the ideal, to see people as Christ does, we begin to understand things in a different way, and then those hard things can become easier to desire, to give and receive."

Luke scoffed. "I need a different way because, right now, all I want to do is seek revenge, to hurt those men and make them feel the pain she felt."

"I get it. Justice is required, and a sense of justice appears to be lost when forgiveness is given, especially when they fail to ask for it and show no remorse. Naturally, we feel they should *pay* for their sins." Tom turned more squarely toward Luke. "Think about forgiveness this way. Forgiveness doesn't excuse the sin or say it's okay. Forgiveness is really the opposite of that, directly pointing out the sin, acknowledging it, and making it the central focus."

"Huh. I would have never thought of that, but it's not helping yet," said Luke, staring down into his half-full cup.

"I understand. Now, by identifying the sin to be forgiven and then forgiving it, justice will be done through God and fulfilled by mercy. That mercy offered has a greater effect on the one offering it, freeing that person from the effects of sin. Mercy is a way for God to remove the hurt and free us to encounter His mercy all the more by forgiving our sins—something we often don't deserve."

"So we make believe nothing happened? That they didn't do what they did to Kathryn?"

"Not at all. Forgiveness doesn't equal reconciliation unless the offender accepts forgiveness after humbly admitting the sin and transforming it into grace. Forgiveness is up to us, but true justice is a two-way street. The offender has a lot of work to do to reconcile themselves to God and us through a sincerely humble and purifying act of remorse to satisfy justice. Our job is to trust God and do our part. God is in charge of ensuring true justice for the offender, who must repent and seek that forgiveness. If we try to do God's job, we become imprisoned in our own sense of vengeance and do nothing to help the ones we love."

Luke raised his head and grumbled. "That's a lot to chew on, brother."

"It's a big one, but one we can probably only grasp by trusting and doing it. Something unexpected happens when we do stuff *with* God versus on our own."

Angelo opened the door and stepped into the kitchen. "I hope I'm not interrupting anything, am I?"

With half a smile, Luke said, "Perfect timing. Tommy's giving me some homework on justice to think about."

Angelo glanced at Tom and back at Luke. "Okay, I guess. I've been thinking more about Harry Simon. They are charging Jon Alpheus with his murder. Either he is being framed for it with all the clues, or else he's trying to make it appear like he is being framed."

Luke pulled out a chair for Angelo, who remained standing. "Angelo, if Alpheus was framed, then the real killer wanted revenge against Harry *and* him, right?"

"Right. Harry changed his name in 1994, but Harry's first wife indicated that some significant event changed him five years after they married, so that would be 1980. I think we need to go back to Alpheus's apartment to see if we missed anything."

Cocking back his head, Tom pleaded, "No, Angelo. No more breaking into people's apartments."

A half-hour later, Tom peered out through the curtained window down toward the street as Angelo picked the lock to Alpheus's desk. The files were as they'd left them on their previous break-in, and Angelo ran his fingers across them, pulling out 1993 through 1995.

"What are we looking for?" whispered Tom.

"Names. Harold Monnot in '93 and '94 and not in '95."

Tom scanned through all the names as Angelo pulled out his phone and took a picture of each page. "I'm not seeing anything here. What about 1980?"

Angelo pulled out files for 1979 and 1980 and scanned them with his flashlight, taking photos of each page. Nothing new with the lists of the staff.

"Angelo, if you have your pictures, we should leave," said Tom.

"Okay," replied Angelo as he returned the files, locked the desk, and headed to the exit before turning back to Tom, who was pulling a book from the shelf. "I thought you were anxious to leave?"

Tom opened the Ovid book *Metamorphosis* to a page bookmarked by a dried flower. He then snapped it shut and tucked it under his arm before passing Angelo at the open door. "I'm just borrowing it, like a library book. It's for a good cause."

Angelo raised his brow as he quietly closed and locked the door.

Back at the rectory, Luke laughed as Tom and Angelo squinted to make out the photos on Angelo's phone. "Let me get those printed for you before you two go blind."

Angelo glanced at Tom. "Smart man."

"Well, he is from my family." As a broad smile made its way to Angelo's face, Tom followed up with, "Yes, and he got the good looks, too."

The three amateur detectives started analyzing each sheet for anything that stood out. "I see nothing new here that would explain why Harry was forced to leave and change his name. Someone on that list probably knows something or might even be involved," said Tom, just as Luke stopped his finger at a specific name on the list he was inspecting.

"Hey, Angelo, who was the man you followed the day of the funeral?"

"Gately, Sam Gately."

Luke turned the sheet on the table for Angelo and Tom to see. His finger was pointing to the name *Samuel Gately*.

Chapter 17

"I think we should check out this Sam Gately," said Angelo as he kept pace with Tom's long strides toward the police station.

"You know how Brooks feels about us intruding on his cases uninvited," replied Tom.

"Technically, he called you to help, and I think he could use some."

Tom held the door, giving Angelo a dubious glance as they entered and approached the front desk. Before he could say a word, Seargent Doherty quipped, "Brooks was just talking about you two."

Flaherty approached from the front entrance. "Why do I feel like you two are here more than me, and I actually work here?"

Tom gave a playful shrug of his shoulder. "We're just here to pass some information onto Brooks. You might be interested as well since you talked to this person."

Brooks stood inside the detective's room, leaning against his desk with his arms folded and eyebrows raised. "Did you drop by to sell tickets to the church quilt raffle, or do you have something of value for me?" He reached back and grabbed an object, handing it to Angelo. "I believe this is yours."

It was the flashlight Angelo had used to search Alpheus's apartment and must have carelessly left behind. "It's a nice flashlight, but I don't know about it being mine."

Brooks offered a sarcastic smile. "Salvato, you know that all ex-cons' fingerprints are in our database, don't you? And that breaking in and trespassing on a crime scene is still a felony? Maybe you miss the pen more than I thought? Okay, so, what do you have that we missed?"

Tom stepped forward. "We know that Harry's first wife said something happened around 1980 that changed him, and we know that Harry was later forced to change his name. We also know he was forced out of a job he loved, teaching swimming at the Y, in 1994."

"Yep, we all know this," retorted Brooks.

"So, what happened in 1980 and then in 1994? Sam Gately's name showed up in 1979 and 1980, and he attended Harry's funeral, leaving abruptly at one point. We don't know if there is any connection, but he may be worth talking to. I thought Brian might be interested since he talked briefly with him before the funeral Mass started."

Brooks's eyes shifted toward Flaherty. "Anything to contribute?"

"Not really," replied Flaherty. "I don't really know him. I saw him a few times at the library and we talked about a book. He's a bit older than me, and I was surprised to see him at Mr. Simon's funeral. He didn't seem like the type who'd have anything to do with a murder."

Brooks shifted his attention back to Tom and Angelo, raising his open palms. "My amateur detectives and trespassers, do you have anything that connects this Gately to the murder?"

Angelo said, "No idea. Father Fitzpatrick wanted you to check it out instead of us interfering."

Tom held out the book he was clutching. "This is from Alpheus's apartment. It's another copy of Ovid's *Metamorphosis*. I grabbed it—"

"You stole it," interrupted Brooks.

"I borrowed it because I was intrigued by the dried iris flower bookmarker. I haven't had much of a chance to analyze it, but I wondered if it has a connection."

Angelo stared with interest at the book Tom hadn't shared with him.

"I didn't know you were a flower kind of guy. What connection do you think there is?" inquired Brooks.

Tom shrugged. "I don't know. The flower bookmarked a story about the Greek god, Olympian, and medicine healer, Apollo, and Hyacinthus is described as a beautiful Spartan youth who loved sports."

As Mullen entered the room, Brooks rolled his eyes. "Where is this going, and what does it have to do with Harry Simon?"

Flaherty picked the book up to see the etchings of Apollo holding an injured Hyacinthus. "What's the story about, Father Tom?"

Tom pointed to the etchings. "There are several versions of the story. One is that Apollo and Hyacinthus were playing with a discus. Apollo tossed it first to *scatter the clouds*, as Ovid puts it, and Hyacinthus ran after it. Another god, Zephyrus, or 'Westwind,' loved the beautiful young man, Hyacinthus, and was highly jealous of their attachment. This envious god blew the winds so that the discus struck Hyacinthus and killed him." Tom moved his finger down to the etching Flaherty was staring at. "Apollo is distraught, holding Hyacinthus and trying to save him to no avail."

Flaherty continued to stare as Brooks inquired, "What does the flower have to do with it?"

"The myth is that Apollo had a flower, most likely an iris with purple leaves and yellow markings, spring from his blood. I didn't see a strong connection, but there was a small index card between these pages as well that read, *Westwind is a danger to the innocent*."

Brooks stood up and played with an unlit cigarette, shaking his head. "You've completely lost me, Padre."

"Like I said, I'm not sure there's any connection, but one of the notes talked about taking away the *innocence of the world*, so I thought it was worth considering. Maybe Sam Gately could shed some light on things?"

Flaherty raised his head. "Detective, I could try to talk to him if you want."

Mullen stepped forward. "I can go with him too if that works for everyone."

Later that evening, there was a rap on the rectory kitchen door while Tom, Luke, and Angelo were cleaning up after dinner. Cold air swept into the room as Tom opened the door to see Detective Mullen standing on the stoop by herself, which surprised Tom. He'd never spent much time with Jan Mullen without Brooks in tow. "Come in. Come in." Tom waved inside as he held the door wider. "Is everything okay?"

Mullen stepped in. "Oh, sure. Everything is fine. I wanted to let you know that Brian— Officer Flaherty—and I talked with this Sam Gately, and it doesn't seem as if he knows anything. He knew Mr. Simon from the Y from years ago and had seen his obituary in the paper, so he attended the funeral out of curiosity more than anything else."

Angelo frowned. "He seemed very upset for someone just curious, and uncomfortable talking to me about it."

Mullen gave a slight nod. "I remember you saying that, but he was pretty relaxed with us and answered all of our questions. I just wanted you to know that we still have Mr. Alpheus in custody, and Detective Brooks wants to move forward with the charges based on the witnessed argument that night, the opportunity, and the evidence collected. We don't know the motive, but he seems like our guy."

Mullen leaned toward Tom. "Father Tom, I have something else I wanted to ask you about."

Angelo glanced at Luke with a momentary silence, and they both said, "We know when we're not wanted." They said good night to Mullen, and Tom waved her toward the table, offering her some tea.

She shook her head. "No, thanks. I just wanted to ask you something about Officer Flaherty. You know him pretty well, don't you?"

Tom said, "Pretty well. I met him at the first parish I was assigned to in the early 90s. He was a great kid, an altar boy, and a very good ballplayer. I lost contact with him for many years until he joined the police force, and we bumped into each other in the precinct. Why do you ask?"

Mullen blushed. "Well, I don't think I've made too much of a secret about liking him. It's hard to meet people working this job, and it's hard for any girl these days to meet a good man. He seems like someone who cares about people, works hard, and—"

"And, isn't bad looking either?"

Her face turned beet red. "No. I think he's quite handsome."

"Based on your own qualities, it looks like you two would be a good match," replied Tom, with his eyes widened.

"I think so, but I get no movement from him. We're friendly and everything, but nothing more. I guess I'm a bit old-fashioned, but it's nice for a girl to be asked out. I thought you might have inside info to help with some advice."

He shook his head. "Sorry, my match-making skills are a bit rusty. I know he's really focused on finishing up his master's program and doing some counseling on the side. That's a lot with a full-time law enforcement gig, as you know better than me. On the sly, I can see what I can find out if you want me to?"

That brought a sudden smile to Mullen's concerned face. "Thank you, Father. I'd appreciate it."

As Tom let her out the door, he said, "Maybe you two could come to Mass together for your first date?"

Mullen turned, embarrassed. "Oh, sure. You can officiate our wedding for our second date, too!" she said as she started down the driveway.

Chapter 18

After saying Mass, Tom sat at the kitchen table with Luke and set down his coffee as he opened the newspaper. "Today?"

Luke asked, "Today, what?"

Tom turned the paper and pointed. "They are holding a preliminary hearing for Jonas Alpheus this morning. I wanted to hear what evidence they are presenting against him and what his defense will be."

"Do you still agree with Angelo that he might be innocent?"

"In my gut, I just don't know. I'm going to the hearing, but I've got to get back for the noon service," replied Tom.

"What's today?"

Tom tilted his head. "Ash Wednesday, my brother."

"Man, I missed Fat Tuesday last night?"

Despite the cold, Tom could feel the sweat on the back of his shirt from his sprint to the courthouse as he slid into the bench, suddenly aware that Brian Flaherty was next to him.

"Fancy meeting you here, Officer Flaherty."

Flaherty turned, seemingly surprised, and reached over to shake Tom's hand. "Hey, what are you doing in court?"

"Still curious about this case, I guess. Do you think this will go long? I need to be back at St. Francis before noon."

"I don't think so. They're just going to submit initial evidence and arguments to see if there are any motions. I have to be here because I was one of the officers at the scene, but Brooks and Mullen are more likely to be called. Hey, you've got a smudge of something on your forehead."

Tom caught himself reaching for his forehead. "Very funny. Those are called ashes, in case you've forgotten. There are plenty of opportunities to get yours today, Officer Flaherty."

Flaherty's face reddened. "I guess I do owe you for your mentoring." He turned and stared directly into Tom's eyes. "And I never forget anything. You must know that."

Tom realized he was talking about an event from their past. He patted Flaherty on the shoulder, and they listened to the proceedings, which offered little information that Tom didn't already know and a very forceful case against Jonas Alpheus. Tom spent most of the ninety minutes watching Alpheus's expressions, sometimes angry as he grimaced at the questions, but most of the time hanging his head, appearing despondent and numb. Conflicted between the sympathetic figure and the weight of the evidence against him stirred strong feelings inside of Tom.

Tom leaned toward Flaherty. "I've got to get going, but promise to let me know if I miss anything interesting."

"Will do, Father Tom, and safe home."

At the noontime Mass, Tom felt encouraged as he gazed out at a packed church, with many standing in the back. "It is so good to see all of you here as we begin this journey of Lent together. Many of you may already know that Ash Wednesday comes from an ancient Jewish tradition of penance and fasting. Ashes symbolize penance and contrition, grief that we have sinned and turned from God. But remember, it is also a reminder that God is loving and merciful to all those who call on Him with repentant hearts. I love the time of Lent because it's a great opportunity to stop, reflect on our lives and priorities, and grow in our relationship with God."

Tom paused as he scanned the faces of the congregants who attentively listened to his words that he hoped the Holy Spirit was guiding. His gaze paused when he noticed Luke sitting to the side next to Angelo. "For each of us, today can be a turning point. It's an opportunity and a moment where we realize something is wrong with our lives, with our hearts. We repent not just to recognize the sins that turn us away from God but because we realize we are called to something more." A broad smile made its way to his face. "God really, really likes us. He loves us more than we can ever fully realize, but we come to know that he has plans for us, not as mediocre people but as His incredibly beautiful and beloved sons and daughters. So, when we receive ashes on our foreheads, notice what shape it is in—the Sign of the Cross. The ashes are to acknowledge our sins, but its shape lets us know that Jesus claims us as His. He says to us, 'You are Mine,' and He was willing to pay the price for us on that cross. So, let this Lent be an opportunity to turn away from sin and turn back toward God."

When Tom stood to give each parishioner ashes on their forehead, he noticed Brian Flaherty stepping forward, peering up at Tom. Tom pressed his thumb into the ashes in the small glass bowl he was holding and made the Sign of the Cross on Flaherty's forehead. "Remember that you are dust, and to dust, you shall return."

Mass ended, and Tom spotted Flaherty standing in the back and pointing to his watch, letting him know that he needed to get going. Tom gave a slight nod and walked down the aisle.

There would be another Mass at 7:00 p.m. for those who couldn't attend the morning or afternoon services. Tom ate an early dinner with Luke and Angelo and then he returned to the church to hear confessions, starting at 5:00 p.m. As he stepped in, the church was no longer crowded. Still, a scattering of people sat in various pews, praying and waiting for him to enter the confessional box for the Sacrament of Reconciliation.

Tom would meet people face-to-face for this sacrament when they desired. Many did these days, and it made conversation easier for some, but others preferred being able to confess their sins without the priest knowing who they were. They felt freer, to be completely honest, or it was just how they grew up, so he would hear confessions in the confessional boxes built with the church. The priest sat in the middle, and there was a compartment on each side for the penitents to enter and kneel until Tom slid the small panel door to the screened window to listen to their confessions.

Tom shifted in his chair and heard someone enter the compartment on his left. He slid the panel aside and said, "I'm glad you came today. In the name of the Father, and of the Son, and of the Holy Spirit."

A young woman's voice replied, "Bless me, Father, for I have sinned. It has been two months since my last confession." She hesitated and then continued, "These are my sins—"

Before the young woman could continue, an ear-piercing shriek came from the other side of the confessional. Tom jumped from his seat, and when the door flew open, he saw an older woman in black on her knees with her face buried in the palms of her hands. He stepped toward her, heard her sobbing, and then she let out another scream as Tom touched her shoulder with his left hand. Everyone in the church gathered around, and she pulled back, extending her shaking finger as she pointed toward the confessional curtain.

The concerned watchers were deadly silent as Tom stepped toward the confessional and slowly pulled back the heavy red curtain that acted as a door. The dim light inside didn't reveal anything until the curtain was pulled completely back, and a mixture of screams and gasps came from the parishioners surrounding the gruesome sight.

Chapter 19

Tom called Detective Brooks. Within fifteen minutes, the scene was taped off, and the parishioners moved to the back of the church to be interviewed about what they may have witnessed. The curtain was fastened back, and a light aimed at the opening to the confessional box.

"What the heck is this?" asked Brooks.

Taking a second look, Tom could see a burlap-type bag next to the kneeler with some markings. On top of the bag was a human head turned backward with a black Jewish-type covering on top. "I have no idea."

Behind him stood Angelo and Luke, staring directly at the decapitated head.

Brooks squatted down to take a closer look. Photos and forensic evidence still needed to be taken, so he was not moving anything inside the compartment. "Do you know what these writings say? I'm guessing this is Jewish or something based on that cap."

Tom peered closer. "I think it's in Hebrew, and that cap or *kippah* appears inside out. Hold on. One of the parishioners that your officers are interviewing grew up in the Jewish tradition before converting, and I believe he knows Hebrew."

Brooks stood and pointed to the older man with white hair and a beard, waving for Officer Spiro to bring him over. The man cautiously approached, his eyes darting around.

Tom said, "Benjamin, this is Detective Brooks, and we were wondering if you might be able to help us interpret something. I think this might be in Hebrew."

Benjamin stepped forward with Detective Brooks and leaned down, adjusting his glasses to read the writings on the burlap-material bag.

אני רק אבק ואפר

In a soft and weary voice, Benjamin said, "Ah, this makes sense."

"What makes sense?" asked Brooks with a strained tone of impatience.

"The verse is from Genesis. '*I am but dust and ashes.*'"

Tom said, "Hmm. Today is Ash Wednesday. We say almost the same thing when we distribute ashes, and this is a day of repentance, so the confessional may be a clue."

Brooks stood and rolled his eyes. "Please, don't tell me this is about religious mumbo-jumbo stuff again."

Benjamin pointed to the cap on the back of the head. "I don't know about the mumbo stuff, but there is definitely a Jewish religious theme here. The cap is called a *kippah*. You've probably heard the term *yamaka*. It's the same thing. It is a religious head covering or a dome above the head, honoring God, who is always above. I can't tell what's in the bag, but that is sackcloth, and there are many verses in Hebrew scripture about wearing sackcloth with ashes over one's head as a visible sign of repentance for sin. This head has ashes on it."

Tom pressed his lips together at the sight. "Yes, it's meant to be an external demonstration of an internal condition made with sincerity. But there's writing on the *kippah*, too."

Benjamin brought his hand to his lips and gave a few slight nods. "Yes. The *kippah* was put on inside out. It's hard to tell if they did that on purpose and if it has some significance, but the writing is in Hebrew as well."

היום הוא יום כפרה לחפים מפשע

"Remember, Hebrew reads from back to front. These characters are not well done, but I believe it says, 'Today,' ahh, okay—'Today is atonement day for the innocent.'"

Tom exchanged a glance with Brooks. "A connection to the Harry Simon case?"

Brooks rubbed the back of his neck before waving the forensics team in to collect their evidence for analysis. Meanwhile, Tom and Brooks thanked Benjamin for his assistance, and Brooks added, "We may need your help again if we find anything else."

As Benjamin walked to the back where the police interviews continued, Tom pulled Brooks aside. "Detective, we've got a Mass scheduled for seven. Do you think you'll be done with your work here?"

Brooks laughed lightly. "Aren't there enough churches in town for people to get their ashes elsewhere?"

Angelo leaned in. "Father Fitzpatrick, most other churches are starting their services at 7:30. Let Luke and I take care of getting the word out."

"Thanks," Tom said as he noticed an open-mouthed Luke pointing behind him. He turned to see the forensic officer gently loosening the sackcloth twine tie and lifting the opening.

Mullen leaned forward. "What are we looking at?"

The forensic officer replied. "I don't know. This bag is full of ashes and bones—and they look human." As the officer lifted the bag, he retrieved something from underneath it.

Brooks carefully took the small antique book into his gloved hand.

Tom recognized the diamond-shaped design on the faded rose fabric cover. "That's T.S. Eliot's poem called 'Ash Wednesday,' right?"

Brooks shifted his gaze to Tom and then back to the book, opening the hardcover to the first page inside. "I've never heard of it. It looks like a first edition published in 1930 and signed by this Eliot guy, and someone called Isaiah."

Tom stepped beside Brooks, spotting the signature of T.S. Eliot with a slash mark underneath. Below that were the other markings. "I think this signature is authentic, but the one below is more recent—wait a minute, it reads *Isaiah 57:21*. That's from the Old Testament."

"Why should I be surprised?" quipped Brooks. "Isaiah fifty-seven-twenty-what?"

Tom pulled a copy of the Bible from his back pocket, but before he could flip to the Scripture verse, Benjamin, who had made his way back to the scene, said, "There is no safety, said my God, for the wicked."

Brooks rolled his eyes. "Are you a prophet now?"

Tom showed Brooks the verse from the Old Testament reading. "No. He's quoting Isaiah 57:21. I guess the murderer was sending a message, possibly, about his victim."

Brooks asked Tom if they could move to the rectory while the analysis was being completed and the remains removed from the church.

In the small kitchen stood Brooks, Mullen, Tom, Angelo, and Luke. "Oh, I don't think you two have ever met my little brother, Luke."

"Luke, my sympathies for your sibling assignment and your prison mate here, too," joked Brooks, motioning his head toward Angelo.

Luke shook hands with Brooks and Mullen. "Somehow, I've managed to survive it so far. Do you think we're dealing with a serial killer?"

Brooks shifted his eyes back to Tom. "*We're* dealing with? I guess he really is your brother. Look, we know nothing at the moment and don't need anyone getting people panicked with hypotheses. I am interested in your thoughts based on what you saw there."

Tom stood with his hands pressed together against his lips. "I almost don't want to say the possibilities running through my mind."

Angelo said, "You mean that there may be five more murders to go if we don't catch this guy?"

Brooks, Mullen, and Luke turned toward Angelo, confusion filling their eyes. "Five more?"

Tom said, holding up his hand, "We shouldn't get ahead of ourselves, but I think Angelo may be thinking that there is too much of a coincidence with these murders. Both were on Holy Days, and both related in some way to two of the seven sacraments: Baptism and Confession."

Brooks shook his head. "This seemed to be related to a Jewish thing, the kippor, or whatever it's called, the sackcloth and ashes, the Old Testament readings. That doesn't sound like a Catholic sacrament thing to me. Let's not start jumping to any wild conspiracies or serial killer theories before we know what we're dealing with!"

Chapter 20

Standing in the kitchen rectory, Brooks tapped an unlit cigarette against the palm of his hand, glimpsing around at Detective Mullen, Tom, Angelo, and Luke. "Look, I already had my Sunday school lessons for the year, but I need to know if any clues can help us with this case. The head with ashes on it. The cap with the message. The sackcloth is full of ashes, bones of who knows who, and then there's the book of poetry under the sack. If these murders are connected, this guy seems like a lunatic."

Angelo pulled the table from the wall and brought two more chairs so the five could sit. "Do you want coffee or a cold drink? You might need some Moxie for this one, Brucato."

"Coffee for me," replied Brooks with a sigh.

Mullen and Luke both raised their hands.

Tom placed a notebook on the table and began jotting down the evidence they had so far. "We don't know if the victim is Jewish, but the cap or kippah and the Hebrew Scripture readings point to the possibility. The strong references to repentance with the sackcloth, dust, and ashes, and the 'Day of Atonement' with the ashes on the head are clear, so the connection to Ash Wednesday makes sense."

"Why the connection to Ash Wednesday?" Mullen sipped her hot coffee.

Tom replied, "Christianity and the Catholic Church come from the Jewish tradition. It's the fulfillment of the whole story of salvation the Jewish people were custodians of and lived. Jesus was Jewish and honored his faith. Jewish Passover is fulfilled in the Eucharist. Yom Kippur is a high holiday and the Day of Atonement for the penitent to turn back to God. That is what Ash Wednesday is all about. Harry Simon's death was surrounded by symbols and clues related to Baptism, and everything I have seen tonight is related to

Confession or Reconciliation—a strong theme of Ash Wednesday."

Brooks scanned the kitchen. "There's no way for me to escape this, is there?"

The shadow of a smile appeared on Angelo's face. "I don't think so. Not if you want to solve this case."

"Okay. Educate me, but keep it as short as possible."

Tom noticed his brother's smirk as he began, "Okay, so Lent starts on Ash Wednesday. It is a time for true self-examination and realizing we have gotten off the track and turned away from God in one way or another. I think that's why Eliot's book was under the sackcloth."

Brooks put down his coffee with a loud clink. "Slow down. I'm getting lost. What does the poem have to do with this?"

"'Ash Wednesday' was a conversion poem for T.S. Eliot. It's about someone who lacked faith and then found it, moving from spiritual barrenness to the hope of human salvation. We turn from a life where we are hollow men, more dead than spiritually alive, and—"

Luke leaned forward. "I get it. When we turn away from God and try to create our own selves, we are less, and it never works. Didn't the poem talk about having wings that are no longer wings to fly? And the ashes symbolize our frailty?"

Tom nodded. "I'm impressed. When we turn away from God and seek our own plans instead of His, we are empty. That may be why the head was turned backward, and there were ashes on top, saying he needed to confess, repent, and turn back to God, who is 'gracious, compassionate, slow to anger and abounding in love,' as Eliot puts it.'"

"Tommy, there's a line about 'dead bones' offered to God, isn't there?" added Luke.

Tom raised his brow. "That's right, and that might explain the bones in the sackcloth. I feel that the person who did this thought the victim would not atone for whatever sin he committed and needed to pay for it. It's hard to tell if the killer was a victim of the dead man or if this was a revenge killing."

There was a rapping sound at the kitchen door. Luke popped up and let in the policeman. Brooks glanced over, and the officer leaned in, whispered something in his ear, and then left. Brooks paused for several moments. "It looks like we have an I.D. of the victim. I can't have anyone letting this out beyond us for now. Do I have your word?"

Everyone nodded.

"The victim's name is Joel Silverman. He was seventy-nine, so no spring chicken, and worked as a psychiatrist in an office at the corner of Tremont and Rutland."

Angelo murmured, "Huh."

"What is it, Salvato? Those *huhs* always mean something," quipped Brooks.

"Harry Simon was a swim instructor, and his death was focused on water and Baptism. What do people do in a psychiatrist's office?"

Tom leaned in. "They examine their lives and confess their innermost secrets, fears, or even their sins to get better. I think Angelo may have something there."

"Yeah, well, that's a stretch I'm not willing to put any money on yet. Officer Spiro did mention one other thing. They found a branch, some type of woody, cedar-smelling tree on top of the confessional box Dr. Silverman was placed in," replied Brooks.

Tom quirked one eyebrow. "Was it a juniper tree?"

Brooks squinted. "How did you know?"

"It's in Eliot's poem—'three white leopards sat under a juniper tree.' I think I remember this being his reference to Dante's *Divine Comedy*, where three beasts represent three types of sin in hell. Let's see. There was a wolf for the malicious sins of fraud and betrayal, the ravenous lion represents the sins of violence, and the leopard symbolizes the lust of the flesh. It's the leopards who eat all the organs and flesh, leaving just the bones."

"What's the point?" asked Mullen.

In the poem, the leopards feed on the poet's legs, liver, heart, and brain, the sources of his energy, anger, passion, and intellect. The leopard represents the sin of lust that has wasted and consumed him. In the Old Testament Scripture, the juniper tree is where Elijah sat to die but receives rest and renewal."

Angelo added, "But for Dr. Silverman, there was 'no safety for the wicked' as the Scripture verse in Isaiah says. This definitely sounds like revenge for justice and a lot of work to leave clues, just like the other case." Angelo turned to Brooks. "Are you sure you've got the right man in custody?"

Brooks snapped back, "Salvato, you know better than anyone how deceptive criminals can be. There are plenty of copycat killers out there, so I'm not jumping from one amateur wild-goose-chasing hypothesis to the next!"

Chapter 21

Luke watched as Angelo made his last move to beat Tom in their chess match for the second time that evening.

"Not that it would have made a difference, but you weren't really concentrating tonight," said Angelo, tipping over Tom's king with his knight.

Tom raised his brow. "Sorry. The game got me thinking about a line from Eliot's poem: 'Shall these bones live?' Funny, chess pieces are sometimes made of bones, and it's almost as if the killer is knocking off the enemy's pieces to avenge some serious wrong. Maybe he sees himself as a knight defending those who can't seek their own justice?"

Luke stared at the knight piece he was now holding in his hand. "Most of the clues seem to point to the sins of the victims and why they deserved their executions. I think you're right, though; it may also say something about victims of those killed or the killer himself or herself—who knows?"

Hours later, Tom lay restlessly in bed, images from the two scenes of murder filling his head, only to be broken by a faint tapping from the kitchen. He rolled to see the glowing numbers of his bedside clock showing 12:15 a.m. and squinted twice to make sure he was reading it correctly before his feet hit the cold floor. The kitchen was dark, lit only by the dim light from the waxing moon through the window over the sink. Tom could see a dark silhouette outside and hesitated.

The figure rapped again.

Tom half-opened the door, and a familiar voice said, "Sorry to drop by so late. I hope I didn't wake you."

Tom ran his fingers through his hair. "Detective Brooks, come in. Don't worry about waking me. I had to get up to answer the door, anyway."

Brooks rolled his eyes as he stepped into the kitchen, rubbing his hands together to warm them from the cold night outside.

"Let me get you something warm to drink."

Brooks nodded, and they sat at the table. "I've been too restless to sleep, worrying about these murders. Look, I'm not so blind that I can't see the real possibility of the same killer involved in these two deaths. That only means the clock is ticking before another body and another set of crazy clues I can't get my head around is found."

Tom squinted as he sipped his hot cup of tea, seeing a different side of Brooks. "You really do care? I don't just mean about the victims, but that people in this town are protected and safe, don't you?"

Brooks raised his head, seemingly taken by Tom's observation. "Of course, no different than you care about the people's souls in this town. I know you do, and it means a lot that you care enough to fight for them."

Tom raised his cup in Brooks's direction. "Maybe we have more in common than we thought. So, what are you thinking?"

Brooks lifted the small book from his coat and placed it on the table. "I don't know what to think. All these religious references are out of my league and hard to get a handle on. I wanted you to take a look at this to see if anything stands out. It's the book that was found under the victim. We've dusted for fingerprints, DNA, and fiber particles so you can handle it now."

Tom held it carefully as he opened the cover to see the reference to the Isaiah verse. "I think it read, 'There is no safety—said my God, for the wicked.' It's a guess, but I think this killer believes he is acting as God's executioner for those who have committed a grave sin and refused to repent."

"Okay, I've got that part, but is there anything else that can lead us to this killer? Can we go into the church again to look over the scene?"

Tom said, "Sure, let me get on my shoes and a coat."

As they walked across the driveway, a myriad of stars shone brightly in the crisp winter sky, adding to the quiet stillness of the night. Tom opened the large wooden door and turned on the light over the confessional box where the remains of Joel Silverman had laid just hours earlier.

Brooks squinted. "Why here? Why the head, the ashes, and the bones? Why that book? We found no fingerprints other than Dr. Silverman's, so the killer knows how to cover his tracks while taking the time to leave all these cryptic messages."

Tom opened T.S. Eliot's book, *Ash Wednesday*, trying to see the connections. He flipped through the pages, stopping at a verse. "Someone underlined verses and left notes. Let's see, *And the light shone in the darkness* has a heavy underline, *silent word* and then, *Our peace in his will*. There's a note in the margin. *No peace for the wicked, but peace for the innocent.* There's that word *innocent* again. Same as with the Harry Simon case."

In the dim light, Brooks glanced at the phrases Tom pointed to. "What stands out?"

"If the killer made these markings, they might believe they are shining a light in the darkness where the victim is silent. The verse *Our peace in his will* is a play on a line in Dante's *Divine Comedy* that starts with the author's journey to hell, then purgatory, and finally heaven, where we realize *In His will is our peace*. I take it from the note in the margin that the killer doesn't believe Joel is going to heaven."

"I doubt the killer will be on that train either."

Tom continued to page through until he spotted another verse underlined. "Let's see, here, they've underlined, *spirit of the fountain, spirit of the garden*. We know Harry was placed in the fountain, and I guess he may be referencing the juniper branch he placed above the confessional as *the garden*? I don't know, but there is a note here too. *But the worthless, every one of them will be thrust away like thorns.*"

"I wonder," said a voice from the darkness startling Tom and Brooks. Angelo stepped into the light, and they both sighed with relief.

"You wonder what, Salvato?" queried Brooks.

"Sorry to interrupt, but I saw the lights on. When I followed Sam Gately after he left the funeral, I ended up at his apartment on Tremont. Harry Simon and Jonas Alpheus both lived in that area, and the Y is one street over, and now we have *the garden*."

Brooks impatiently asked, "Can you make some sense?"

"It didn't hit me until I bedded down for the night. When I was walking down Tremont, I remembered that corner at Rutland Street. There was a small office building called The Garden, and the front was full of rose plantings. Nothing is blooming this time of year, but I know roses well enough. One of the signs in front said, 'Rose and Silverman Psychiatric.' Maybe that's why the killer left his head, because he was a shrink, a head doctor?"

"I wish I had your eyes and memory, Angelo," said Tom. "That note about *thrusting away the thorns* is a Hebrew scriptural reference. And I found another set of verses underlined in this book.

The single Rose
Is now the Garden
Where all loves end
Terminate torment

"The first lines are supposed to be about the union of divine and human love, but the *terminate torment* line is heavily underscored. Do you think the reference to the *single Rose* is highlighted to point to Dr. Silverman's partner in the practice? Maybe something bad about Dr. Rose spread through the garden and needed to be cut out?"

Brooks held out his hand for Tom to hand the book back. "There's one way to find out—and don't you two start breaking into dead doctor's offices. I think it's still illegal these days."

As he handed back the book, Tom pointed to the publishing date on the inside page. "Maybe it's a coincidence, but the killer may have picked this book for multiple reasons. This book is a 1930 edition, the same year Joel Silverman was born, and he also died on this book. The killer may somehow know Silverman pretty well, but the question is how he came to know him."

Smirking, Brooks said, "And maybe Silverman just bought the book because it was published in his birth year? Don't get into too many conspiracy theories. Leave the analysis to the experts."

Angelo curled his lip. "The initials on the inside cover are *J.C.A* versus *J.S.*, and the book focused on Catholic and Anglican themes. If he was a devout Jew, it may not have been high on his list to own and engrave it with someone else's initials. Just a thought."

The dim light hid most of the sudden flush to Brooks's face. "Wiseguy, and how many J.C.A.'s do you know?"

"Jonas Christos Alpheus might be one," replied Angelo.

"Nice work, Angelo!" said Tom as he gave him a pat on the back.

Brooks rolled his eyes. "And I bet you always did your best work in the middle of the night."

After Brooks left, Tom turned to Angelo and narrowed his eyes at him. "I'm not going to be talked into it. Ask me seventy times seven, and the answer will be no every time. Okay?"

With a long hesitation and a deep sigh, Angelo replied with noticeable reluctance in his voice, "Okay, chief."

Chapter 22

Later that Thursday morning, Brooks entered the police station. Seargent Doherty motioned toward the bench where Tom and Angelo sat. Brooks' gaze shifted toward the ceiling as if praying their presence was an illusion. Without a word, he waved them toward the front entrance, where he pulled out a cigarette and took a long drag. "Please, don't tell me you broke into the doctor's office after I left."

Tom put his hand on Brooks' shoulder. "That would be illegal. You know that, Detective. We were just curious if you had any news."

Brooks exhaled smoke from his pursed lips. "You both know you don't work here, right?" There was a long pause as he rubbed his palm across his forehead. "Look, I know you guys want to help and have helped. I truly appreciate it, but some things are confidential police business."

"So, you got the files from Silverman's office and found some names," said Angelo.

"Maybe."

Tom and Angelo moved closer.

Brooks stared up and then sighed. "Okay, but this goes nowhere, or I'm on the street with a tin cup. We got a warrant for Silverman's files and found two names of interest. He saw Sam Gately for many sessions in 1980 and then again in 1991, and finally, he was part of a group therapy between 2005 and 2007."

Nodding, Tom said, "Wow. That's a very interesting connection, and don't worry about confidentiality. What was the other name?"

Brooks eyed Angelo and then Tom with a long hesitation in his reply. "Alpheus. He saw him in 1980 and then again in 1994 for several sessions. Also, Silverman's partner's name was Dr. Aviel Rose. The two of them have been at that location for over thirty years and often covered for each other's clients or customers or whatever you guys call them."

Angelo inquired, "Did you talk with Rose?"

"Not yet. Later today. We have a warrant to search his office and apartment, as well. If you come back this afternoon, we may have some more pieces to this holy puzzle," replied Brooks as he blew another puff of smoke.

Tom smirked. "I heard those might not be too good for you, Detective. Thanks for the invite, though."

Tom and Angelo started back to the rectory when Angelo took an unexpected turn down Tremont Street. "Angelo, we can't be going to the doctor's office while the police are searching it."

"Who's going to the doctor's office? I think we should try to talk with Sam Gately to see if there is any connection to Silverman. I heard he works at a coffee and bagel shop down the street here, so we may be able to catch him." Angelo's pace picked up as they searched for the shop. A hundred yards down the road, he pointed. "There it is."

Tom glanced up to see the *Cup-O-Joe* sign where the *O* was an artistically painted bagel. "I'm getting hungry."

Angelo and Tom entered the coffee shop, sat at a table tucked in a back corner, and glanced around for any signs of Sam Gately. Tom volunteered to order some coffee and bagels at the counter and spotted Sam sitting at a small table near the employee-only door. He was wearing the same Cup-O-Joe's shirt as the other employees and must have been taking a break, since he was reading a book. After ordering, Tom approached Sam's table. "Hi, Sam."

Sam looked up, his eyes widening. "Ah, hi. You're that priest."

"Well, I'm one of them. Are you on a break?"

He nodded.

"Would you like to join us? I can buy you a bagel."

Sam squinted cautiously, clearing his throat. "Why do you want to talk to me?"

Tom's eyes softened as they peered into Sam's piercing blue eyes. "Just being neighborly. How do you like working here?"

Sam shrugged, slid from his seat, picked up his cup and book, and followed Tom. "It's okay. I haven't been here all that long." He stopped short and stepped back as he spotted Angelo at the table. "He followed me. Why is he here?" He rubbed his hand through his overgrown curly red hair.

Tom pulled out a chair. "Sam, this is Angelo. He's a good guy, and you're not in any trouble. We're here as friends."

Setting his book aside, Sam sat, staring down into his cup of coffee. "I don't know what you want to talk about."

Tom gave a reassuring smile. "We just wanted to know how you're doing. You seemed upset at the funeral. It was a terrible thing that happened to Harry."

Sam's head jerked back, his voice stronger. "I guess that depends on your perspective. Maybe someone thought Mr. Mon—Simon deserved it?"

Tom glanced down at the old book Sam was holding. "You like to read?"

Sam's face relaxed at the question.

Tom pointed. "Is that Yeats?"

His eyes widened as if talking about an old friend. "Yeah. 'The Second Coming' is my favorite after 'Leda and the Swan.' Do you know it?"

"Things fall apart; the centre cannot hold;
Mere anarchy is loosed upon the world,
The blood-dimmed tide is loosed, and everywhere
The ceremony of innocence is drowned;
The best lack all conviction, while the worst
Are full of passionate intensity," recited Tom.

A broad smile made its way to Sam's face. "You do know it! Few seem to these days, and few appreciate poetry and literature."

Tom opened the book to the inside cover. "Hey, this is a first edition. You're a lucky man with good taste. For Yeats, in 1919, with World War I, the turmoil in Ireland, and chaos in the world, the signs of the second coming of Christ must have seemed to be very much at hand."

Sam's eyes drifted to his cup again.

Tom said softly, "I was always struck by the thought that one's center cannot hold and innocence is drowned. It has to be such an overwhelming feeling."

Sam abruptly stood up, excusing himself, his eyes narrowed in anger. "I-I have to go. I have to go back to work now. Please leave me alone. I just want peace." He quickly disappeared around the corner.

A waitress came to the table to deliver their coffee and bagels. Tom spied the name on her tag. "Thank you, Alyce. That looks great. Have you worked here long?"

"Almost four years. I'm a senior at Northeastern."

"And the question I'm sure no one has ever asked you—what is your major?"

"Occupational therapy. I have a practicum at Beth Israel, too," she replied.

"Well, an early congratulations and the best of luck. We talked with Sam Gately while he was on his break."

Alyce stiffened a bit. "Yeah, Sam has been here for a few months."

"Has he been any different lately?" asked Angelo.

"He's always different," replied Alyce. After a pause, rubbing her fingers across her lips. "He has seemed a little agitated, even angry lately. He didn't show up for work on Wednesday, but I'm not the boss. Speaking of work, I've got to get back. I hope you enjoy your Cup-O-Joe."

Angelo whispered to Tom. "That was interesting."

Tom bit into his bagel and added, "Do you know what else was interesting? There were initials on the inside cover of Sam's book. *J.C.A.*"

Chapter 23

Later that afternoon, Tom approached the church's side entrance to see Angelo clearing some ice on the steps. "I'm heading to the station to see if they've talked to Dr. Rose yet. Are you interested?"

Angelo shrugged. "I am interested, but I think I'll let you check it out alone. Brooks is a bit suspicious of me and might be more open to sharing information about a psychiatrist's patients without me in the picture."

"I can't disagree with your logic. I'll let you know what I find out," Tom replied before trekking to the Harrison Avenue station.

When Tom entered, Seargent Doherty waved him to the desk. "Brooks was asking if you had dropped by yet. They're bringing that shrink doctor into the interrogation room for questioning now. They want me to take you into the viewing room if you're up for it."

"Sure," replied Tom as he followed Doherty to the now-familiar two-way mirror. He sat and waited. Suddenly, Mullen opened the interrogation room door, and in walked a large balding man wearing a tweed-type jacket and a peeved expression in his eyes.

Brooks lifted his head. "Mr. Rose?"

"*Doctor* Rose. For what possible reason have I been brought down here as if I were some common criminal?" chided Rose.

"Dr. Rose, please sit. We just need to ask you some simple questions, and all you have to do is tell us what you know—truthfully," Brooks replied as Mullen pulled out a chair for him to sit. "Do you know Dr. Joel Silverman?"

Rose furrowed his forehead. "Of course I do! He's been my partner for over thirty years. What has he done?"

Mullen leaned forward to make eye contact. "I don't know if anyone has informed you, but we found his—well, we found him dead. Murdered, actually."

The chair squealed as he stood, and the leg scraped across the floor. "What? You must be mistaken! I just saw him."

"When did you see him?"

"Yesterday. Today is my day off, and he's probably seeing patients right now. Obviously, this is a mistake," replied Rose, now glancing nervously around the room.

"Dr. Rose, we have confirmation that the victim was your partner, Dr. Joel Silverman. If you can sit back down, we just need your help on some things," implored Brooks as he pointed to the empty chair.

Rose slumped back down, adjusting his shirt collar. "This can't be right. When, where—how did this happen?"

"Could you tell us about your partner, Joel Silverman?" asked Mullen as she held her pen over an open notebook.

"I have never known a better doctor or a better man. No one would ever have any reason to hurt—never mind kill—him. He helped so many people, so many troubled people. He was a loving man, not a religious man, but a good man. Oh, God. I can't believe this," replied Rose, staring down at the table. "*Baruch Dayan HaEmet.*"

"Can you tell us about your day yesterday?" asked Brooks as he pulled the cigarette box from his coat and held it.

Rose ran his hands across the desk. "Yesterday? Ah, yes. Wednesday is Dr. Silverman's day off, and I am in the office."

"So, he did not come to the office on Wednesday?"

"Not normally, but he did come in the morning. He must have had an emergency request for a session. As I remember, it was quite loud, and I stayed in my office to avoid making the client uncomfortable when they left."

Brooks pulled a cigarette from the carton, bringing it close to his nostril. "Did you talk with him?"

"The client?"

"No. Dr. Silverman."

"I don't believe so. I was busy, and I think he left without saying anything."

"What time did he leave?"

"It was an early appointment, so maybe around ten. I don't really know."

Mullen jotted on her notebook. "Dr. Rose, did you stay in the office the entire afternoon?"

"I don't take clients on Wednesdays since I use that day to review my sessions and do paperwork. I did go out for a few hours, sometime mid-afternoon. Are you asking for any particular reason? I hope you don't think I could be responsible for this murder?" Rose turned to each detective. "Do you?!"

"We just need to be thorough. I hope you appreciate that." Brooks held onto the cigarette as if he wanted to take a drag.

Tom watched Rose's body language and listened to his voice change as he was told about Silverman's death or asked uncomfortable questions about his whereabouts. He pulled a small notebook from his coat pocket and quickly jotted something down. He waved to the officer at the door, tore off the small sheet, and handed it to him. "Can you take this to Detective Brooks or Mullen?"

The officer took the note, and several seconds later, Tom watched him enter the interrogation room and hand Brooks the paper, who quickly read it and raised his head. "Dr. Rose, do you know a Jonas Alpheus?"

Rose stared at the mirrored wall and shifted uncomfortably in his seat. "Sure. I think he came to our practice for help a few times."

"Did he see you or Dr. Silverman?"

"I think we both saw him at different times and compared notes."

Brooks leaned forward. "Compared notes?"

"Confidentially, of course. He had some difficult struggles to talk through. That's why we are here—to help those who need help."

"And did you know a Sam Gately?"

Rose scratched the sparse hair on the side of his scalp. "Gately? Gately? Maybe. The name does sound familiar. I would have to check the files."

Brooks placed the cigarette between his lips, pressing down. "We've already checked Dr. Silverman's files, and we should know about yours shortly."

Rose's head snapped back, and he jumped to his feet. His face turned red as his eyes widened in anger. "What? I came here to help, and you are trespassing in my office without my permission? My files are confidential. This is outrageous!"

"No, it's called a warrant. Sit down, Mr. Rose."

"It's *Doctor* Rose! And I want to see my lawyer."

Mullen lifted her hand. "Dr. Rose, you are not under arrest or being charged with anything. We are looking for information to help find out what happened to your partner." Brooks slid the notepaper to Mullen, who said, "Just two more questions, Dr. Rose. Have you ever met Harry Simon or Harold Monnot?"

Rose continued standing. "Monnot? Dr. Silverman saw him. I think he felt forced into therapy sessions and was never cooperative if I remember correctly. That was long ago, so I would have to check his notes."

"And the final question for now," said Mullen as she squinted and re-read the note. "Do you think T.S. Eliot is overrated?"

Rose stiffened and his eyes squinted as if he was confused by the question. "What?"

"Do you think T.S. Eliot is overrated?"

"That is the silliest thing I've ever heard. He was a giant of modern literature, maybe the greatest poet of all time. How can you ask that?"

Brooks stood up, directly facing Rose, who may have been four inches taller than him. "I always forget, but was it Eliot or that other guy who wrote that silly 'Ash Wednesday' poem? It hardly even rhymes."

Rose turned to the door. "I want my lawyer."

Chapter 24

At the station, the large detectives' room was buzzing with activity. Next to Brooks' old wooden desk, Tom sat on a hard chair, waiting for Brooks and Mullen to arrive. A detective sporting a full crop of hair, a beard, and a leather jacket, walked up to him. "Hey, Father, did you punch in when you got here? You know they don't pay you around here if you don't clock your time!"

A few of the guys burst out laughing as Tom nodded. "Funny, God works the same way, but thanks for the friendly tip. I'll have to remember that."

"Good one, Father," quipped one of the guys. "I didn't know that God had a sense of humor."

"You'd better hope that he does!" bantered another, handing Tom a cup of coffee.

Finally, Brooks and Mullen entered the room. Mullen approached the whiteboard, which was covered with photos of the victims and associates, and took a blue marker to draw connections between Dr. Rose and Silverman, Alpheus, Gately, and a dotted line to Harry Simon. "Thanks for those questions, Father Tom. What made you ask that one about Eliot?"

Tom set the coffee cup down on Brooks' desk. "I was curious if he knew his work intimately or not. He seemed very uncomfortable with the questions. I mean, anyone would be uncomfortable, but he seemed easily agitated for a man who has practiced psychiatry for so many years."

Mullen turned on the desk to face Tom and squinted with curiosity. "Do you think he is capable of doing something like this—to a friend?"

Tom raised his eyebrows. "I have a hard time thinking anyone could do something like this, but we're all capable. You never really know what lies beneath the surface of someone you think you know, someone you think could never do evil to another. I have no idea if he could or would do this, but I think you need to check him out."

Mullen furrowed her brow. "Hmmm. Do you know what Dr. Rose said when we told him about Silverman's death? Was it Jewish?"

"*Baruch Dayan HaEmet*, if I have that right. It means 'Blessed is the Judge of Truth.' It's hard to say if he was referring to Silverman or himself."

Brooks lifted several plastic bags. "Well, forensics is still scouring the two offices of Silverman and Rose, but these are a few items they retrieved from Rose's apartment on Comm Ave. I guess it's a very nice place. Very clean, especially when we got there, but some things may have been overlooked."

Tom tilted his head to see if he could identify the contents. "What did you find?"

"Specs of blood in the bathroom corners where the grout meets the tile. The tub, floor tiles, and several rows of wall tiles were obviously scrubbed recently, but spatters can travel farther than you might think. We're running DNA tests on the samples. We also found residue of ash in the fireplace. Not a lot since that had been cleaned as well, but we are checking it out."

Tom furrowed his brow. "What do you have in those bags?"

Brooks held out one bag. "This contains small hardcover books very similar to Eliot's *Ash Wednesday* found under the victim in your church. Eliot, some guy named Ezra Pound, let's see Yeats, Blake, Auden. We want to see if any forensic evidence, fibers, prints, or markings are similar to the *Ash Wednesday* book."

"Did any have initials inside the cover?"

Brooks smiled, "You mean like J.C.A.? Just the book by Pound. Don't worry, Father Brown, we're catching up to your shrewd observational expertise."

Smiling, Tom pointed at the bag. "And what's in that?"

Turning the bag toward himself, Brooks replied, "This? This is confidential, but it looks like Silverman's notes about a counseling group he ran for several years. It appears that the group met at some other location and was the same group in which Sam Gately participated. We need some ruling on our rights to review this."

"Interesting. I understand the confidentiality requirement and appreciate that you guys actually respect that."

Brooks grunted. "It looks as if Silverman sent a note to Rose in a panic that he could no longer facilitate the group and asked Rose to step in."

"Did the note say why?"

"Nope. Rose just jotted on the note—*Don't worry. I'll make sure no one knows.*"

Tom pointed. "You've got one more bag there. Can I ask?"

Laying the bag on the desk, Tom stood to take a closer look. Through the thick plastic, he could see a fillet knife with the same type of handle as the boning knife found in Alpheus's apartment that could have been used to cut out Harry Simon's heart. Was this used to slice Joel Silverman's body parts from its bones? "Are you starting to think there might be a connection between the two murders?"

Mullen eyed Brooks. "There are definitely connections, but no solid leads to be sure."

Tom scanned the whiteboard with the names and faces of the victims and possible suspects. "Angelo and I talked with Sam Gately for a bit at the coffee shop where he works."

Brooks stared up at the ceiling in apparent disbelief. "Any chance you would let the actual police do these interviews?"

Tom raised his eyebrows.

Brooks sighed. "What do you have?"

"Nothing, really. He seemed awkward, possibly had a troubled past. He definitely thought Harry Simon deserved what he got and became angry when the topic came up. One of the girls who work there thought he seemed more agitated or quick to anger recently. She also thought he always seemed 'different.'"

"I don't think *different* gets you convicted of anything these days. Is that it?" queried Brooks.

Nodding, Tom said, "Pretty much. There was a reason he came to a funeral for someone he believed deserved to die like that. Oh, yeah. He was reading a book of poems by William Butler Yeats on his break."

"Yippee, more poetry. I don't think that's against the law these days, but I'll check that out for you."

"The book was an antique, like the Eliot book found with Silverman, and—"

Brooks held out his hand. "And?"

"And it had the same initials inside the cover. *J.C.A.*"

Brooks leaned back in his chair. "Our friend, Alpheus, does seem to get around, doesn't he?"

"At least his books do," replied Tom as he stood. "Thanks for letting me listen in. I think I'll be heading back to the monastery."

"Let me walk you out," said Brooks as he accompanied Tom into the brisk winter air. "Father, Tom, you still do a lot of psychology work, right?"

"Whenever people need an ear or some advice. Yes. Why?"

Brooks pulled a cigarette out from his coat pocket to light it. "Do any of these characters seem to you as if they could scheme these murders and actually do it?"

Tom held out his hands to shield the match from the breeze and then rubbed the back of his neck. "I've been asking myself the same question. Like I said before, you think you know someone, and I mean really know them, and then they turn out to be completely different inside, capable of doing something you'd bet your life against them ever doing. Some people present an outer persona to the world, but underneath is the real person, often hurt or even the victim of some traumatic event that harbors deep fear and anger. The farther apart our outer self is from our inner self, the more volatile that protective anger can be. We may even fantasize about doing things that the public persona would never do."

Brooks exhaled smoke, a billowing cloud rising into the clean air. "I guess you're right, but what does your instinct tell you?"

Pursing his lips, Tom paused. "It tells me not to guess until we know more."

"Maybe you are more suited to be a cop than a priest?" quipped Brooks with a laugh. They stood in silence for a moment as Brooks glanced around. "I don't want to give you a heart attack or anything, but I have a lot of respect for you and how genuine you are about your work."

Tom relaxed, and his eyes widened a bit. "I appreciate that. I could say the same thing about you, but—I know you wouldn't want me to. Are you telling me this for a reason?"

Brooks squinted as he rubbed his hands to stay warm. "Do I need a reason? Okay, you make me think about stuff. You know. Stuff about my life and what the point is to it all." He glanced up at Tom and seemed to become uncomfortable. "Look. I've got to get going. I just wanted to thank you, that's all." Brooks headed into the precinct without another word or glance, leaving Tom speechless but very happy.

Chapter 25

The winter chill had taken a break for an unseasonably mild Saturday morning. Tom stood with Angelo under a tree in the Baker Street Jewish Cemetery. He peered across the multitude of gravestones, noticing that the sun had melted most of the snow, though there were still patches in shadier spots. On the other side of him stood Brian Flaherty, who whispered, "I've never been to a Jewish funeral before. Brooks asked if I could come to see if any familiar faces attended. There aren't a lot of people here."

Tom leaned over. "The family will arrive with Dr. Silverman's body and the rabbi. It's not hugely different than other burial services, but this is considered a holy act and this holy cemetery ground."

"What are you guys doing here?" asked Flaherty, staring at his feet as if to wonder if where he was standing was okay.

"Just amateur curiosity," replied Angelo as he pointed to the black car from the funeral home pulling up and several people dressed in black getting out. Dr. Aviel Rose and Rabbi Moshe emerged from the second car. Tom had met the rabbi on previous occasions.

Several pallbearers, including Rose, another older man, and a younger man probably from the family, joined in carrying the plain wooden casket toward the gravesite, stopping several times to pray. Finally, the family stood next to the graveside while more family and friends gathered behind them in support. The rabbi said prayers in Hebrew, and the few who knew their faith responded.

Tom observed but was distracted by some movement behind another tree. He tapped Flaherty's shoulder and motioned with this head toward the tree, whispering, "Is that Sam? Sam Gately over there with someone?"

One of the mourners turned toward Tom, squinting in disapproval at his talking, and he felt his cheeks turn beet red as he motioned for her attention back toward the rabbi.

Fallen Graces

"Let me check," replied Flaherty, who quietly made his way towards the tree.

Tom wondered if the other family members were Silverman's brother or sister, son, and wife. Before lowering the casket, Rose stepped forward, thanking everyone for paying their respects to Silverman. He opened his coat and reached his hand over his left shirt side and tore it, then said he wanted to read a poem that was a favorite of the deceased.

Tom listened as Rose recited the verses,
"We shall not cease from exploration
And the end of all our exploring
Will be to arrive where we started
And know the place for the first time."

Trying to identify the poem, he remembered just as Rose was completing the final verse,
"And all shall be well and
All manner of thing shall be well
When the tongues of flame are in-folded
Into the crowned knot of fire
And the fire and the rose are one."

Leaning toward Angelo, Tom whispered, "That's from T.S. Eliot's *Four Quartets*."

The same woman turned again with a nastier scowl as she gave Tom another burning stare. Angelo handed Tom a handkerchief for him to feign some tears as he tried not to acknowledge her admonishing look. The family gathered around the grave to watch the casket's lowering and shoveled dirt onto it to help bring closure. Tom thought of the ashes over Silverman's head found in the confessional box only three days earlier.

As the family turned to leave, the others formed two lines to show support as they passed through, and recited, "May the Almighty comfort you among all the mourners of Zion and Jerusalem."

Finally, the mourners dispersed, and Tom noticed Flaherty approaching him. "I think you were right that someone was there, but I couldn't see anyone when I reached the tree. I don't think they blended in with the mourners since most of the people attending were pretty old."

Tom turned toward Angelo, but he was nowhere in sight. Turning back to Flaherty, Tom smiled. "I think you might have hurt his feelings."

Flaherty paused. "Oh, sorry about that." They started walking together down the path as the cemetery workers gathered to complete the burial work. "Father Tom, I'm hearing some buzz that there might be some connection between the Simon and the Silverman murders. Do you think there is?"

"I can't tell, but there are a lot of connections between people who knew the victims. That Sam Gately guy you talked with at Harry Simon's funeral, do you think he has more than just a curious interest?" Tom turned to glance around the cemetery. "I was almost certain that I saw him here earlier."

Flaherty stopped walking and paused for a moment. "I guess I don't know him enough to say." He shook his head. "I don't know why he might do it, and it doesn't seem to be in his psyche. Do you think he could be a strong suspect?"

Tom started walking again. "I think he's worth talking to a bit more."

"More? Have you and Angelo been running your own personal detective interrogations again?"

"No. Just an interest to see justice done and understand the motives."

"I can see that," said Flaherty. "I guess you never really know."

"That's what I was just telling Brooks."

As their paths diverged, Flaherty said, "Brooks is good. He'll figure it out sooner or later."

"I hope sooner than later is the answer." Tom waved and headed back.

When Tom approached the driveway between St. Francis Church and the rectory, he heard the sound of chipping ice and turned the corner to find Angelo making sure the side entrance was safe for the Saturday evening Mass. "And where did you disappear to, Mr. Houdini?"

Continuing to chip away at the hardened ice that had built up from the sun-melted snow on the roof above, Angelo replied, "You were right."

"Right about what? And why do you seem so surprised that I could be right? Angelo, what is it?"

"That was Sam Gately at the cemetery this morning," said Angelo as he finally peered up and leaned on the handle of the ice chopper. "And he was with another man, early thirties, stocky, balding in the back."

Tom rubbed his chin. "What was he doing at Silverman's funeral?"

"What was he doing at Harry Simon's funeral?"

"You're right. That's as important a question. Who was this other guy with him, and why did they leave so abruptly when Brian headed in their direction?"

Angelo scratched the back of his scalp. "Len Weitz."

"Len Weitz?"

"That was the other guy he was with. I followed them back to his apartment, where they talked outside for a while. Weitz seemed very animated and emotional as Gately tried to calm him down. I couldn't hear any of the conversation, but Gately left, and Weitz went up to his apartment."

"Angelo, how do you know his name was Len Weitz?"

"I got close enough to see which mailbox he retrieved his mail from inside the front security door. When he went upstairs, it was easy for me to get the door open and match up the mailbox with the name on his apartment number. He teaches middle school math."

Tom smirked. "How would you know that? Wait, do I want to know?"

"I took a chance and buzzed the intercom for his apartment. I said I was there to inspect the smoke detectors, which let me see each room—lots of books, videos, sketchbooks, and a pet bird. No pictures of any family, and I think he spends a lot of time in his apartment based on the wear on his chair. He had several extra locks on the door and was very uncomfortable having me in the apartment, pacing the entire time I was there. I tried to ask him questions, but he wasn't interested in talking. When I finished, I thanked him, stopped at the birdcage in his living room, and said, "'Because these wings are no longer wings to fly, but merely vans to beat the air.'"

"Angelo! I'm impressed. That's from the Eliot 'Ash Wednesday' poem we discussed."

"Well, Mr. Weitz wasn't so impressed. His head snapped back, and it was clear he was shaken and angry as he opened the door for me to leave. I started to say one more thing, but the door slammed shut."

"That's more than suspicious and raises even more questions about Gately being there with him." Tom glanced down at his watch and said, "I've got to get ready for the four o'clock Mass." He carefully stepped over the remaining ice and entered the side door next to the sacristy.

Standing in his path was the five-foot Sister Helen. She peered up at him and, with her Irish brogue, said, "Father, do you think it's safe to be havin' Mass here with everything that's happened?"

"I think we'll be okay. I think they used the church as a backdrop to send a message about the victim versus a threat against anyone here. If it makes you feel any better, Detective Brooks promised some police presence inside and outside the church for tonight and tomorrow's Masses."

"Maybe a little, but Harry Simon was a parishioner here even if Dr. Silverman wasn't. I just worry about the people and especially any children coming to Mass. It's unsettling, to say the least, and I just hope the Holy Spirit sends some extra guardian angels."

Tom peered into her eyes with a comforting gaze. "We'll be okay—but keep praying."

"To be sure, I will."

When Tom entered the sacristy, he watched the altar boy, Billy McGuire, hustling to attend to his chores in readying for Mass. Tom smiled at his earnestness. Tom grew up a lukewarm Protestant, so he never got to experience being an altar server, but he appreciated all that they did to assist before, during, and after Mass. Sister Helen's words of caution finally hit home as he watched this innocent boy scurrying back and forth. "William McGuire!" spouted Tom.

Billy stopped short; eyes widened with apparent worry. "Yes, Father. What did I miss?"

Tom grinned, placing his hand on Billy's shoulder. "I guess we'll find out, but I just wanted to thank you for being here and helping me out with Mass."

Billy's face turned a bright red as he blushed. "I like helping out," he replied as his eyes widened, now with panic, as he turned for the lighter in the corner. "I almost forgot the candles!"

Tom's laugh was cut short as he peered at the nave of the church and then at the confessional, recalling the awful scene from just a few days ago. He looked back towards Billy, thinking a young boy should never even have to think about something like that, never mind being potentially at risk. It hit him that he had no idea what type of murderer they were dealing with, never mind predicting what they might or might not do—and more disturbingly, why?

Chapter 26

For the next forty days, Tom focused on the season of Lent, preparing meaningful sermons, delivering Lenten programs intended to offer parishioners opportunities to grow in their faith, and tending to the increased number of people attending the Sacrament of Confession. Holy Week would begin with Palm Sunday and end with the Triduum—Holy Thursday, Good Friday, and Easter, with both an Easter Vigil and Sunday Mass celebration.

He realized being busy kept him from feeling frustrated by the lack of new developments with the murders, but a few earlier leads had come to fruition. Flaherty dropped by to tell them that Dr. Aviel Rose had been booked for Joel Silverman's murder. The detectives found additional traces of Silverman's blood and residue of ash in Rose's car and a note in Silverman's office from Rose saying he "couldn't cover for him any longer." When confronted about the note, Rose declined to offer any explanation of what Silverman was referring to. As in the case of Jonas Alpheus being charged with Harry Simon's murder, there was no feeling of closure for Tom or Angelo.

The following Wednesday dawned warm with a balmy spring breeze, so Tom decided to take a walk. The school was out for Holy Week, and the next three days would be full in many ways for him, so the free time was a welcomed break. As he let himself feel the sun and the gentle breeze on his face, there was a sudden light honk of a horn from the street. He took no notice until he heard, "You know, you could get arrested smiling that much in public."

Tom spotted Brooks in the car and pointed to a rare parking spot for him to pull over. Getting out of the car, Brooks said, "Yes, I missed you, and I think I owe you a lunch if I remember right."

"I don't remember that, but I'll trust you," said Tom as he shook Brooks' hand. "How have you been?"

"Pretty good. I know a great deli around the corner where we can get a sandwich and talk."

As they approached the Jewish grocery, Tom laughed. "You are kidding, right?"

Brooks held the door and opened his mouth until it became obvious with the noisy bustle of the jam-packed grocery.

"You know what time of year this is, don't you?"

"I heard it was spring. What's with the crowd on a Wednesday?"

Tom replied, "It's Passover, and every Jewish person in town is here getting their food for the Seder meal. It's got to be kosher and certified by a rabbi."

They maneuvered their way through the crowd. "Hey, speaking of rabbis. Rabbi Moshe!"

Despite the crowd pushing in from all sides, Rabbi Moshe seemed happy to see Tom, yelling above the other voices, "Greetings, Father Fitzpatrick, and happy Holy Week to you."

"*Chag pesach sameach*, to you and your family." Tom turned to Brooks, and raised his voice. "Detective Brooks, this is Rabbi Moshe. He officiated at the funeral service for Dr. Silverman; God bless his soul. Rabbi—"

Rabbi Moshe nodded. "Detective Brooks and I have discussed the case many times. I told him all I knew about both Joel and Avi. I still can't believe Joel is dead, nor that Avi could have done this. They worked together for so long." He turned suddenly, raised his hand, and yelled over the heads of the people ahead of him, "Miriam! Mir—make sure you get the brisket—a nice brisket. He knows who we are. And the lamb shank bone!" He turned back to Tom and Brooks. "I'm sorry about that. So much to do, and we still have to finish the *chametz* search. They make the best matzo ball soup here, and the gefilte fish and potato latkes are unmatched."

Tom glanced down to see the rabbi's basket full of Seder meal preparations, including the wine and horseradish.

Tom peered directly into Rabbi Moshe's eyes. "How certain are you that Dr. Rose couldn't have done this?"

Rabbi Moshe curled his lower lip and bobbed his head up and down. "It's just my gut, but we can never be so certain when it comes to people."

Tom nodded. "One question, Rabbi. I'm not as familiar with Jewish customs, but at the funeral, I noticed that Dr. Rose was the only one who tore his clothing at the gravesite. Is that normal?"

The rabbi leaned toward Tom. "Usually, only the family would perform the *Kirah*, tearing the left side of the garment over their heart as a tangible expression of grief and anger in the face of death for a loved one. I thought it was odd for Avi to do that at the gravesite, so I assume they were closer than I thought. The family was not so thrilled with Joel over the years for some reason. Joel and his wife lost a son when he was only ten, so there has been grief. When Avi performed the *Kirah*, the family didn't even say the traditional, '*Barukh atah Adonai Eloheinu melekh ha'olam dayan haEmet*' or 'Blessed are You, Adonai Our God, Ruler of the Universe, the True Judge.' They seemed almost cold about the services and the shiva for the seven days following the burial."

"Huh. That is odd. Well, we don't want to hold you up."

"The Exodus from Egypt was easier than getting out of here will be today," joked the rabbi.

"You may be right. I'll try to stop by the temple sometime. Oh, one question—what's *chametz*? Did I say that right?"

Rabbi Moshe laughed. "You must have taken some Hebrew with that Latin. Sure, *chametz* is food in the house that has leaven or could rise. Any *chametz* must be found and burned before the Passover celebration."

Tom said goodbye and turned to Brooks. "We're never getting a corned beef on rye here today. How about if I treat you at Dempsey's?"

They entered the old Irish pub to be greeted by Dempsey's broad smile. "Well, well, well, look what the cat dragged in. Did Detective Brooks *collar* you, Father?" He laughed at his own joke and pointed to an open booth for them to take.

Tom slid into the worn wooden bench. "Demps, how long have you been saving that one up for?"

The grin hadn't left Dempsey's red cheeks. "Not long enough, I'm guessing. I'll bring you two Guinnesses while you decide if you want burgers, burgers, or burgers."

After Dempsey returned and set down the two foamy stouts, Tom tipped his glass with Brooks. "So, how have you been since we talked last? Have you had a fruitful Lent?"

Brooks squinted and took a long sip of his beer. "What's a fruitful Lent?" He held up his free hand. "Never mind. We've been moving forward with the cases against Alpheus and Rose. I think the fact that things have been quiet shows that we've got the right guys off the street."

Tom raised his eyebrows.

Tilting his head, Brooks asked, "You still don't buy that they are the killers, do you? We keep finding more evidence pointing to these guys, and they offer absolutely no answers or plausible alibis to raise any doubts. I guess that you and 'Detective' Salvato have fallen in love with the intrigue of complex conspiracy theories, but, in the real world, murders are almost always more simple and more personal."

"I know. I know. I just feel as if there's more to these murders than we can see on the surface."

Brooks raised his hands. "I need evidence, not the feelings of amateurs."

"I know. I really do. You know your business, and I trust your professional instincts." Tom paused and then asked, "When you're not at work, how have things been going for you?"

Raising his head, Brooks replied, "Funny, no one ever asks me that. I'm okay. I love my job, but it can wear you down, and it's become pretty much all I do these days. I keep thinking there must be more to life."

Tom's eyes widened. "I think you're onto something."

Glancing around the pub, Brooks said, "Look, I don't want to get all philosophical or anything, but I get a feeling that you have a deep sense of purpose and peace that goes beyond what a job can give you. It just makes me think a little bit—well, a lot, lately. I guess I'm getting old enough to stop and think about what life's supposed to be about, and I'd like to feel the way I think you do. Don't let this get around, but I admire that about you, or maybe I'm jealous. I don't know. I'm probably not making any sense."

"From my vantage point, you're making perfect sense. Like I said, I think you're onto something, and I wouldn't dismiss it." Tom paused for several moments, staring into his half-empty beer glass.

Brooks asked, "What is it?"

"*Chametz*," mumbled Tom.

"Ch-what? What are you thinking about?"

Tom replied, "I've been thinking about this all wrong. Holy smoke, tomorrow is Holy Thursday!"

"Hey, if you have to go—"

"No. No. Rabbi Moshe said he had to go home to find any *chametz* in the house before the Passover Seder meal."

"And what's *chametz*?"

"It's any leavened food. The Torah says the Hebrews left Egypt with such haste that there was no time to allow baked bread to rise; thus, flat, unleavened bread or matzo is a reminder of the rapid departure of the Exodus."

"So?"

"So, the rabbi said it must be found, burned, and turned into ashes before the Passover Seder."

"So?"

"Tomorrow is Holy Thursday, the Last Supper. Jesus was celebrating Passover with His apostles, and He would have shared unleavened bread with them."

Shaking his head, Brooks blurted, "You are completely losing me. What are you talking about?"

Tom lifted his head. "Sorry, I'm rambling. The first two murders pointed to a Catholic sacrament, right?"

"Yeah, but you're talking Jewish Passovers."

"I know. The Jewish Testament prophesied the New Testament or Covenant Christ brings. They mirror each other. Harry Simon's death was all about Baptism. Joel Silverman's demise was about Confession. The next sacrament is what?"

"I don't know. Uhm, Communion?"

"Right! Holy Eucharist. The simplest, most banal-looking, and tasteless thing in the world is transformed into the Body of Christ, the Lamb of God, the most amazing person to ever happen to all of us. I truly hope there are no more murders, but the Sacrament of Communion would be next on the list if the killer were still out there."

Brooks squeezed his eyes tight. "Well, they're not, so you can relax." They sat silently until Dempsey took their order for two burgers, and then Brooks turned back to Tom. "What were you thinking?"

"I was originally thinking they might strike on the Feast of Corpus Christi—but now I'm wondering if Holy Thursday, the Feast of the Last Supper, might not be the target."

"Tomorrow night? Passover. The Last Supper. This is getting crazy. And where is this grand murder supposed to take place?"

Tom pursed his lips. "I don't know. I hope it's not at St. Francis again."

Brooks grunted, and there was silence as Dempsey brought over their burgers. "Who died?" Tom peered up without a word, and Dempsey placed their plates in front of them. "Enjoy your burgers, boys. Extra-burnt, as you ordered."

As Dempsey headed back to the bar, Brooks shook his head and quipped, "Burnt anything isn't exactly helping my appetite these days. Let me ask you something. First, you said Christ is the unleavened bread in Communion, and then you said He's the Lamb of God. Isn't that confusing to people?"

"Maybe. The Jews had been making a sacrifice of their lambs to God, but it was an imperfect sacrifice by humans. Jesus became the perfect sacrifice to atone for our sins, the Lamb of God. In the New Covenant brought by Jesus, he gives us Himself in the living bread from Heaven—to become one with God."

"So, the Jews sacrificed and ate a roasted lamb for Passover, but why was Rabbi Moshe having brisket instead of lamb? He only ordered a lamb shank bone."

Tom smiled. "Ahh. You are very observant for a detective. The custom of sacrificing lambs on the eve of Passover and eating the meat ended with the destruction of the Temple in 70 A.D. Without the Temple, there was no place to make the sacrifice, so modern Jews do not eat roasted lamb for Passover. For Christians, the Passover Lamb's sacrifice is considered fulfilled by the crucifixion and death of Jesus, the Lamb of God. So no more sacrifices are required, and the Word of God is complete. That perfect sacrifice is now only celebrated and made present with thanksgiving in the Mass at the Eucharist, Holy Communion."

"You are going way over my head, Padre." They remained silent as they ate until Brooks said, "We'll have some officers assigned to St. Francis for Mass tonight."

Mouth full, Tom lifted his head. "I appreciate it. I just hope I'm wrong."

Chapter 27

Celebrating Holy Thursday Mass was something Tom looked forward to each year. This was the night Jesus would spend His last supper with His apostles and friends before offering Himself out of love and mercy on the Cross the next day. The church was overflowing with parishioners coming to celebrate a Mass in which all their senses would be captivated and elevated. Despite the beauty and power of the moment, Tom gazed out at the congregation with some protective concern. He trusted God's ultimate justice to avoid anxiety but was concerned as he noted police officers at the side exits. The entrance hymn evoked a sense of peace, which was boosted when his eye caught Detective Brooks and Officer Flaherty at the back of the church by the baptismal font.

Tom prayed for the Spirit to remain immersed in the celebration through the Scripture readings, washing of the feet, setting the altar table, and sharing in Holy Communion. Normally, nothing would take his full attention away from the moment when the simple gifts of bread and wine were changed into something or someone extraordinary as Christ poured out Himself fully as a gift for us to become one in Him. Still, tonight he held his breath and prayed that no one at church tonight would become a victim of a mysterious killer if he was still at large.

Tom breathed a sigh of relief as he said, "The Mass is ended, go in peace, glorifying the Lord by your life." There were no signs from the police that anything he'd feared had happened. Parishioners greeted each other and talked as they filed out of the church, thanking Tom for a beautiful celebration to start the Holy Triduum. As he stepped back into the church to approach a waiting Brooks, he caught sight of something in the corner under a carved relief of the Last Supper.

Brooks tightened his brow. "What is it? What are you looking at?"

Tom took several steps closer as Angelo made his way up the side aisle. "It looks like a dead animal was placed here sometime during Mass."

Angelo tilted his head. "It's ah—It's an owl."

Brooks squatted down, removing a pen from inside his coat; he lifted the bird's head. "A dead owl." He squinted and leaned in as he lifted the feathered carcass a little higher. "There's a bloodied piece of paper underneath with some writing on it I can't make out."

Tom lifted his vestment to kneel beside Brooks, leaning over to read the written message. "Huh."

"It doesn't say, *huh*. What do you see?" implored Brooks.

"Well, it says, *Heugh! Heugh! Heugh!*"

Brooks let down the carcass. "Are you trying to say, *Whoo*?"

Standing back up, Tom tried to think of a connection to Communion as he scratched his scalp. "It's from old English folklore. I'm trying to recall it. Let's see, Jesus walked into a baker's shop."

Rolling his eyes, Brooks stood. "This is no time for jokes."

"I know. I know. Okay. Let's see. In the story, Jesus, disguised as a beggar, walks into a baker's shop and begs for some bread to eat. The mistress of the shop took pity on the hungry man and quickly put some dough into the large oven to bake for him."

"And, this has something to do with a dead owl?"

"I don't know, but the daughter reprimands her mother, insisting the piece of dough is too large, reduces it, and then reduces it again to a very small size. But, once in the oven, it expands to an enormous size, pushing the doors open, and the girl shrieks, 'Heugh, heugh, heugh,' sounding like an owl. Supposedly, Jesus turned her into an owl for her stinginess."

Shaking his head, Brooks muttered, "You know, whenever I think you're going to help me solve a case, I get useless gibberish. Does this mean anything to you?"

Tom stared down at the lifeless bird. "Owl feathers were also brought to a dying person to help with their flight to heaven, but, obviously, these feathers weren't brought to a dying person." Tom turned to Angelo. "Baker?"

Angelo nodded.

Tom said, "Detective, I think you should check out the bakeries in this area."

Brooks rubbed his hand across this forehead as he motioned to one of the officers to tape off the area around the dead bird. "Bakeries? What are you two dreaming up now?"

Tom answered, "Unleavened bread for Passover. The Bread of Life in Holy Communion at the Last Supper. The folklore about the baker and his daughter has to do with Jesus and bread on Holy Thursday. I admit it's just a hunch, but Harry Simon was a swim instructor, and his death was connected to water and Baptism. Joel Silverman was a psychiatrist, someone you trust to 'confess' your inner secrets or even your sins to, and his death was tied to Confession. Holy Communion has to do with bread, and this folklore clue points to a baker or his daughter."

"All right. All right. We'll waste our evening visiting bakeries."

Brooks turned as Flaherty hurried toward him and whispered something in his ear. Brooks glared and turned to Tom. "I think we've narrowed down our search."

"What is it?" asked Tom.

Flaherty glanced toward Brooks, who motioned. "Go ahead."

Flaherty replied, "La Provence Bakery off of Tremont. A neighbor heard screams from inside and found the baker's wife in tears."

"What happened?"

"I'm not sure, but I think her husband was cooked alive in one of the ovens."

Within minutes, Tom and Angelo were at La Provence Bakery with Brooks, Mullen, Flaherty, and the forensic team. The old-style bakery had been in the same location for decades, but Tom had only dropped in a few times for dessert or roasted chicken and lamb. With the increased demand for prepared meals, the bakery purchased an oven to offer roasted meats along with their baked goods.

Tom walked toward a woman who was shaking and sobbing by the counter. "Mrs. Boulanger." She glanced up, eyes puffy and reddened, mascara running down her cheeks with the tears that wouldn't stop.

One of the officers interviewed her, and Tom joined Angelo as the police inspected the scene. Tom recoiled at the sight. They saw part of the blackened corpse lying flat inside the large roasting oven. Tom assumed it must be her husband, the baker, Peter Boulanger. Angelo pointed Tom to writing above the opening to the roasting oven.

Dieu lui-même rejettera l'agneau.

Brooks squinted to follow the path of Angelo's finger. "What's this?"

Tom answered, "I believe it's French. I think the first word is *God*, but I'm not sure. Mrs. Boulanger may know, but I don't know if she's in any condition to see this again."

As Tom spoke, Angelo had written down the letters on a small notepad and torn off the page. Tom approached her with the note. "Mrs. Boulanger, I'm Father Tom Fitzpatrick."

She wiped the sides of her cheeks with the wet tissues clutched tightly in her hand. In a shaking voice, she replied, "I know who you are. I remember you coming in a few times, but we aren't religious."

He handed her the note. "I was wondering if you knew what this says. It's in French, correct?"

She wiped her nose and then placed her glasses on. "Uhm. It says, 'God Himself will reject the lamb.' I don't know what that means."

"That's okay. Thank you, and my prayers are with you and your husband." Tom turned away and then back again. "Do you have any children, a daughter?"

"Yes, we have a daughter. Why?"

"Just curious. My sympathies to her as well."

"She will be devastated. She was always much closer to Pierre than to me. You just never know with children, but then again, she's no longer a child."

Tom caught a glimpse of a book on the desk in front of the baker's wife. "Could I ask if that is your book, Mrs. Boulanger?"

She shook her head, and an officer lifted the book with his gloved hand. Tom could see the antique binding title that read *Hamlet* by William Shakespeare. Tom asked the officer to open the book, and on the inside cover, he noted the handwritten initials *J.C.A.*

Brooks pulled Tom and Angelo aside. "Thanks for coming over, but I think we should let the experts do their work to see if we can find any fingerprints, DNA, or other forensic evidence. I just can't believe this is happening."

As they stepped outside the bakery, Brooks lit a cigarette and took a deep drag. "I'll have to tell you that I'm getting tired of this game and these cryptic clues. What the heck is going on here?"

Tom placed his hand on Brooks' shoulder, "I can empathize with you. You know, I used to think you were professional but almost indifferent. Hearing you lately, I can tell you're not indifferent. I can tell you who else isn't indifferent."

Brooks rolled his eyes toward Tom. "Who's that?"

"This killer isn't indifferent. I think he's on a mission. Revenge. Justice. I don't know, but he's trying to send a strong message with each victim." Tom watched his breath drift into the cold air. "I'm sure you saw that there was another antique book left behind."

Brooks lifted his head. "Eliot, again?"

"No. Shakespeare's *Hamlet* with the initials J.C.A. on the inside cover, again. There was something else written inside that cover as well. *But you, that are polluted with your lusts, Stain'd with the guiltless blood of innocents, Corrupt and tainted with a thousand vices.* It's from another Shakespeare story. I don't recall which one, but all three murders have reference to the innocent, possibly as justification for their executions."

Brooks took a deep drag, then replied as the smoke drifted from his lips. "Just what we need. A self-appointed executioner."

Angelo asked, "Isn't there a Feast of the Holy Innocents?"

"Yes, but that was after Jesus was born when King Herod ordered the killing of all male babies, age two and under. Passover celebrates the Israelite's freedom from slavery in Egypt and the 'passing over' of the households marked with the blood of the lamb, sparing the firstborns on the eve of the Exodus, the last of ten plagues sent by God."

Brooks let out a deep sigh. "I know I'm going to regret this, but what does this have to do with our roasted victim in there?"

Tom rubbed his chin. "I don't know. There are powerful events connected to both the Jewish Passover and the Last Supper of Jesus. The French writing over the oven is another change of scriptural text. Instead of saying, 'God Himself will provide the Lamb,' it says, '*God Himself will reject the lamb.*' I'm assuming the latter applies to Mr. Boulanger if that's who's in that oven."

"I'm glad you're not jumping to any conclusions."

Angelo said, "Huh, so Jesus turned the baker's daughter into an owl because of what she did, and God will reject the baker for something he did. What's the commonality between the lamb at Passover and the Last Supper?"

Tom replied, "Ah, it's incredibly huge. Jesus was a devoutly religious man and came to Jerusalem for Passover. You probably remember Him entering on a donkey on Palm Sunday. Well, this is the same time that Jews would bring in their lambs to be inspected for the Passover sacrifice. Only those lambs deemed unblemished would be acceptable for the sacrifice. If you remember back to the time of Abraham, God tested him. He instructed Abraham to take his son Isaac to Mount Moriah to make a burnt offering of him to God. Abraham loved his only son but trusted in God and took his son up the mountain. When Isaac asked his father where the lamb was for the sacrifice, his father said—"

Angelo jumped in, "I'm guessing he said, 'God Himself will provide the Lamb.'"

"Very good. Just as Abraham was about to kill his son, an angel stopped him and blessed him for his obedience and trust, unlike Adam and Eve. Mount Moriah is where Solomon built the Temple in Jerusalem and is believed to be the site of Creation itself. So, when Jesus arrived, he was to be—"

"The ultimate sacrificial Lamb who submits to the will of His Father," said Angelo.

"Right, God loved us so much that He was willing to sacrifice His only Son for us. Jesus was inspected by Pilate and found to be innocent, the unblemished Passover Lamb who would die for our sins," replied Tom.

Brooks dropped his cigarette butt and crushed his heel on it. "Where is this going?"

"I'm just saying what comes to mind. Jesus sacrificed his life for our sins, and it appears the murderer, here, sacrificed Mr. Boulanger for his sins against an innocent, just like Simon and Silverman."

Brooks rubbed his forehead. "I'm getting a headache." He turned to an officer who came up with photos of Hamlet's pages with underlined verses.

-Get thee to a nunnery. Why wouldst thou be a breeder of sinners?

-accuse me of such things that it were better my mother had not borne me
-O wicked wit and gifts, that have the power
So to seduce!—won to his shameful lust
-Cut off even in the blossoms of my sin, Unhousled, disappointed, unaneled,
No reckoning made, but sent to my account, With all my imperfections on my head.

"This just sounds like jibberish. What does any of it mean?" quipped Brooks.

Tom squinted as he read the lines. "No pun, but Shakespeare would make a play of words. By *nunnery*, he meant for Ophelia to get to a brothel for tempting Hamlet. It seems like the focus is on seduction, shameful lust, and being *cut off* while still sinning."

Angelo leaned in. "What about *unhousled*? Did I say that right?"

"Let's see. *Unhousled* means not having received the Eucharist. I think 'disappointed' refers to being unprepared, probably referring to his soul not being in a good place for death. And *unaneled* would mean without the Sacrament of the Sick. These lines seem to indicate the victim's sin and connect with the words over the oven saying that God would reject this 'lamb.'" Tom glanced back at the photo. "I think there's one more verse underlined."

They say the owl was a baker's daughter. Lord, we know what we are but know not what we may be. God be at your table!

"Owls and bakers, again," quipped Brooks.

"And daughters. Do you know where the daughter is tonight? With the dead owl and this line saying that Jesus has more power over what we will be than us, I'm worried her life may be in danger—or worse," replied Tom with a furrowed brow.

Chapter 28

Good Friday and Easter services were celebrated peacefully, without any unusual events. Tom woke on Monday morning drained of energy but also restless about the three murders and the possible connections with St. Francis. He sat with Luke at the kitchen table, sharing a cup of coffee and having scrambled eggs for breakfast, recounting the scene of horror at La Provence Bakery and cringing at the thought of the charred body of Peter Boulanger.

Angelo entered from the kitchen door with warm pastries. "Are you two finally up?"

"What is this for? These smell fresh," said Tom.

Angelo's eyes widened. "Fresh from La Provence Bakery."

Luke quipped, "They're open?"

"Almost as if nothing had happened. Boulanger's wife was very busy, working alone."

"Huh. What about Boulanger's daughter, Olivia? I wonder if Brooks has talked with her yet?" Tom wondered.

"I don't think so," responded Angelo.

"Why is that?"

"Mrs. Boulanger was all business when I asked how she was. When I asked about her daughter, she became more agitated and finally admitted that she hadn't seen her since days before her husband's death."

Luke sat up straighter. "She isn't worried about her? Her husband has been murdered, and her daughter's missing!"

Angelo nodded. "When I asked her if she was concerned, she froze. She said her husband and daughter had a pretty tense argument about something several days before the murder, and Olivia stormed out, and that was the last she'd seen of her. Mrs. Boulanger went to the back room and then gave me this note from Olivia. It's been obviously crumpled more than once."

Tom asked, "What does it say?"

"*I was the more deceived, and now you will rue the day that you stole my life, my love, and our innocence!* Mrs. Boulanger said it was in Olivia's handwriting and broke into tears when she said she was afraid to give it to the police—afraid of what it might mean."

Luke gasped at him. "She thinks Olivia may have killed her own father?!"

Tom stared down at the table. "I hate to think any family member could do that, but—"

"But what?"

"Could just be coincidence, but the note has lines from Hamlet in it. *I was the more deceived*, and *rue* is the flower of bitterness and repentance that the despondent Ophelia held. Ophelia's father had forbidden her to see Hamlet, which might connect to her comments about Olivia's stolen life and love. I don't know. I'm just tossing stuff out."

Angelo tapped his fingers on the table. "It is too much of a coincidence. We need to find her and what all these connections mean."

The silence was interrupted by the wall phone ringing. "Hello, this is Father Tom."

"It's Brooks. I hate to bother you, but would you be available to meet me at the Mount Hope Cemetery? Do you know it?"

"I do, and I can be there in a few minutes. What is it?"

"I'll let you know when you get there. Thanks." A click completed their conversation.

Despite the traffic, Tom and Angelo reached the cemetery inside of fifteen minutes and spotted the flashing blue lights surrounding a section of the burial grounds. As they made their way between the officers on the scene, Tom caught Brooks staring at a body on the ground—a young woman in a long white dress with flowers in her hair. He approached the scene, and a deep sense of disappointment and sadness filled him. A blood stain spread out from where a dagger had pierced her heart, her hand wrapped around the hilt of the knife.

"Is this—"

"Olivia Boulanger," replied Brooks as he ran his hand across his mouth. "It appears she or someone else plunged that dagger into her chest several days ago. This area is out of sight from most of the walking paths, and the grounds crew was off for Easter weekend, so they didn't find the body until this morning. It looks like she was dressed for her wedding with those flowers and dress," replied Brooks.

Angelo pointed to her other hand. "What is she clutching in her left hand?"

Tom squatted down. "It looks to be daisies and violets. Daisies represent innocence, and violets faithfulness and fidelity. Detective, I think she is clutching something else."

Brooks instructed the forensic officer to open her hand to retrieve a tightly rolled paper. Gently unrolling it, a note inside seemed to match the writing on the crumpled paper Mrs. Boulanger had given to Angelo.

Shall I believe that unsubstantial death is amorous, and that the lean abhorred monster keeps thee here in dark to be his paramour? Why I descend into this bed of death is partly to behold the face of my only love forbidden by that monster. Some shall be pardon'd, and some punished, for never was a story of more woe.

Brooks walked Tom and Angelo away from the scene. "What is this? More Shakespeare?"

"Most of it is from Shakespeare. I was trying to understand it in the context of another note she wrote that Mrs. Boulanger found and gave to Angelo. She said it was in Olivia's handwriting."

Brooks lowered his forehead into the palm of his hand. "What? What is the victim's wife doing giving evidence to a con? What did it say?"

Angelo unfolded the crumpled note for them to read.

I was the more deceived, and now you will rue the day that you stole my life, my love, and our innocence!

Tom said, "This is from *Romeo and Juliet*, and you can see the reference to *innocence* again. It seems as if she felt deceived, possibly by her father, and he would rue the day for what he did. The last part of the note we just looked at seems to indicate that she died to join her only true love that was forbidden to her, but the first part points to a monster keeping that person in the grave as its lover. It's very hard to tell without asking questions, but the lines are mostly pieced together from someone who knows this story."

Brooks peered out over the sea of headstones. Without turning back, he said, "We've been looking all over for this woman. Did she kill her father in revenge, and for what? Did she kill herself for what she did?"

Angelo said, "Mrs. Boulanger said that she had a pretty nasty argument with her father and then disappeared a few days before his murder. Based on the note, her mother was afraid of what it might have meant."

Brooks spun around. "Well, it would be nice if someone would tell the police all these little details. She never mentioned this to us, only saying that she hadn't seen her daughter. Great! We had some evidence pointing to her as a possible suspect, but we may never know the full truth of Miss *Owl'livia*, if you can pardon my gallows humor."

Tom stepped back toward the gravesite where Olivia's body lay. The forensic team carefully took samples from the area and inspected her lifeless body. The headstone behind her caught his eye. It read:

Rowan Montecchi
Born May 13, 1978
Died Jan 2, 2009

As he noted the teardrop carving on the top of the stone, Tom thought, *Who was Rowan Montecchi to Olivia that she would breathe her last breath on his grave?* "Did she see herself as Ophelia or Juliet in this tragedy?" he murmured. "Ophelia's tragedy lies in the way she loses her innocence through no fault of her own. Did she blame her father for keeping them apart or something worse?"

Angelo stepped forward. "I keep wondering what the common thread is that ties these murders together. Sam

Gately was connected to Harry Simon and Jonas Alpheus, and then he shows up at Joel Silverman's funeral talking to Len Weitz. Both had been seen by the Rose and Silverman practice for counseling."

Brooks tilted his head. "What would a French baker and his suicidal daughter have to do with doctors and teachers? It is possible that she saw these other two murders and tried to mimic them when she had a heated row with her father and then regretted it enough to do herself in. You have to think of all the possibilities."

Angelo raised his eyebrows. "Hmmm. I'll try to factor them in when I think of *J.C.A.* as just a coincidence."

Leaning in toward Brooks, Tom whispered, "He's got a point. How many people know about the initials in the book? It might be a good idea to find out how this Rowan Montecchi died and what his relationship with Olivia or her father may have been."

"I know. I know. This thing is getting way too complicated to get a handle on without some more pieces of this growing puzzle filled in," quipped Brooks.

"Seven weeks," added Tom as he stared down at the flowers in Olivia's flowing hair.

"No more riddles," pleaded Brooks. "Seven weeks for what?"

Tom peered up into Brooks's eyes. "Seven weeks until Pentecost. The Sacrament of Confirmation is the special outpouring of the Holy Spirit granted first to the apostles on the day of Pentecost. It's on May 31 this year, and we may only have seven weeks to figure out who the next potential victim might be."

Chapter 29

Dr. Franks sat at his desk, tapping a newly sharpened pencil on his notebook, waiting for the next client. Daniel had never been late, so the fifteen minutes before the client finally arrived felt much longer.

The young man rushed into the office, winded and with sweat on his brow. "I'm sorry, Dr. Franks. I had an appointment that took longer than expected."

"No problem at all. It's your time," replied Dr. Franks as he sat in his usual leather chair and motioned toward the couch. "Can I get you anything to drink? Coffee? Water?"

"No. No. I'm all set. So, what should we talk about today?"

Dr. Franks squinted. "That is really up to you." He opened his notebook to scan a few notes he had jotted down from earlier sessions. "We've spent time discussing your father and what losing him meant to you, but you feel you've worked through that. Is there anything in that relationship that has come to the surface since the last time we talked?"

Daniel appeared unphased by the topic. "Not really. It's sad to think about, but it's not healthy to live in the past or feel like a victim."

"So, no part of you feels wounded or like a victim even though you know it would be understandable?" asked Dr. Franks as he studied the relaxed expression on his client's face.

He shook his head again. "No. No wounds or scars that I'm aware of. Why? Do you think it seems as if I haven't worked through this? Ah, 'Everyone can master a grief, but he that has it,' is that it?"

Dr. Franks tilted his head. "That sounds familiar. Is it a quote or your own philosophy?"

Daniel jotted a few notes into his own spiral notebook. "I guess it could be both. It's from *Much Ado About Nothing*. I don't think I have any baggage or unresolved skeletons in my closet, but your questions are good ones."

"That's what I'm here for," replied Dr. Franks. He sighed and half-smiled as he gazed upon this young man. "In our first sessions, I think we said we can feel we've resolved or faced everything from our past that impacts us today, but I've never met anyone who has."

"Maybe, until now," replied the man with a light laugh. "Do you really feel we can repress significant events from our past to the extent that we don't even remember them?"

"Sure. Sometimes, the more traumatic they are, the more we avoid going near them, even wiping them totally from our conscious memory."

Daniel squinted as if to ponder the reality of that dynamic. "Huh. I'm having a hard time believing it's possible to put a lid on something like that forever, especially if it was a big thing."

Dr. Franks turned to note the time on the wall clock. "Daniel, I agree. A bad memory always seems to rear its ugly head one way or the other. The more we repress traumatic events and avoid dealing with them, the more likely they are to negatively distort our thinking, how we view ourselves and our relationships with others. Usually, it's not the negative things that happen to us that impact us as much as avoiding dealing with them. That avoidance can cause all kinds of issues and effects on us."

"Hmm. I'm kind of the type of person who would want to know and then deal with it instead of dealing with a lifetime of avoiding the truth. I don't like living in fear, so I think I'd be more likely to act."

Dr. Franks nodded. "That's a good sign, as long as your actions are justified and healing."

Daniel straightened himself. "Justified? Of course. I hope you don't think I'm someone who would ever do anything that wasn't justified or right." He paused. "It's important you know that."

Glancing back down at his watch, he gave Daniel a friendly nod. "Of course. I am sorry, this was a bit of a shorter session than usual, but I have another person waiting. Can we pick this up next time?"

Daniel finished jotting down some final notes and stood up. "Hey, I'm the one who was late, so no apologies necessary. I appreciate your being generous with your time. I'll see you in two weeks."

Chapter 30

Several weeks had passed since the death of Olivia and her father. The last update Tom had from Brooks was that the evidence in the Boulanger death seemed to point to a murder-suicide by the daughter after the heated exchange. Some additional notes and forensic evidence led them to no other alternative scenarios.

Rowan Montecchi had worked at the bakery when he was fourteen and Olivia was thirteen. Her mother said her daughter had a crush on Rowan that never left her, but the father had forbidden them from seeing each other and fired him from the bakery. Brooks said the mother had become oddly cold about her husband's death but remained very emotional about losing her daughter. Her alibi for that evening was airtight—she was attending a class at Mass Art.

With the end of May and the Feast of Pentecost approaching in a few weeks, Tom was getting antsy about figuring out who the killer or the next intended victim might be. As he headed toward the precinct to check in with Brooks, Tom's eyes widened when he spotted a young man approaching him pushing a cart with large baskets on each side full of cans he had collected alongside the streets that day. "Joey, I haven't seen you in a while. How have you been doing? I hope the winter wasn't too hard on you this year."

He never knew Joey's real name. Everyone called him Joey "Donuts" because he always hung out in front of the Dunkin Donuts, and people would bring him out coffee and his favorite coconut donuts or some spare change.

Joey ran his hand through his long unruly beard. For a young man who was probably only thirty, if that, his face showed the wear of living on the streets in Boston's harsh winters. He often stayed at the Pine Street Inn shelter. They provided meals, medical, and a cot for the evening to sober people in need, if they got there early enough on a frigid night.

Wrapping his tattered coat tighter, Joey replied, "Hey, Father Tom. We've had worse winters. How about you?" His smile revealed a recently lost tooth.

"I've been well. Thanks for asking. It's been a tough winter, though, with these awful murders in town. Have you heard about them?"

Joey reached up with his ragged gloved hand and adjusted the green woolen hat on his head, something not needed on these warmer days of May but a signature hat Joey had worn for many years. "Heard about them? Who hasn't? You never know when that vigilante will strike next."

"Vigilante? What makes you think the killer is a vigilante?" queried Tom.

"Oh, uhm. That's the word on the street. He doesn't rob them or anything, so there's got to be a reason. Maybe these guys deserved it or something?"

Tom paused. "Joey, can I ask you something?"

Joey hesitated for a moment. "Shoot."

"I can tell you're intelligent and young and fairly healthy for living your life. I'm sure you could be successful at doing a lot of things if you wanted to. Do you ever think about giving something you like a shot? I'm always available if you want any help getting started."

Joey glanced downward. "You've always been kind to me. You look me in the eye when you see me; and most people just look away or through me, like I don't exist. I guess I haven't wanted them to see me either. I haven't wanted to exist, but maybe—" He stopped short.

As he pointed to Joey, a broad grin made its way to Tom's face. "Ahh. Ahh. Maybe? I'll take that for a start."

Nodding, Joey returned the smile. "I'll think on it."

"Deal and take good care of yourself," said Tom as he held out a twenty-dollar bill.

Joey hesitated, then put out his hand and gazed directly into Tom's eyes. "Thank you. I may pay you back someday."

Tom returned the nod and patted Joey on the shoulder. "Come to Mass, and we'll call it even."

Joey laughed. "I've never been, but no one's ever invited me before!"

"Well, now you're invited."

As Tom approached the Harrison Street precinct, Flaherty yelled out. "Are you finally turning yourself in?"

Tom turned to catch the broad smile on Flaherty's face. "Brian, you look happy."

Flaherty approached. "Just finished my last finals, and the weather's getting nice enough for getting out on the water. What could be better?"

"Hey, congratulations on school. When did you get a boat?"

He laughed. "I wish. A friend of mine has a nice ketch over on the corner of Mystic and Charles, and he's letting me use it. He wanted to call it the *Sea Warrior*, but I convinced him to name it *Cuan Sábháilte*. I can sleep on board on my nights off," said Flaherty sporting a broad smile.

"I like it. Talk about freedom. I'm glad for you. You've worked hard, and you deserve it. Do you know if there have been any updates on the string of murders Brooks was investigating?"

Flaherty shrugged. "I haven't seen too much of him. It's been a while, so I assume they're hoping there won't be any more and all the bad guys have been taken care of. Hey, how has your brother, Luke, been?"

Tom gave a subtle shrug. "He's doing okay. He's still struggling with losing his wife so violently and is consumed with these men being brought to justice. He has good days and bad days, but thanks for asking."

Brian sighed. "I feel for him. A crime like that would eat anyone up. Does he want to go back to South America?"

"I know it's constantly on his mind, but I hope he can let it go someday. I'm not sure what he will do about going back."

"I don't know how you could ever let that go. I know I'm a novice counselor, but the big things never seem to take care of themselves," replied Flaherty.

"Hmmm. I know, but I don't think seeking revenge is the answer."

Flaherty tilted his head. "I've gotcha, there. I guess it's either one demon or another. Well, I've got to get back on my beat. Say hello to Brooks for me."

Tom never caught up with Brooks that day or over the next several weeks as time ticked away to the last day of May, the Feast of Pentecost.

Chapter 31

Dr. Franks opened the notebook on his crossed leg. "Daniel, we've had some good discussions, but, so far, they've been more removed and academic in nature. I was wondering if you'd feel comfortable diving a little deeper today. Well, I should ask if you mind exploring things that might feel uncomfortable at first?"

Adjusting his position on the couch, the young man replied, "I can't think of anything that would be uncomfortable to talk about, but, sure—I'm open to wherever you want to go. Exactly, what were you thinking about?"

Dr. Franks lifted his head after moving his finger down the notes on the page. "Well, despite a less-than-ideal childhood, I've admired how much you've maintained a positive attitude and what you've accomplished in life. Unfortunately, many do not cope as well."

Daniel squinted. "Well, thanks. It wasn't as if my father abused me or anything. I guess he was just indifferent and abandoned us emotionally. Who knows what challenges he faced?"

"Hmm. From what you've told me so far, Daniel, you've poured yourself into your work and self-improvement. Does that sound right to you?"

He scratched his head. "I guess you could say that, but that's not a bad thing. I always tell other guys not to be a victim, to take control of their own lives, and make things right. You know, don't wait for others to take care of what only you can take care of to move on in life."

Nodding, Dr. Franks offered a half-smile. "I don't hear you talk at all about relationships. Family. Girlfriends. Marriage. Even close friendships. Why do you think that is?"

Daniel exhaled and shifted in his seat. "Uhm. I wish the days were longer, but there is only so much time, and it's been pretty busy lately."

"Don't answer anything you don't feel comfortable answering, but have you ever thought about marriage, a family, an intimate relationship in your life? We tend to fill our time with where we put our priorities, but, sometimes, to avoid uncomfortable things, things that scare us inside."

"I don't think that's my issue," he snapped.

"How close were you to your mother? Was she affectionate toward you?"

"What do you mean by that?"

"Children crave affection. They want to know they are loved, that they are worth loving. We know you didn't get that important message from your father, which can create a higher demand for emotional availability from your mother. Did you feel she was there for you?"

Daniel stood abruptly and paced the floor, then turned to Dr. Franks. "She didn't leave us. You have to give her credit for that. Look, I don't know where this is going."

Jotting a quick note, Dr. Franks replied, "The fact that this topic invokes discomfort could be important information for you. Remember when I said that our instincts will tell us to run in the other direction, to avoid going deeper into these dark corners that frighten us."

"Nothing frightens me—anymore," he said with a glare.

"Daniel, have you ever had any physical intimacy in your life?"

His eyes squeezed tight, his brow furrowed as a painful expression made its way to his face, and his hands clutched into his fists.

"Daniel, don't try to think; just tell me what you felt—what memories were invoked?"

He rubbed his forehead with the tips of his fingers, and then the palms of his hands ran down his face. "There's nothing. I don't know what you're talking about. I have no memories or feelings that come to mind, so let's move on!"

Dr. Franks stood up and approached him with one arm extended toward him. The young man pulled back. "What are you doing?" he demanded.

Stepping back to create more space, Dr. Franks responded, "Daniel, I'm sorry. You were closing down. I couldn't tell if you were panicking, and I just wanted to calm you. You deserve a place to feel safe and loved."

Suddenly, Daniel shot a wary glare at Dr. Franks. "I'm going to go. Sorry, but I can't do this right now. I can't." Leaving his jacket on the couch, he took several quick strides and opened the door to the back stairs. Without turning back, he paused. "I'll be okay. I just need some space right now. I'm sorry."

Dr. Franks watched as he hurried down the flight of narrow stairs. A light entered the bottom landing as the door opened, slammed shut and the area darkened.

He sat at his desk and jotted several notes about the session and his client's reaction.

Chapter 32

"When the time for Pentecost was fulfilled, they were all in one place together.

"And suddenly there came from the sky a noise like a strong driving wind, and it filled the entire house in which they were. Then there appeared to them tongues as of fire, which parted and came to rest on each one of them. And they were all filled with the Holy Spirit and began to speak in different tongues, as the Spirit enabled them to proclaim. Now there were devout Jews from every nation under heaven staying in Jerusalem. At this sound, they gathered in a large crowd, but they were confused because each one heard them speaking in his own language," said Tom as he read the Gospel for the Mass celebrating the Feast of Pentecost.

The red vestments he wore symbolized the shedding of blood by Christ and his apostles. He peered out at the overflowing crowd as he explained to the parishioners that the color red also signified the burning fire of God's love on Pentecost when the Holy Spirit descended on the apostles and tongues of fire rested on their heads. "We are all challenged to become witnesses for Christ with the help of the Holy Spirit."

It wasn't until Tom had said, "The Mass has ended, go forth in peace to spread the Good News," and the closing hymn began that a long, loud shriek came from the back of the church. Everyone turned toward the back as a woman, tightly clutching the collar of her coat with one hand, pointed toward a bronze relief of the apostles receiving the Holy Spirit at Pentecost.

Tom made his way to the back to calm the woman as he peered ahead and saw blood on the head of the figure of one apostle. Tom moved closer, closing his eyes when he recognized what it was.

Within thirty minutes, the police had cleared the church and cordoned off the back area as Brooks stood with hands in his coat pockets, staring at the sight in front of him. "I guess you're going to tell me something about the poetic significance of a bloody tongue on this statue?"

Tom stood next to Angelo and Luke, pondering the sight and letting out an extended sigh. "The Holy Spirit rested 'tongues of fire' on the head of each apostle. I think this is about the Sacrament of Confirmation."

The forensic officer gently lifted the severed tongue with a thin metal rod. "This organ appears to have been frozen." She pulled out a thin plastic sleeve covered in blood from underneath. "It looks like a note of some sort inside."

Rolling his eyes, Brooks mumbled, "Should I be surprised?"

With a pair of tweezers, the officer removed the note and unfolded it on a tray she pulled from her equipment.

Tom stepped forward with Brooks to inspect the writing. "I think it's Blake."

"The victim?"

"No, William Blake, the poet. Let's see. *O Rose thou art sick. The invisible worm. That flies in the night, In the howling storm: Has found out thy bed, Of crimson joy; And his dark secret 'love,' Does thy life destroy.* The poem is called 'The Sick Rose.'"

"And?" demanded the impatient detective.

Tom shrugged as he thought. "I don't know. Every clue the killer leaves is the opposite of what was intended by God and about the loss of innocence. The rose should symbolize love, pure love, but here it is sick. The worm destroys it and its innocence. There are references to this being in the cover of night—in shame and secrecy, crimson for lust, and he puts *love* in quotes as if to indicate it's not real love but one that destroys the victim's life and innocence."

"I'm getting confused, but what's new?" quipped Brooks.

The forensic officer took the tweezers and turned over the paper, showing additional words typed out.

THE SICK ROSE, THE HANDS, AND FEET OF HIS CREATOR ARE NOW THE SCATTERED PRIDE OF MAN,

SOMETHING TO NOW STOP THEM FROM DOING WHATEVER THEY PRESUME TO DO, FROM BABELING AND MAKING A NAME FOR HIMSELF AND BUILDING WITH HIS BRICKS. UNLESS THE TONGUE CATCH FIRE, THE GOD WILL NOT BE NAMED, AND IT WOULD BE BETTER FOR HIM TO HAVE A GREAT MILLSTONE FASTENED ROUND HIS NECK AND TO BE DROWNED IN THE DEPTH OF THE SEA.

Brooks shook his head, "What the heck—"

Officer Spiro quickly approached and interrupted, "You have to see this!"

In each corner of the church was tucked either a severed hand or foot, possibly from the same victim as the tongue.

"Did you find the body?"

Spiro shook his head. "Not yet."

Angelo said, "You might want to check the harbors near any millstones if that note was a clue."

"Probably over by Haymarket," said Spiro.

Brooks squinted. "Why Haymarket?"

"Someone reported that old Boston Stone—you know, near the Union Oyster—went missing the other day. It's a millstone. There's a larger one near Fanueil Market, but that's got to weigh a ton, and this one is smaller—and missing," replied Spiro, removing his hat and scratching his head.

"Get some guys out to Long Wharf, Columbus Park, and that area to see if there are any signs of it," ordered Brooks to Mullen, who started out right away. He rubbed his head again. "Okay, let's let these officers do their work. Can we sit in the front and talk this out?"

Tom said, "Sure," as he walked them to the front pew facing the altar, where he genuflected and removed his vestments, laying them over the back of the pew before sitting with Brooks and Angelo.

"What do we have besides poems and body parts?" snapped Brooks.

Tom gazed up at the cross to calm himself and think. "Okay. The Sacrament of Confirmation is connected to Pentecost and some Old Testament events. I think they are both worked into the back of that note. Not to give you another Sunday school lesson, but we have to think in the context of what this killer is writing."

"Everything seems connected except for figuring this case out. What's the context you think is so important?" asked Brooks as he started to pace with nervous energy.

Tom responded, "The whole story of salvation starts from the very beginning. God willed Adam and Eve into existence out of nothing but love and had a plan for them—"

Brooks interrupted, holding out his hand. "Not the whole Bible, please."

Tom tilted his head. "I'll be short. Despite having everything, they didn't trust fully in God's plan and chose their own with the help of Satan. Fast forward to the time of Noah—"

Brooks mumbled with a roll of his eyes. "He is doing the whole thing."

"Well, the note makes specific references to the people of Babel. Instead of writing for the victim to stop *babbling*, he wrote, *babeling*. The people of Babel trusted in their own plan. They used man-made bricks instead of stones made by God. They thought they could reach heaven on their own by building a tall enough tower, and they also wanted to make a name for themselves versus honoring God's name. It was a sin of pride, and God said, '*nothing will later stop them from doing whatever they presume to do,*' and he confused their language so they could no longer understand each other and scattered them."

"Like this poor victim's body parts are scattered," said Brooks.

"Right. They turned away from God and inward on themselves to achieve a false oneness. Jesus saves us, makes us one, and reverses all this at Pentecost. For the Jews, seven weeks after Passover is the Shavout, when God gave the Torah to the children of Israel. Now, seven weeks after Easter, the Holy Spirit gave the apostles the power to speak God's word. The burning tongues gave them the gift of speaking in tongues so that everyone would understand them in their own language. Instead of being confused and scattered, they could understand God's plan and be one in Him. The Sacrament of Confirmation is when we commit to that faith, to His plan, and receive the gifts of the Holy Spirit."

Brooks quirked one eyebrow. "I'll have to admit that I've never heard that before. It's almost as if it's one story that makes sense versus—well, never mind. So we have languages, sacraments, and a millstone. What's that all about?"

Tom turned to the back of the church, where the forensic team was still attending to the severed tongue and other body parts. "That part comes from Matthew and might reference how this victim didn't follow God's plan." He pulled out a small Bible from his back pocket and opened it to Matthew 18:5: "*Whoever causes one of these little ones who believe in Me to sin, it would be better for him to have a great millstone fastened round his neck and to be drowned in the depth of the sea.* That might be why the tongue was frozen versus on fire. He references a line from another William Blake poem about Pentecost. *If the tongue does not catch fire, the God will not be named.*'"

"A language teacher," said Angelo as he sat staring at the floor, his forearms on his knees.

Brooks shook his head. "What are you babbling about, Salvato?"

"Ahh. Definitely a strong possibility. Detective, each of the killings has been connected to a sacrament by the profession of the victim. The emphasis here has been on tongues and language."

Office Spiro quickly approached with beads of sweat pouring down his forehead as he whispered into Brooks' ear.

Brooks squinted as he turned toward Salvato, nodding with the news. "I'd better not find out this wasn't more than a guess from you. They found the victim submerged in the harbor across from Columbus Park. He had the stone tied around his neck by a rope secured to the pier. Nice of our murderer to make it easy to find him."

Tom asked, "Do you have an identity?"

"Confirming, but the license and info in his wallet are of a Jared Costello, a language teacher at Boston Academy. They found this note in his pocket," replied Brooks as he held out the plastic-sealed note.

Per i più piccoli senza un principale guida.

Angelo sighed. "Huh."

"Another 'huh,' Salvato?"

"It's Italian and says, *For the little ones without a guiding principal*. If they meant *principle*, it would have been spelled *principio* instead of *principale*."

"Well, maybe here the murderer doesn't know his Italian or is a bad speller?"

Angelo shrugged. "So far, that hasn't been the case. He's been very intentional with his language and clues left behind. You might want to check out Boston Academy's principal just to ensure all the bases are covered."

"We know how to cover our bases."

Angelo nodded respectfully. "One more question. Is Dr. Rose still in custody? Just curious since the poem references a 'sick Rose.'"

Brooks ran his hand through his hair. "He's been out on bail."

Chapter 33

Evidence found at the scene and the apartment of the dismembered Jared Costello pointed to the principal at Boston Academy, where Jared had taught Latin, Italian, Spanish, and French. Detective Brooks left Tom with a strong sense that he wasn't feeling comfortable with the evidence being so neatly packaged for each murder—murders connected to an orderly and righteous theme. Who were the innocent victims, and what was the common connection each of them shared?

Tom approached Angelo as he tended to the garden behind the rectory. It was Tom's favorite place to sit and pray when the weather was nice, and Angelo had a knack for mixing the roses and other flowers with his tomatoes, peppers, and herbs. Tom stood beside Angelo as he tilled the soil around some beautiful pink and red blossoming flowers. "These roses are looking great this year."

Angelo laughed. "These are peonies. The blossoms do look like big roses, but the good thing is they don't have thorns. I'm guessing you aren't here to talk about flowers, though, are you?"

With a scratch of his head, Tom replied, "You know me too well. I've been thinking about—"

"What else?"

"Right. I don't know. Maybe this murderer isn't going to do all seven sacraments."

"And maybe he is."

"Right, again. I don't know which one would be next; Marriage, Holy Orders, or Last Rites which we call Sacrament of the Sick these days. And we don't know what day the killer will choose the way we could hypothesize with the first four. I'm hoping and praying he is done with his vengeance murders if that's what this is about."

Angelo stood. "I don't think so. It feels as if he wants more closure or a sense of public justice. You mentioned that

Brooks found more notes going back and forth between Rose and Silverman?"

Tom replied, "Yeah, it seems as if they were arguing a lot before the murder. Rose was telling Silverman things like, 'This has to stop,' 'We can't cover this any longer,' and 'You've got to end this, now.' They also found monthly payments of five-thousand dollars coming from the business account Rose referred to in his notes—and then they suddenly stopped in late December."

"Do they know who the recipient was?"

"A woman from the neighborhood named Mildred Goldshore."

Angelo brushed off his sleeves. "Maybe we should pay her a quick visit?"

Tom stared at Angelo until it was clear that his friend was going with or without him.

Mildred Goldshore's address was listed on Newland Street, just around the corner from Rose and Silverman's office. Tom kept up with Angelo's quick pace. "Angelo. What are we doing? What are we going to ask her?"

They approached the single- and two-story brick family homes that lined the street. "Here it is." Angelo pointed to the names next to the buzzer. "Look at this. Ms. M. Goldshore and Mr. L. Weitz."

Tom squinted as he read the names. "What about it?"

"L. Weitz. Lenny Weitz was the man at Joel Silverman's funeral. He was talking with Sam Gately and disappeared when Flaherty tried to approach them. It seems too coincidental. Rose was at his partner's funeral, who was making monthly payments to this woman. Rose and Silverman argue that they stop these payments, they stop, and months later, Silverman is dead."

A middle-aged woman answered the door, holding a lit cigarette and adjusting the kerchief tying back her hair. "Do I know you? What do you want?"

"Mrs. Goldshore—" started Tom.

"There's no mister, so there's no missus."

"Ms. Goldshore. We just saw Len Weitz."

She took a long drag from her cigarette and let the smoke slowly drift out as she responded. "Lenny? What would you be seeing my son about?"

"Well, we saw him at Dr. Silverman's funeral, and—"

Her face flushed deep red. "Silverman! That bastard deserves to be in the ground. Lenny would never go to his funeral after what he did. Never! Why do you make things up like this? You, a priest and all. Who are you two?"

Angelo kept a calm, straight face. "Ms. Goldshore, we're on your side. We saw that Rose and Silverman were sending you money for years, and then it stopped. Could you tell us why it stopped?"

Mildred squinted as she took another long drag. "Who told you? Look, those two were no good. Ask Silverman's family what they thought of the good doctor. I know exactly when it happened. Nineteen years ago! That boy and my son have never been the same. No amount of money could take away the damage they did, but they owed me. Thinking they can just stop when nothing has really been paid back—bah. They are both bastards in my book. Jail or the grave is the only place for them."

She started to close the door when Tom asked, "How well does Lenny know Sam Gately?"

She glanced up at Tom. "Why do you want to know?"

"If your son has been through a lot, it is good to know he has support and friendship."

She squinted, and her face tightened. "They've got that group. I don't know what kind of friends they are, but they are thick as thieves since that poor Rowan ki—died."

"Rowan Montecchi?"

"That's it. That was sad. Sad, he thought that was the only way he could finally take control of his life. There are other ways. Look, I've got things to do," snapped Mildred as she pushed the door shut without a goodbye.

Turning toward Angelo, Tom asked, "Did we learn anything?"

"Probably a lot. I have a feeling the clue we need is on that list."

"Which list?"

"Rose and Silverman did some group counseling. We know that Sam Gately saw Silverman, and when I followed him after Harry Simon's funeral, he said that he 'had *that* covered.' I took that to mean he was still seeing someone now."

"So, you think there's a group still meeting, and they may be responsible for these murders? Victims seeking revenge justice from these men? There is certainly a lot of pain and damage evident, especially when someone takes his own life," said Tom with a long sigh.

"I don't know what to think, but I do know that something or someone connects all these murder victims and the nicely packaged clues to implicate the killer."

Tom stopped. "Do you think all of the charged suspects and, I guess, Olivia are innocent?"

Rubbing his sparse scalp, Angelo replied, "Either that or one of them is guilty and framing the others to give him cover. I wonder what Ms. Goldshore meant when she mentioned something that happened nineteen years ago. Was there another boy Lenny knew, and if so, what happened? Lenny would have been about twelve, so I wonder if he was seeing Silverman at that time."

"So, you think either Alpheus, Rose, or the principal—what's his name?—could be the murderer and he framed himself along with the others to eventually escape the charges?"

"The principal is Charles Noyes," Angelo replied. "They found blood in the trunk of his car and on a pair of his shoes, both of which had been recently cleaned. I heard that they also found a letter in Jared Costello's apartment from Principal Noyes threatening to fire him and that he couldn't cover for him any longer," responded Angelo, his eyes shifting as they did when plotting his strategy while playing chess with Tom.

"And then there are these innocents mentioned at each murder. Are they the victims finally seeking revenge?"

Chapter 34

On the following day, after morning Mass, Angelo met Tom coming out of the side door of the church and asked, "Can I treat you to a Cup-O-Joe's?"

"Are you thinking of seeing Sam Gately again?"

"I've seen him enough. I was thinking more about talking to him."

Tom opened the door to the rectory and led Angelo into the kitchen. "Wait. Have you seen him again?"

Angelo responded. "A few times, but I haven't been able to approach him. Yesterday, I saw him with that Lenny Weitz again. They were in front of Dr. Rose's office, talking with another guy."

"Do you know who it was?"

Angelo raised his hands. "Nope, but I did hear Lenny call him 'JoDo' when I got close enough to hear. He looked like he lived on the streets."

"All right. We can go and see him—"

Angelo raised his brow.

"Okay, talk with him, but what are we going to ask him this time? Are you the Boston Sacramental Serial Killer we've been looking for?"

Angelo handed Tom his jacket. "I have no idea what connects the victims in this case, but I think he might."

As they entered the busy coffee shop, Tom recognized the girl who had worked there last time and waved when she spotted him in line and smiled back. When they reached the counter, Tom said, "It's Alyce, right?"

She glanced up. "Good memory."

"How does it feel to have your classes over and done with?"

"Good, but I still have my practicum, and I'll probably always be learning new things, one way or another. So, is this going to become your regular coffee spot?"

Tom laughed. "You can't beat the friendly service. Do you know if Sam Gately is supposed to be working today?"

Alyce shook her head. "Supposed to be? Oh, yeah. Is he here? Nope. He missed yesterday, too, and that's why I'm doing an extra shift. Why are you so interested in Sam, anyway?"

Tom glanced at Angelo, who said, "We're just concerned with how he is doing. Hopefully, he has friends around."

"Huh. I think he does. Some people have come around several times. You know, guys around his age, and this older guy dropped by a few times to talk with him." As a line queued behind them, she asked, "Did you want to order anything?"

Tom replied, "Sure, two coffees and two of those 'everything' bagels. By the way, was the older guy a large man, balding, possibly with a tweed jacket?"

"Yeah, that was him. I'll get your order."

Tom whispered to Angelo, "Dr. Rose, I presume?"

"I think you're right, Stanley," replied Angelo through tight lips.

Holding the bag of coffees and bagels, Tom stood with Angelo outside of Cup-O-Joe's. "We need to think about what this might mean."

Angelo raised his hand to his lips. "What about if we enjoy the good weather and breakfast on a bench in the Common?"

"Sounds good," said Tom as they navigated the handful of streets until they reached an open bench by the Park Street station next to the Brewer Fountain, watching some kids scooping water from it. "Why would Gately be meeting with Dr. Rose, or the other way around? I wonder if the other people coming to see him were Len Weitz and this 'JoDo' you overheard?"

Sipping his coffee and watching the birds flock to the top basin of the running fountain, Angelo replied, "Gately doesn't seem like the friendly type, so I don't imagine his social circle is that broad. I guess it's possible Rose wanted to get rid of a five-thousand-dollar monthly extortion payment and Joel Silverman at the same time. It sounds as if they had a few heated arguments about the payments and covering for him."

"Hmm. Gately could have wanted Harry Simon dead, and it sounds as if Len Weitz, or at least his mother, had something against Joel Silverman. But why kill Boulanger, the baker, and Costello, the teacher?" asked Tom.

"That's a very important question. I would think Rose would have been privy to many skeletons and grievances through his counseling sessions. What if there was a group of men with painful grievances, and they decided it was time for justice? Time to take control?" asked Angelo.

"And Rose might be empowering them to take that control, even if he didn't intend it to go that far? Or maybe he is directly involved? Huh. I think we might be getting ahead of ourselves," replied Tom as he spotted an older woman wearing a heavy coat and hat lifting something from the trash. He stood up and walked over toward her, making her jump when she realized he was next to her. "Mary?"

She seemed relieved when she peered up and realized who it was. "Father, you gave me a fright."

"Mary Quill. You are looking good, and I'm glad the weather has been warmer. It was nice of you to drop off money for staying at the convent that cold night, but it wasn't necessary. I want to give it back to you."

Mary shook her head. "I don't want no handouts. I've got my pride."

Nodding, Tom said, "You are a proud woman, Mary. We appreciate it, but can I treat you to a nice dinner for your birthday? That's okay, right?" asked Tom as he offered a twenty-dollar bill.

She hesitated, staring at the bill for several moments before she nodded and let him drop it in her hand. "My birthday isn't for two months, so I'll save it until then. I think it would be rude to refuse a birthday gift, right?"

Tom's eyes softened as he noticed Mary turning to the fountain. "It makes me happy that you accept my humble gift to a beautiful woman. That must have been a rough night here at the fountain last January."

Mary squinted and pursed her lips. "I don't like to think about it." Her eyes closed tight. "No. I don't want to see it."

"I understand, but you did help the police by telling them all you know."

Her eyes opened as she glanced up at Tom and then back down, slowly shaking her head back and forth without a word.

"Mary, did you tell them everything you saw that night?"

Her lips pressed together as she stared downward, appearing to ponder his question.

"Mary, are you afraid of someone if you say anything? Did you see someone here in the Common that night?"

She mumbled as she started to move slowly away from Tom. "I promised."

Tom called out, "Mary, what did you promise? Who did you see?"

Her back to Tom, she continued to distance herself and did not respond to Tom.

"Mary, did he have curly reddish hair?"

She looked back at Tom, her eyes full of fear.

Chapter 35

Tom plopped down on the park bench next to Angelo. "I have a feeling Sam Gately may be more than a funeral attendee."

Angelo didn't respond but continued to read the newspaper that had been left rolled up on the bench.

"Angelo, what is it?"

Angelo turned the paper back to the front page to show the headline for the day.

WILL GRACE SAVE US FROM SACRAMENTAL MURDERER?

Tom shook his head. "Oh, boy. They might scare more people to death than the murderer himself. We'd better get over to Brooks." Standing up, Tom turned back to Angelo, who was still sitting. "Are you coming?"

Angelo motioned behind Tom. "Why go to the police station when they come to you?"

Tom turned to see Brooks and Mullen approaching. Brooks scoffed, "Did you guys miss something on your Freedom Trail stroll the other day?"

"Detective Brooks, I think you need to talk to Sam Gately and possibly Dr. Rose again."

Brooks gave a sarcastic half-smile. "We do this for a living, you know."

"We've been watching Gately's apartment," said Mullen. "No sign of him, but we searched it today and found one of the walls in his bedroom plastered with the articles from different papers on the murders—all in order by sacrament."

"That's certainly suspicious," said Tom.

Mullen added, "That's not all. He had three sections marked off and titled Holy Orders, Marriage, and Last Rites. And—"

Tom leaned forward, "And?"

"And a printed photo of the Brewer Fountain—"

Angelo interjected, "He could be just fascinated with the case."

Brooks quipped, "It was date-stamped 1:44 a.m. on the morning of January 12—"

"The morning of the first murder. Was the body visible in the photo?" inquired Tom.

Mullen said, "It was pretty grainy, but we could make out the hand. We just need to find his camera or phone to get a cleaner look, but all that work was unlikely accomplished in the sixteen minutes before Mary Quill found the body."

"And it's not likely he was just passing by doing late-night photography of Boston fountains for a hobby," said Tom. "Speaking of Mary Quill, it sounds like she may have seen someone in the Common that night."

"What?" quipped Brooks.

"She definitely didn't want to talk about it. She mumbled something about a promise, but when I asked if she saw someone with curly red hair, she became frightened and scurried away," recounted Tom.

"And you let her go?" snapped Brooks. He pivoted to Mullen. "We should be able to track down an old homeless woman with a bad leg and see if we can't bring Rose and Gately in for questioning."

Tom peered up at the upper basin of the fountain. "I hope you find them soon."

Brooks patted his jacket as if to feel for his pack of cigarettes. "Can you meet me at the station?"

"Sure, we can come down," replied Tom.

"I didn't mean *you* as in *you two*."

Angelo eyed Tom and said, "No problem. I'd just get in the way, plus there's something about police stations that gives me the creeps."

Tom rode back to the station with Brooks, entering one of the interrogation rooms. "Do you want a cup of coffee or anything?"

"What else do you have?" asked Tom.

"Nothing, just bad coffee."

"I'll pass. What's on your mind?" asked Tom as he sat in the room he had only seen from the other side of the mirror.

Brooks placed his notebook in front of him as he ran his hand across his forehead, pausing to answer. "Look, I don't know if this is going to be a sensitive topic, but I need to ask you a few questions."

"Sure, sure. I'm more than happy to talk about anything that can help," said Tom, wondering what would come next.

"Ahh. Look. A lot of the case files in Rose and Silverman's office had to do with young men that were abused as kids. I can't talk about any specifics, and I'm not allowed to see the names, but I've been thinking a lot about this case. What's driving these murders? What are these clues about? What wrong is being righted, in the mind of the murderer, with these sick killings?"

Tom sighed. "I've been thinking a lot about this, too. Four men killed because of their sins against the innocents. You think it might be sexual abuse against minors, right?"

Brooks stared down at the table. "I do."

Tom rubbed his forefingers against his lips. "What do you want to ask me?"

"I know this is a sensitive topic for the Church after the scandal was exposed seven years ago. The abuse. The coverups. The lack of accountability."

Tom nodded. "It's...uhm—"

"It's the worst thing you can do to a kid," snapped Brooks. "I'm still pissed about it, and it may be why I haven't gone back to church in a while." He let out a long sigh. "I'm not one of those guys who thinks every priest is a pedophile. I know the reality. Ninety-eight percent of priests are clean and still get looked at sideways. Most cases happened during the fifties through the eighties, and there are much higher abuse rates in other professions, but you do have some rotten priests."

Frozen for a moment, Tom replied, "There are. The abuse is criminal, and the enablers are criminal. Even though we've got a ton of protective measures in place today, and the kids are safe, there is no excuse for any cases. It's the opposite of what the Church is about, so I feel ashamed about it. Actually, I feel damn angry about it most of the time."

"So, you can imagine how angry a killer bent on revenge against these monsters might be."

"I can."

Brooks leaned forward. "I figured you would. If the next sacrament on that list is Holy Orders, then we might be looking for a pedophile priest still on the loose. Someone who hasn't been held accountable. Someone who hasn't been found out yet and has a protector. How are we going to find this priest before the next hit?"

"Well, I'm guessing that these incidents all happened ten to twenty years ago. So far, all the victims are local to that area, so we might be able to focus on churches in the area and go back through the history of priests assigned to those parishes that are still alive," replied Tom, his stomach in knots at the possibilities.

Brooks was writing in his notebook. "Good idea. I just can't figure out the whole pedophilia thing. How can anyone do that to a child?"

Tom pursed his lips and paused. "I think I'll have that bad cup of coffee now if you don't mind."

Brooks came back with a coffee-filled paper cup. "Have you ever counseled anyone who's been sexually assaulted as a kid?"

"Not that I know of. Keep in mind that there is a wide range of abuse, from inappropriate touching to rape. From what we know about the priest scandal, the vast majority of the cases were not pedophilia."

"What does that mean?" demanded Brooks.

"Pedophilia is an attraction to prepubescent boys or girls. Hebephilia is the attraction to pubescent minors."

"And that makes it okay?!" shot back Brooks.

"Absolutely not. But it's a different dynamic and psychology on the part of the perp. I think it's important to know the dynamics, what you're dealing with, and who the victims might be."

Standing up and pacing, Brooks grumbled, "What is it? I can't figure out what's up with these guys."

Tom stared down at the table, lost in his thoughts. "Things fall apart; the center cannot hold. Control."

"What center? What control?"

Tom's eyes narrowed. "Most abusers experienced some type of traumatic event in their own childhood. About a third were sexually abused themselves, and many never formed a healthy attachment to a parent. They may feel as if they're going to disintegrate. They may crave affection. Whatever it is that leads them down this path, subconsciously, it's a situation they can finally control."

Brooks slapped the table with the palm of his hand. "If you were molested as a child, how could you ever do that to another kid? You would think it would be the last thing they would do."

Tom continued to stare down at the table in front of him. "Yeah. Well, as children, they could not control their situation. By sexually assaulting children, they attempt to re-live the trauma they experienced to learn how to master it. The role reversal gives them the upper hand, the power to prevent themselves from being victimized. The control they didn't have."

"So, we're looking for a screwed-up social misfit priest who has a traumatized past and takes it out on vulnerable boys who may have been looking for a trustworthy adult?"

Tom sighed. "Maybe, but this is a complex thing. Many abusers have a hard time developing intimate adult relationships, so they can become fixated on children—often thinking they are doing nothing wrong and that they are actually loving the child."

"What? How can they possibly think that?"

"Like I said, their thinking is distorted, and these relationships often happen over time. Only a small minority are aware repeat predators, and many don't even realize they hurt a child until they are in therapy," replied Tom in a serious tone.

There was a sudden knock on the door, and Mullen peeked in. "We've got Dr. Rose in for questioning, but no sign of Gately."

Chapter 36

Tom slipped into the viewing room while Mullen brought Dr. Rose into the interrogation room, where Brooks sat without making eye contact with the suspect.

"Why are you harassing me like this?" demanded Rose.

"All you have to do is convince us that you're not involved in these murders in any way, and you'll never see us again. So far, you look like the prime suspect to me, and there's plenty of evidence to back that up. You know that, right?" grilled Brooks.

The door opened again, and a thin man with glasses and wearing a suit and carrying a worn leather suitcase walked in. "Why do you have my client here? This is harassment. My client is completely innocent. We'll be suing the Boston Police Department for serious damage to his reputation."

"If you want to give speeches, do it in the hall. If you want to sit and listen, you can sit and listen." Brooks peered up at Rose. "If you're innocent, why did you feel a need to bring your lawyer in?"

Rose stared back but did not respond.

Tapping his hand on the table in front of him, Brooks opened the file folder. "Dr. Rose, can you tell us about your relationship with Sam Gately?"

"What are you asking me?"

"Do you know a Sam Gately?"

"His name sounds familiar. I think he may have seen Dr. Silverstein or myself a few times."

Brooks pulled out a large photo and slid it across the table in front of Rose and pointed to one of the men in the photo. "This was taken from a surveillance camera in front of your office. Is this Sam Gately?"

Rose gave a slight nod.

Moving his finger, Brooks asked, "And is this you?"

"Possibly. The quality of the photo is poor," replied Rose as he pulled back in his chair.

"Possibly?" Brooks said in a sarcastic tone. "This photo was taken a day before the murder of a Mr. Harry Simon." Pulling another photo out, Brooks said, "And another meeting the day before your partner's murder. Who is this other man in the photo?"

"I have no idea."

"You should. It's Leonard Weitz. He and his mother have been receiving payments, maybe blackmail payoffs, from your office, each month for years. These payments suddenly stopped after arguments between you and Silverman, and then your partner was dead a short time later. I don't believe in coincidences, Dr. Rose."

Rose's lawyer chided, "Detective, this type of questioning is out of line. I must protest."

Brooks turned toward the lawyer, anger rising as the muscles in his neck tightened. "Sit in the corner and make yourself a sign and protest all you want. I need to know the truth." Turning back to Rose, he said, "I think you and Silverman saw a lot of men with abuse issues, possibly sexual abuse. I think you either worked with them or empowered them to finally seek justice for the abuser's damage to their lives. I think you had a specific group of men that may have plotted a revenge plan against those abusers, coordinated through you, or possibly, they were helping you."

"You are grasping, Detective. I think you are panicking because you haven't found any evidence to lead you to the real killer, so you are trying to use me as a scapegoat with this wild conspiracy theory. I took you for a hard-facts kind of guy, but you are obviously not." Rose turned to his lawyer. "Do I have to put up with these slanderous accusations?"

"Detective Brooks. I have to ask for this inquisition to end right now!" demanded the lawyer.

Brooks continued to drill his stare directly into Rose's eyes. "So, you deny that you know Len Weitz?"

"Dr. Silverman was the main facilitator of that group, and Mr. Weitz wasn't even part of it when Joel ran it."

"So, you do know Len Weitz? And that was him with Gately talking with you in the photo?" demanded Brooks.

Rose glanced toward his lawyer but did not respond.

"Did you know a Mr. Rowan Montecchi?"

No response.

Brooks shot up, the seat squealing back behind him. "Which priest is the next victim on your list?!"

Mullen grabbed Brooks' shoulder to hold him back as Rose's lawyer shouted, "This so-called interview is over."

As they left the room, Tom noticed Rose turn back and give an arrogant glance at Brooks that seemed to say, "You're not good enough to catch me." It seemed like such an odd glance for anyone who was either innocent and being falsely accused or deadly guilty.

Chapter 37

The week had passed quickly, and there were no breaks in the case, no sign of either Sam Gately or Len Weitz. Rowan Montecchi was dead, and the only Boston Academy student connection with Jared Costello was a young man named George Stroupe. Despite bristling at the name of Costello, he offered no help or insights. George lived on his own, close to Tremont Street, and outside of a failed attempt at marriage that only lasted two weeks, there was nothing remarkable about his quiet existence.

As the days passed, Tom became increasingly concerned about the possible murder of a fellow priest, even if the murderer believed he deserved punishment for his crime. Tom worked with Brooks and the archdiocese to identify priests who served at the parishes in that part of Boston, even if they seemed above reproach. Police details were assigned to each parish, but all remained quiet.

The rectory phone rang, and Luke picked up the phone from the kitchen wall. "St. Francis. This is Father Tom's butler. May I help you?"

Tom grabbed the phone from him. "This is Father Tom. How may I help you?"

"It's Brooks."

"Dear God, what is it?"

"It looks like our killer or killers have struck again."

The names and faces of all the priests on the lists they had assembled and talked with over the past week ran through Tom's head. He took a deep breath and asked, "Who was it?"

"This is not public knowledge yet, so keep it to yourself. The victim was a doctor. His office is a few doors down from Boston Medical if you're available to look at a few things."

Tom said, "Sure, Detective. I can be there in a few minutes."

When he arrived at the scene, one of the officers escorted him into the examination room. Brooks stood next to a doctor who said, "It looks like a case of induced pulmonary edema."

"Speak English to me, Doc."

"Well," the doctor replied as he closed up his medical bag, "someone tied him down to this examining table and most likely injected an illicit drug into his system that made his lungs fill with fluid, literally making him drown until his last breath."

Brooks looked closer. "What's with the oil all over his body?"

"I don't know. My guess is it's olive oil that had gone rancid."

"How can you tell it's rancid?"

"A good olive oil will have a fresh fruit or vegetable scent. Rancid olive oil will have a waxy smell, like a crayon or putty."

"Thanks, Doc. Let me know when you have a read on what type of drug was used and how long he's been dead," requested Brooks as he turned and spotted Tom standing by the door.

Brooks walked the doctor to the outer office, where a nurse sat sobbing uncontrollably, and Mullen attended to her. Brooks motioned Tom to the outside waiting area.

Tom asked, "Do you think this is linked to the others? That's not a priest in there, is it?"

Brooks shook his head. "No." He handed Tom a folded piece of paper.

Unfolding it, Tom saw the heading, *'Last Rites,' by Francis Reginald Scott*. "I see. I assume that man inside is Dr. Alfred Finkle, as it states on the door, and this is connected to the Sacrament of Last Rites or what we call today, the Sacrament of the Sick." The poem was long, and Tom noted the words highlighted in yellow marker. *Twenty-four years Within his tent of pain and oxygen, Nurse will fail, Death will block The channels of her aid, But nurse will stare This evil in the face, will not accept, And I who watch this rightness and these rites, I see my father in the dying man.*

"What do you think?" inquired Brooks reading the highlighted sections with Tom.

"Hmm. I'm not familiar with this poet. *Twenty-four years* is penciled in while the rest of the poem is typed and some verses highlighted, so I'm not sure if something happened in 1985 that caused the *tent of pain*. A lot of focus is on the nurse failing *in her aid* as she stares *this evil in the face*. All the other murders had clues pointing directly to someone else they wanted to be punished. Maybe some of the victims were those who 'aided' or enabled the sins of the one who deserved the death penalty."

Brooks wrote a few notes in his book. "What about the last line highlighted? *I see my father in the dying man*. Do you think Finkle would be the killer's father?"

Tom scratched his scalp. "I don't think so. I think the murderer may be taking this out on Dr. Finkle because of his own father. I don't know if that will narrow things down since a lot of possible suspects have had issues with absent or abusive dads. Was there anything else left?"

"Now that you mention it." Brooks pulled out a small black leather book. On the jacket was a gold embossed print that read, *PASTORAL CARE OF THE SICK: Rights of Anointing and Viaticum.*

A sudden warmth made its way to Tom's face as he opened the cover and saw the name written inside. *Father Tom Fitzpatrick*. "This was in there?"

"Yup," said Brooks. "Can you explain why?"

"It's been missing for a while, but I thought I had just misplaced it."

Brooks asked, "Do you keep it in the church?"

"No, the rectory."

"So, assuming you aren't the killer, he's been inside your house. Are those your yellow tabs in the pages?"

Shaking his head, Tom opened to the prayers for the Anointing of the Sick. Over the first prayer was taped a handwritten version that read, *Through this unholy anointing may the Lord in his justice judge you. May the*

Lord condemn you for your sins against the innocent and never raise you up. The final tabbed prayer page marked also had a handwritten note that read, *This is the Lamb of God who takes away the sins of the world. Happy are only those who are called to his supper.*

"It seems as if this executioner is taking God's place for judgment, justice, and final condemnation," remarked Brooks as he took the book back. "I hope you don't mind if I hold onto this. I may need a statement from you on when you lost it."

Nodding, Tom said, "Understood."

"Hey, what's with the rancid oil?"

"Probably to do the opposite of the sacrament. Holy Oil is used as a visible sign of grace for Baptism, Confirmation, and the Sacrament of the Sick. The killer wanted the opposite of healing, forgiveness, and salvation for his victim," said Tom, noticing Angelo had joined them.

"You're too late, Salvato," quipped Brooks.

"I guess we all are. I heard most of what you said, and I wonder if the 'evidence' will point to the nurse and if there is another person in that group that Rose and Silverman facilitated who was a patient of the deceased doctor when he was a young boy? You know, about the age of the group that Gately and Weitz were in."

"Funny thing about that group. Weitz was seen by Silverman when he was twelve but was not part of the group counseling. I can understand why he wouldn't want to be connected with Rose or Silverman. The other thing is that there are only five men listed in that group, not seven. We've had five murders, so I don't know if there's one more or he's done. Maybe, hopefully, they were only intending the five." said Brooks, taking out a cigarette and waving it under his nose to inhale the aroma.

Tom and Angelo sat in the detective's room next to Brooks' desk, watching Mullen fill out additional pieces of the puzzle on the whiteboard, with a large question mark at the top.

Victim		Profession	Suspect	Group Member
Baptism	Harry Simon	Swim Inst	Jon Alpheus	Sam Gately
Confession	Joel Silverman	Psychiatrist	Avil Rose	Len Weitz (No)
Communion	Peter Boulanger	Baker	Olivia Boulanger	Rowan Montecchi
Confirmation	Jared Costello	Teacher	Chuck Noyes	George Stroupe
Last Rites	Alfred Finkle	Doctor	Wendy Morse	Terry Rivers

Brooks entered the room with coffee in hand. "So, my volunteer squad. We have five bodies, five murders tied to Catholic sacraments, all with neatly packaged evidence pointing to five suspects, and five dysfunctional young men all tied to them, but only four in this group. Oh, yeah, and all the suspects seemed to be hiding something about the victims."

Mullen pointed to the last two names. "We had a hard time locating George Stroupe and Terry Rivers, but both had very little to offer about the victims. They were actually very cold about them, and neither had a good alibi for the time of the killings. We still haven't located Gately and Weitz, and we know that Rowan won't be talking anytime soon. The other name is Daniel Murphy, but we have no record of him in Boston."

Angelo approached the board. "All these suspects have a ton of evidence pointing to them, almost professionally staged—not too easy, but all very findable. If these people in this suspect column aren't guilty, then there must be a good reason they've been set up."

Brooks grunted. "There is still the strong possibility that Rose is behind this and framed himself just like the others to ultimately get off. Who knows what goes on in the mind of a psychiatrist?" Brooks said, glaring at Tom. "You know, my mom told me to avoid dating psych majors because there's always something going on inside them that they're trying to figure out. Did your mom tell you that too?"

Angelo wisecracked, "Funny, my mom always told me to watch out for cops. The troublemakers in the neighborhood always went into law enforcement."

"Very funny. My mom also told me—"

Mullen held up her hand. "Okay, that's enough, boys. We've got a case to crack."

Angelo straightened. "My money is on Gately or someone in the group orchestrating this. We've got to find Gately or Weitz."

Chapter 38

Standing outside the station with Angelo, Tom said, "I don't think this is going anywhere without talking to some of these key players."

Flaherty opened the precinct door, stepped outside and jested, "Are you two off of your shift?"

"We asked for a raise, and Brooks fired us on the spot. He probably should have gotten rid of us long ago based on the help we've provided so far," replied Tom.

Deep in thought, Angelo lifted his head. "Alpheus. We should try to talk with Jon Alpheus."

"Why is that?" asked Flaherty.

"Well, if he's being framed for killing Harry Simon, he must have come up with some ideas on why. He's being held at Walpole right now, isn't he?" asked Angelo.

Flaherty paused. "I think you're right. He didn't have bail, and they are holding him for trial. I can call ahead to get permission to visit if you want."

Tom sat next to Angelo in the prison waiting area. "Do you miss it?"

Angelo rolled his eyes. "I miss my dear friend, but never the bars—or the food."

A half-hour later, the prison officer brought them to the visiting booth; thick fiberglass partitions stood between them and the prisoner.

Jonas Alpheus was escorted to the chair on the other side of the partition, scowling at the floor. "What are you two doing here?"

Tom raised his hand. "Jonas, you say that you are an innocent man."

"I didn't say that. I said I didn't kill Harold Monnot."

"Okay, well, we're on your side to help find out who did and get you out of here," said Tom, trying to catch Alpheus' eye.

He pursed his lips as he continued staring at the floor. "I can't do much about that in here."

"Well, maybe we can. What do you know about Sam Gately?"

Alpheus's face flushed at the name. "Why?"

"Do you remember him from all those years back?"

"Hmm. Of course. He was a twelve-year-old boy who came to us for lessons. I still remember his eyes, piercing but so vulnerable and tentative. I knew something wasn't right at home for him, and it pained me to see that in his eyes. So handsome, so smart, and so afraid."

Angelo asked, "What do you think he was afraid of?"

Shaking his head, Alpheus replied, "I don't know. His mother would drop him off, hoping, I think, that we could help him somehow. I don't know the exact situation with his father outside of drinking and physical abuse. Thank God he left them."

"Who taught Sam's swimming lessons?"

"I started with him, but Harold was a newer teacher who asked to take over. Monnot was a good teacher. He worked well with Sam, and I watched him develop trust and confidence." There was a long pause.

Angelo studied Alpheus's changing expressions. "They became close?"

Alpheus squinted tight at the question. He seemed to hesitate and drift off in thought.

Tom said, "Jon, are you saying they developed a friendship?"

"At first, but I had to talk with Monnot several times about getting too personal in his relationships with the students, especially with Sam."

"Is that why you had to let him go?" asked Angelo.

"That was fifteen years later. We argued many times about Sam and other boys, but then—" Alpheus stopped short as anguish rippled over his face, and a tear appeared in the corner of his eye.

Angelo leaned forward. "Do you think something happened to Sam that would make him capable of killing Harry? Sam left after that year."

"I can say nothing."

"And Harry had to change his name after you let him go, so I have a feeling there is more you aren't telling us."

Alpheus rubbed his brow. "I think it's time you left."

Tom stood as Alpheus did. "Jon, we didn't want to upset you. I had one last question. Who is the young boy in the picture on the wall of your apartment?"

Alpheus turned back to Tom with a glare in his eye and then left the visiting area without responding.

On the quiet ride back to Boston from Walpole Prison, Angelo said, "Why did you ask about the picture in his apartment?"

Tom replied, "Do you remember the clues left at Harry Simon's murder? The story of the jealous Cyclops and the Greek lovers. And then the story of Zephyrus, or 'Westwind,' who loved the beautiful young Hyacinthus and was highly jealous of Apollo's attachment to him, enough to kill the boy. I think that picture of the boy with the curly red hair is Sam Gately, and Jonas was very taken with him. I don't know what happened between Harry and Sam, but it was enough to make Jonas angry and eventually fire Harry from the job he loved to do. There was also something big enough for Harry to change his name and break up his marriage."

Angelo mumbled, "Interesting. Speaking of marriages, the last two sacraments are Holy Matrimony and Holy Orders. I guess every married couple and priest with a skeleton in their closet should be worried about what happens next."

Chapter 39

Dr. Franks stared at his client, Daniel Murphy, for several moments. In the heaviness of the silence, he could tell that Daniel was on the edge of an emotional breakthrough, and the reaction was never predictable. "Close your eyes for a moment and think of yourself as a young boy, whatever age strikes you."

Daniel closed his eyes and went with the exercise. His head began to nod. "Okay."

"Where are you?"

His eyes squeezed tight, and he let out a long breath. "On my front steps."

"What do you hear and see?"

"I don't know. A group of kids is playing down the street. Uhm, I hear yelling from inside the house."

"Are your parents arguing?"

He nodded.

"The kids down the street. Did you want to be included?"

He fidgeted on the leather couch.

"What are your parents arguing about?"

"I don't know. I just knew—" He stopped and folded his arms.

"What did it make you afraid of, Daniel?"

His eyes and face tightened. "He would get so angry that he would leave."

"Leave your mother?"

His body shook, and he mumbled, "No, me. I would never see him again."

"If you could have anything at that moment, what would it be?"

"No, it feels too risky to wish."

Dr. Franks jotted short notes. "What if there were no risk to wish? Don't think about it. What would you want from him at that very moment?"

One tear fell, and then another. His arms folded and wrapped tighter around the other.

"Would you want him to come out and sit next to you? To put his arm around you and let you know how much you mean to him?"

More tears fell without any words.

"To tell you he loved you? To spend time with you and teach you how to play ball?"

"I wanted him to love me. I wanted him to look me in the eye once to let me know he would never leave."

Dr. Franks let the moment sit. "It's okay, Daniel. We all need affection. We all need to know we are loved and wanted. You deserved it."

He shook his head. "If I deserved it, he would have wanted me."

"Growing up, did you have any place where you felt valued?"

His eyes shut again, almost as if retreating to a calm place.

"Did you have any male mentors, men who could teach you and see you?"

He grinned a bit, nodding. "One place."

"How did that make you feel?"

"Like I mattered."

Dr. Franks stared at him, wondering where this would go. "What happened?"

He opened his eyes and peered back. "What do you mean, what happened?"

"This man who made you feel as if you mattered, what happened next? Do you still stay in contact with him?"

"I don't know what you mean. Nothing happened. I don't know what happened next. I don't even remember who it was."

"Okay. So you didn't know this person very long, then?"

His gaze drifted off. "I didn't say that. I just don't remember. It seems like—"

"Daniel, it's okay. You don't have to go anywhere you're not ready to go. Do you remember any happy or safe moments in this friendship?"

His eyes closed with a long quiet pause before finally nodding.

"Daniel, sometimes we can repress certain memories in our past. They may feel overwhelming or too frightening to recall, but they still live inside, keeping us prisoner. I want to ask you something."

He opened his eyes. "What?"

"Do you feel strong enough to explore this a bit further in our next session?"

Chapter 40

Tom and Angelo headed over to the police station to catch Brooks, but he was already gone. On their trek back, they stopped in front of a pub. Tom glanced at Angelo. "I heard this was a good pub with great pizza or a great pub with good pizza."

"If the pizza is great, I'll buy you a good beer," jested Angelo.

In a matter of minutes, they had grabbed a table by the open window, sipping beers, and watching the world pass by on a pleasant evening.

Tom sighed. "All these secrets and people dying or disappearing. It's such a difficult case to get a handle on."

Angelo took another sip. "I know. I've got to put the word out to see if we can track down Gately or Weitz. I think they're key to opening this up."

"You might be right. Brooks said there were five men in that group, and it stopped two years ago."

Angelo tipped his head forward. "Or maybe it didn't stop?"

Tom followed Angelo's gaze and spotted a group of men exiting the South End Library, a small branch of the Boston Public Library. His eyes widened when he spotted Sam Gately and Len Weitz, with the four other men conversing. "Do you think the group continued after Silverman stopped it?"

Angelo raised his brow. "Maybe. Maybe he stopped it because Len Weitz was joining it."

"That would make a lot of sense. Let's see if we can make out the other four. There was George Stroupe, Terry Rivers, and another name I don't recall."

"Daniel Murphy," said Angelo. "Maybe that guy with the coat and hat is Daniel."

"No, no. I think I recognize him. I think that's Joey."

"Who's Joey? Brooks didn't mention anyone named Joey."

"Joey 'Donuts.' I'm embarrassed that I don't know his last name, but I think he has lived on the street since he was a kid. I've talked with him several times. Intelligent, thoughtful, and a mystery in a lot of ways."

Angelo propped his head on his hand. "Huh. Maybe he escaped a bad situation as a kid, and he's still trying to work through it?" Suddenly, the man at the center of the group turned as they began to break up. "Flaherty?"

"Angelo, what did you say?"

"It's Officer Flaherty, and he's crossing the street."

Tom raised his hand and called out, "Brian. Brian Flaherty!"

Flaherty glanced up.

Tom waved him over. "Do you have time for a beer?"

"Have I ever turned down an offer for a free beer?" replied Flaherty.

As he made his way to their table, Tom joked, "We were hoping you might treat us. Sit down and have a slice while we order. Do you want a Guinness?"

Flaherty gave an enthusiastic nod and sat. "Is this a regular spot for you guys?"

"First time. We were coming back from our visit to Alpheus. Thanks for greasing the skids on a quick approval for the visit."

"I hope it was worth the trip. Did you gain any insights?"

Tom shook his head. "Not a lot. He was definitely not willing to talk about Harry Simon. Maybe he made a promise he is committed to keeping, but I think Sam Gately fits into this somehow. Speaking of which, was that Sam we saw with you and the group coming out of the library a few minutes ago?"

Flaherty paused.

"Wait. You said you were running a counseling group for your studies. Do I remember correctly?"

"Look, Father Tom. You know about confidentiality in this work. I feel pretty strongly about it. That's why I could only say that I didn't know Sam Gately very well."

Angelo said, "Lenny Weitz was there as well. If the group met here, is it possible that he tried to join the group without knowing Joel Silverman was leading it, and that's why Silverman abruptly stopped leading the group?"

Tom leaned forward. "You said you've been facilitating this group for about two years."

Flaherty sighed. "Len was hurting and looking for a place to figure things out. I understand he showed up to this group one night, and Silverman never showed up, or maybe he did and recognized him. These guys were left without anyone to help them. I used to come here to study at night and saw them meeting every Tuesday night. The next Tuesday, they returned, and I heard them trying to figure out what to do, so I approached them. We talked about it, and I told them I could facilitate for a while if they were open to a novice. That was just over two years ago, and they are the best group of guys I've ever met."

A smile came to Tom's face. "You're a good man, Dr. Flaherty."

"Hey, don't get ahead of yourself. I've learned a ton from these guys, and I don't want to violate their confidence. I need you guys to honor that as well."

"Of course," said Tom. "Of course. If I ask a question that you're uncomfortable with, just tell me. I'm pretty sure I recognized a guy named Joey in your group."

"Joey Duggan?"

"Is that his name? I've only known him as Joey 'Donuts.' Was he part of Silverman's group?"

Flaherty replied, "No. I've known Joey for many years from my beat, and I invited him to join us about a year ago. He's a smart and perceptive guy. Not what you'd expect from someone collecting bottles and cans for a living on the streets. He left home when he was ten and has been hiding on these streets for twenty years. His parents searched for him and don't even know he's alive, so please don't reveal his last name to anyone."

Tom replied, "We promise."

"I don't think I should be talking anymore about people in the group."

"I certainly understand and respect that," replied Tom, pausing for a few seconds to take a bite from his pizza. "From a professional perspective, how do you approach counseling a group?"

Flaherty rubbed his chin. "I guess that's more of a generic question. I think I was fumbling for a long time. I listened a lot, trying to figure out how to help. I think you know that we lost someone in the group. Rowan was such a great person, but he was in so much pain that he committed suicide about six months ago. I was pretty shaken up—still am—about it, but when Sam said he thought it was the only way Rowan could finally take control of his situation, to be the one to decide, that hit me."

Tom said, "Did you help to empower them? Make them feel less like victims without control over their destiny?"

"Yeah. How did you know?"

"It makes sense. I've done the same thing, but I've had to be careful about how each person was processing it. If they had a deep reservoir of unresolved pain and resentment, their idea of taking control might be translated into taking revenge to right the wrong."

Flaherty dropped back in his chair, appearing to process what Tom had just told him. He ran his hand through his hair a few times. "No. I don't think that's possible. These are good guys who had a bum ride in their childhood."

For the rest of the pizza and beer, they talked about the Celtics playoffs, the Red Sox, sailing, and anything but the case, but Flaherty had become quieter than usual during parts of the conversation. Tom thought that he might be wondering if he had caused more harm than good in how he was counseling the members of this group to take charge of their lives, to become empowered and in control, and to seek justice.

Chapter 41

Over the next week, Tom spent most of his time attending to his duties at St. Francis School. He stood in the corridor with a broad smile as he watched the energy of the kids in the hallway. Sister Helen came up beside him. "Sure, it's good to see you rememberin' your day job. The students have missed you."

"Now, it hasn't been that bad. And wasn't it you who said that you wanted the kids to be safe from, what do they call him, the Sacramental Killer?"

"Ah, so you're tellin' me you've caught him already?"

Tom paused. "Well, not yet."

"I see. Maybe if you were here more, they would feel safer? Just a thought," said Sister Helen as she strode down the hall, stopping to help one of the girls with her backpack as she peered back at Tom.

"She may have a point," came a voice from behind.

"Angelo. How do you sneak up on me like that? It's like your chess moves that I never see coming. You look as if you're up to something."

Angelo nodded. "Well, I spent most of the week tracking down Sam Gately and Len Weitz."

"And?"

"I found them, and I think we should try to talk with them."

Glancing toward the ceiling, Tom murmured, "And just when I was getting back into Sister Helen's good graces."

"Don't get your hopes up too high there."

Tom started up his Honda hatchback on the third try. "Where are we headed?"

"North End."

'Ah, you're making me hungry. I could go for some good food right now." Tom licked his lips.

Angelo peered out the window as Tom maneuvered around parked cars in the narrow Italian neighborhood. "Here. Head down Clark Road to the harbor."

Tom pulled down the oneway street and took a left along the harbor until Angelo pointed to some condominiums on the wharf. "Hey, I don't know if they'll let me park this car here," joked Tom as he pulled into an open visitor's spot before proceeding along the harbor by foot.

"Here it is."

"Angelo, these apartments are expensive. Are you sure Sam lives here?"

"It's Rowan Montecchi's place. I guess he did very well, but the apartment isn't doing him much good now that he's dead. Sam and Len have been staying here for the past few weeks, hiding out from something or someone."

Tom glanced at a bench by a grassy area overlooking Boston Harbor. He grabbed Angelo's shoulder and pointed, "Isn't that Sam on the bench?"

Sam turned, spotted them, and stood, ready to run.

Tom called out, "Sam! We're not here to harass you or turn you in."

He slowed to a stop, hung his head, breathing heavily, almost as if he were tired of a lifetime of running. He rubbed his forehead with the back of his hand and turned as Tom and Angelo approached him, a silhouette against the bright sun behind him. "What do you want?"

"Sam, a lot of people are looking for you. We've got to stop these murders!"

He squinted. "Do you think I've killed all those perv—whatever they are?"

Angelo said, "We know these killings seem to have a connection to the members of your Tuesday group. You've attended several of the funerals, and the police found the wall in your apartment plastered with news clippings of each murder organized by sacrament with sections left open for those remaining out of the seven, the same number of people in your group."

Tom said, "And they also found a photo of the Brewer Fountain taken around the time of the murder of Harry Simon. You can see how this might look bad for you, so help us understand so that we can help you."

Sam's eyes shifted as he hesitated. "There's nothing I can tell you. I didn't kill anyone."

"Why did Silverman stop facilitating your group counseling sessions two years ago?" asked Angelo.

"Why do you think?"

"I think it might be because he realized Lenny Weitz was going to join the group that met at the library, a group Weitz didn't realize Silverman was running. I think Silverman panicked when he saw Weitz and never showed up again. Does that sound right?" asked Angelo.

Sam stared down.

Tom leaned forward. "Sam, I sense that you guys bonded in friendship around a painful reality that no child or young person should ever experience."

Sam's eyes shut, wincing at the comment.

"Sam, I think you were very close to these men, especially Rowan. When he took his life at the end of last year, I think that hit everyone in the group very hard," said Tom softly.

Sam's face tightened, and his eyes closed. "He was the best person I had ever known. I had no real friends growing up, but he didn't care. He gave everything he had to others but couldn't give himself what he needed, what was robbed from him. He was a successful man on the outside, but there was so much pain inside." Sam paused. "Rowan worked for everything he got. He was from the Old Colony Projects in the Lower End of Southie, on welfare after his father ditched him and his mother. She got him out of the crime and poverty of those projects, working the counters at Filene's, like my mom, just to squeak by, but it was always a struggle. I never had a better friend. That was his book you saw me with."

Tom paused to remember. "Oh, yeah. Yeat's 'Second Coming,' right?"

Sam nodded. "I would read that poem to him, and when I got to that line you recited at the coffee shop, he couldn't cope anymore."

"*Things fall apart; the centre cannot hold; Mere anarchy is loosed upon the world,*" recited Tom.

A tear rolled down Sam's cheek. "That's it. He felt no control over his so-called life. It was only in the act of suicide did he finally feel he had control."

"Sam, I'm so sorry. I really am. I can personally empathize with losing someone you care about so deeply that it throws you into a complete loss of hope and desperation."

Sam peered up at Tom and squinted. "We can't dwell on the past. We can be dragged down by our hurts. We need to take control of our own lives and move forward."

Angelo stepped up. "Sam, the book by Yeats. It was Jonas Alpheus's book."

Sam nodded. "He gave it to me many years ago, and I gave it to Rowan."

"How do you feel about him?" asked Angelo.

"I don't know. He was always trying to be my friend, but I don't think he was ever a true friend. He knew. He knew things and never lifted a finger. That's not what a friend does. Friends don't enable sick people."

Tom placed his hand on Sam's shoulder, and Sam jerked away. "I'm sorry. Sam, how did you get that photograph of the fountain around the time Harry Simon was murdered?"

Sam glared at Tom. "I didn't kill that bastard! D— someone sent me a note that he had taken care of things for me, and I went to find out what that meant. I was glad he was dead. He finally paid for what he did."

"So, you were in the Common that night? You saw the dead body in the fountain. And you told Mary Quill to be quiet about seeing you. Is that right?"

Sam stared at the ground and didn't reply.

"Who is this person? Is it Daniel? Is he the man responsible for these killings?"

"Responsible!" Sam threw his arms in the air, his face contorted as he screamed, "Who has ever been responsible when it counted? You should talk. Don't talk to me about being responsible. Why should those who were—"

Sam turned and ran.

"Sam, Sam," called Tom.

"Leave me alone! I need to be alone!"

Chapter 42

The office of the pastoral bishop for the Boston parishes was modest and plain.

"Would you like a cup of coffee while you wait for Bishop John?" asked the administrative assistant.

Tom sat on one of the wood chairs across from her desk, noticing the photo of her family and an image of Jesus. "That would be great, Emily. Thank you. Do you know if he'll be long or what he wanted to see me about?"

She raised her brow. "I love Bishop John, but he's not great about letting me know everything. I had to move several meetings around to fit you in."

Tom had developed a good relationship with Bishop John years ago when the bishop was a local pastor like himself. Cardinal Sean O'Malley had been brought in during the sex abuse scandal to clean up the mess, regain trust and integrity, and put protective measures for the kids in place. Tom was impressed with his humility, sincerity, and the initial act of moving out of the mansion of his predecessor to a modest apartment and office. Bishop John Connors was one of the first priests elevated to a bishop's role to help foster his vision for rebuilding the Boston Archdiocese. In Tom's opinion, he was a great model of Christ in his friendly and loving approach to his ministry, but he was also a strong leader with a purpose for everything he did.

Normally, it was Tom who worked to get onto the bishop's calendar, but this was the first time he had been called for a one-on-one meeting with no indication of the subject matter.

Tom glanced up in surprise when Bishop John showed up at the office doorway with someone else.

"Tom. Sorry to keep you waiting. I think you know Detective Brooks," said the bishop as he stepped aside and closed the door behind him.

Tom stood perplexed, smiling nervously, and nodded to Brooks. "If you guys are going to ask me to choose between being a priest or a cop, I can—"

"Why don't you sit down, Tom," said Bishop John.

Tom noticed that Brooks wouldn't look him in the eye, and the bishop was more business-like than usual. "I can tell something's not right. What's wrong?"

Bishop John sat on the edge of his desk and let out a long sigh. "Tom, you know how hard we've worked to ensure every child in our parishes is safe. And you know we've worked to screen out any clergy that might present a risk—basically, a zero-tolerance policy."

Nodding, Tom said, "Absolutely. That is doubly important with a parish and a school at St. Francis. How can I help?"

"Tom, Detective Brooks and I had a visit from a Dr. Franks. You may know him. He is a psychiatrist with an office off Tremont Street."

"Okay. I'm not familiar with him."

"Well—" Bishop John paused for several seconds. "He's, uhm, he's brought forward some credible and disturbing allegations from a client he has been working with, and—those allegations named you as—"

Brooks interrupted. "I trusted you. He claims you sexually assaulted him fifteen years ago, and—"

"And there is a witness," said Bishop John, followed by a long sigh.

Tom felt lightheaded as he began to shake. "I don't understand. Who is this? I would never do this. You know that. You both know that," Tom pleaded.

Brooks seemed almost angry. "You once told me that we never really know another person or what they are capable of doing. Up until the other day, I would never have believed that, but if this is true, then I don't know what to think."

Tom stood up, rubbing his temple with one hand as he paced the small office. "I don't know how to respond. You have to believe that I wouldn't do this. I love the kids. Fifteen years ago? I was just ordained that year."

Bishop John said, "I know. I was at your ordination. You were assigned to St. Bridget's over on River Street. Sadly, that was one of the churches closed down during the consolidation."

"That's why it wasn't on the list of churches we checked for possible predator priests," said Brooks. "Look, I want to believe you, but Dr. Franks is pretty convinced this client of his was abused as a minor, buried the memory of this trauma for years, and is now telling his story. If it wasn't for the witness, another altar boy at the time, I'd be more skeptical of relying only on a reclaimed memory."

Tom shook his head. "I can't—I can't process this. How do I respond to something that never happened?"

Bishop John said, "I want to believe you, Tom. There will be an investigation by both the Church and the police on this, but I have to relieve you of all your duties at St. Francis. You can collect your things today with a police escort and stay in an apartment we can offer that is out of the zone of any parish or school. I'm sorry about this, but the kids have to be the priority until we resolve this one way or the other."

For the first time, Brooks made eye contact with Tom. "I'm going to need you to come by the station to answer questions and make a statement. I would give anything to find out this isn't true. Maybe it is, and you've buried it yourself or changed somehow. I don't know. I just think of all the damage done to these kids and all the traumatized adults walking around today like zombies because of what no kid should ever experience. Depression, suicide, broken relationships, some crippled with anxiety and can't hold down a job. It's not a one-time thing for them."

Tom had never heard this level of compassion and depth of empathy from Brooks before, but he was in such a daze that he couldn't fully absorb it at that moment.

Officer Spiro escorted Tom to the rectory so he could pack his things and let people know that he was under an investigative suspension from his pastoral duties at St.

Francis. Sister Helen, Angelo, and Luke talked in the kitchen while Tom packed his things. When he re-entered the kitchen, there was silence from three people who were all in shock. The look in their eyes expressed their belief in him.

At the thought of having to walk out that door to leave the parish and school he had loved from the first moment he was assigned there, Tom began to cry.

Luke paced, shaking his head. "This is wrong. Don't they know this isn't possible? This is a mistake. Tom, tell them this is a huge mistake."

Sister Helen stared at him, tears in her eyes.

He knew the tears in her eyes showed her pain for him, but her inability to say anything spoke to her instinctive priority to protect all the children in her school.

Angelo's lips were pressed into a thin line as his eyes watered. "Don't give up. We'll find the truth."

Tom nodded.

His brother stepped forward and gave him a long hug. "I can come and stay with you, Tommy."

Tom wiped his cheeks. "I need some time to think. I just feel so disoriented now; I need to be alone for a bit. I love you, Luke."

Tom felt the comforting hand of Sister Helen on his arm as he approached the door. He looked back, gave her an unconvincing half-smile, and left St. Francis, knowing he may never set foot there again.

On his way down the driveway, Tom turned to Officer Spiro and motioned to the church's front doors. "Do you mind?"

Spiro hesitated, following Tom in through large wooden doors. Tom breathed in the faint smell of incense and gazed up at the expanse of beautiful arches and columns. Despite his own feelings, there was nothing empty about the beauty and holiness of this space. The wooden pews built and donated by poor immigrants, the Stations of the Cross reliefs brought from Europe, and the large crucifix over the altar reminded him of how much Christ loved him and was willing to endure for him. He genuflected toward the tabernacle that held the Body of Christ. He stayed on one knee as he prayed for God to be with him during this time. He offered up this trial and prayed for the strength to accept whatever happened.

When he stood, he turned to peer up at the sun pouring in through the captivating rose window above the entrance. He closed his eyes to remember how many times he pointed out that center, holding an image of Jesus. It was a constant reminder to trust and put God at the center of our lives, which gave him strength and, at the same time, brought tears to his eyes.

Chapter 43

Tom moved as if he were in a fog. He was still dazed as he put down his bags in the sterile feeling apartment that had a bedroom, a small kitchen, and a sitting area. The view out the two windows was of the brick building next door that stood no more than eighteen inches away. For the first time in many years, he felt alone, disoriented, and depressed. What would come next in this unexpected turn in the road?

He carried his bags into the Spartan-looking bedroom, where a crucifix hung over the bed. He knelt to pray, not knowing what to say other than, "Please help show me the way."

Outside the door stood Officer Spiro, who waited to take him to the police station. Their walk was short and silent until they reached the front door. "Sorry about this, Father Tom. If you will see Sergeant Doherty at the desk, he can direct you."

Tom glanced up at Spiro, but the officer had turned to head back to his beat. As Tom approached the front desk, Sergeant Doherty raised his head with an expression of mixed emotions. "Brooks is expecting you," he said, pointing his pen down the corridor to the interrogation rooms.

Tom forced a grin and walked down the empty corridor, where he caught a glimpse of Mullen sitting alone.

She waved him in and motioned for him to take the open chair across from her. "Do you need anything to drink?"

Tom sat. "Maybe, but I don't think you have it in stock here."

The joke brought a brief smile to her face. "We're going to have to ask you a lot of very uncomfortable questions. Guilty or innocent, they're going to be difficult for both of us."

He nodded. "I understand. We both want the same thing. Don't worry about doing your job."

"Thanks," she replied as Brooks entered the room.

His entrance brought an awkward chill and silence to the room as Brooks shut the door and sat next to Mullen, clearing his throat several times. "Look, as far as this process goes, we don't know each other. But—" he cleared his throat again. "As far as I go, I feel angry and deceived." He held up his hand. "I'm not saying I have the right to feel that way, but I wanted to just get that out of the way. I admired you in too many ways not to feel pretty upset about you and the kids."

Nodding, Tom said, "Thanks for being honest. I understand why you'd feel that way, but I'm, ahh, disappointed people are assuming I'm guilty until proven innocent."

"I guess when it comes to the kids, we may be stuck with that reality. Prove yourself innocent," pleaded Brooks staring directly into Tom's eyes. "I want you to."

"I don't even know what the charges are."

Mullen opened the folder in front of her and turned the stapled pages toward Tom. "This is a report from Dr. Franks. He came into the station yesterday, and we sat with him for several hours to discuss the revelations from a series of sessions from one of his clients that was an altar boy at St. Bridget's Parish in 1994, the same time you had been assigned to that parish as a new priest."

Elbows on the table, Tom rested his chin on his folded hands. "I was there. Who are we talking about?"

Brooks snapped, "Names aren't important here! I understand you were close to the kids at the parish."

With raised eyebrows, Tom replied, "Sure. I was younger than the other priests and could relate with middle school and high school kids, so they put me in charge of youth programs."

"How did you treat the kids?"

"What do you mean? I loved working with them and getting to know them. Not all of them had the best home circumstances, and several had no fathers at all. I could tell when there were victims of abuse or neglect at home and how much some of these boys craved any type of encouragement or affection."

Mullen asked, "Do you think any of these boys could have misread your relationship with them? Were you physically affectionate?"

Staring down at the table, Tom ran his hand across the surface. "I don't know. I would give them a pat on the back or even put my arm around them, but there was nothing inappropriate or sexual about it. Hurting any of those kids would have been the last thing I would do. I would have done anything to protect them."

Brooks pulled out a sheet from the folder. "Let me read something to you. It's an interview with a pedophile. *All along, I had known it was wrong legally, but part of my fantasy was that this was love. This was acceptance. This is nothing bad. I'm helping these children.* It wasn't until many years later when he was confronted in therapy by a fellow inmate who'd been repeatedly raped as a child that he finally began to understand the consequences of his acts and to feel regret. He said, *'That was the first time I realized that what I had done does hurt children. I had never had that thought before.'*"

"I would never hurt or abuse any kids. I didn't, and I wouldn't," replied Tom, frustration cracking his voice.

Brooks motioned Mullen to take over.

"Father Tom. As I said, we spent a great deal of time with Dr. Franks. He's been practicing for over forty years, often dealing with abuse victims. He is convinced that this man he has been counseling was the victim of a difficult childhood and sexual abuse at the hands of a priest. When the client first came to him, that client didn't believe anything had happened to him and that he had worked out the grief of an absent father in his childhood and a distant mother who enabled that father's abuse and alcoholism when he was at home."

Tom listened intently to Mullen.

"As he put it, it took many sessions to 'painfully peel back the onion' and for his client to recognize that traumatic things had happened to him and he had repressed and buried those memories so deep that he didn't know they existed. In the last several extended sessions, there was a total breakdown of this wall that separated this painful reality from his life, which was commendably productive and positive. Dr. Franks said that he could tell there was a deep reservoir of resentment and anger that would force its way to the surface to protect the client, so he would pull back, but they continued to dig while trying to avoid causing a total collapse of his sense of self."

"The center cannot hold," mumbled Tom.

"What?" asked Brooks.

"Nothing. Just a line in a poem. Keep going."

Mullen turned the page of the report. "They had several sessions where the client could not proceed, breaking down in tears and his body shaking uncontrollably. Under several sessions of hypnosis, the client began to recall bits and pieces of scenes, mostly at the church. They started with peaceful memories. He felt as if he belonged, people cared about him, and he had hope. He recalled spending more time at the church, helping the priests with Mass, youth group activities, movies, trips to the beach, boating, talks about life. It felt like family."

Brooks squinted. "Is this sounding familiar so far?"

Tom did not respond, waiting for Mullen to continue.

Mullen sighed as she turned to the next page. "Dr. Franks said his client would physically pull back when a memory became uncomfortable, but they forged on, and he started describing the physicality of the relationship." Mullen turned the sheet towards Tom that included explicit descriptions of these examples.

Tom shook his head.

Mullen continued, "Dr. Franks said that there was a reclaimed memory breakthrough of a major event during their most recent session. In that breakthrough, he finally saw you as the priest who molested him."

"This can't be. I've never molested anyone," pleaded Tom.

"We have spoken to a witness that saw you two. A credible witness," Brooks added. "Now you know why I feel the way I do."

For hours, they went over and over Tom's tenure at St. Bridget's and his interactions with the youth program, but there were no admissions of guilt or behavior that could have been misunderstood.

When he returned to his apartment, Tom spent the rest of the day feeling lost and disoriented as he kneeled for hours in prayer, listening and then pleading for guidance and help. He knew he wasn't ever alone, but that was exactly how he felt—until a knock came on the door.

Chapter 44

Angelo and Luke were at the door. Luke gazed into Tom's eyes, "Remember what you always told me?"

Tom shook his head.

"Anytime, anywhere, and for any reason—I'm your brother, and you can always call for help. Well, you didn't call, but I'm still here."

Angelo reached up to put his work-callused hands on Tom's shoulder. "So am I."

Choking up, Tom tried to get out a few words. "Come in." He opened the door and motioned to chairs at the table. "I guess I don't have any food or drink to offer you."

Luke held up two brown bags with Chinese writing on the side. "We've got you covered from all sides."

As they sat at the small table, Tom told them all he could remember from the session with Brooks and Mullen. He admitted that he was in a daze for much of it, but they got the main gist of the evidence.

"Tommy, this is crazy talk. Everybody knows you couldn't be guilty of something like this," said Luke.

Tom couldn't offer a response.

Luke added, "Right?"

"Right," said Angelo. "Now, let's talk about St. Bridget's. Could they have confused you with anyone else? Could the accuser have a reason to be vindictive or be crazy?"

"I don't know who this person is or even could be."

"Let's go over there," said Luke.

Tom glanced at Luke. "The church was decommissioned about five years ago and torn down. It's that ugly parking garage over on River Street now."

"You don't have to convince me of that. I saw it today," said Angelo. "I did check it out. The pastor in 1994 was Father Paul Feeney, and there was a deacon named—"

"Alex Stodder," said Tom.

"Right. I don't know where he is, but Father Feeney is around. He's the senior priest at the Immaculate Conception in Salem," replied Angelo.

Tom gave a half-smile. "How do you do this? I lost contact with Father Paul Feeney about ten years ago. He was a sweet man. No one could tell me where he went, but he must have come back to the Boston area."

Angelo said, "We pushed that thing you call a car over here. If we can get it started, we can pay Father Feeney a visit."

Luke reached over to grab one of the takeout boxes for *chow mein*. "After we eat."

The historic seaport town of Salem, famous for its seventeenth-century witch trials, was forty minutes north of Boston. Tom drove down several streets lined with old brick buildings, and Angelo pointed ahead. "There it is."

"I don't know if I should be even doing this," said Tom as he leaned down to see the steeple of the old wooden church.

Pulling himself forward from his backseat position, Luke said, "You always told me when searching for the truth to keep going and don't stop halfway."

Tom got out of the car and shut the door. He leaned down with his arm on the open window. "Are you telling me that you've actually been listening all these years?"

"Uh-huh."

Tom grinned. "You are full of surprises, brother."

Tom approached alone and rapped on the rectory door. No answer. He knocked again and noticed the curtain on the door pull back a bit, and then the door opened. Despite the gray hair and glasses, the priest still had the same familiar smile.

"Father Paul?"

"Father Tom. It's good to see your face after so many years and miles. I had a call from Bishop Connors earlier today. I was surprised to see you at the door, though. Why don't we go for a walk?"

"I appreciate it. I have a feeling I'm seen as a leper now. Don't get too close."

Father Paul shook his head. "I don't see you that way. We're all children of God, even when we fall—but you should know that I told the bishop I didn't think you could ever be guilty of this accusation. That was your first assignment, right? I could tell you were going to be an exceptional priest."

"Your confidence humbles me. I'm certainly not perfect."

"None of us are. We act *in persona Christi* at the Mass, and He's the perfect example we aim for, falling many times along the way. The important thing is that we keep getting up and heading in the right direction on that road." On their walk, Father Paul paused by the town Common. "What can I help you with, Tom?"

"I, um, I don't even know where to start. I don't know who it is that's accusing me of this. When I saw the complaint filed, those fields were blacked out. I could barely make out the tops of the first initials of his or her first and last name. Can you think of anyone who would be a likely candidate? Someone who you thought might have been abused?"

Father Paul replied, "You know, I've been racking my brain ever since the bishop called me." He paused to think. "There were several of the boys who came from difficult home situations. I never heard of any sexual abuse, and I didn't notice any significant difference in anyone after you left. It was such a long time ago for this aging brain of mine, but I can still see most of their faces. Isn't that funny? I have to work on their names, but I can see their faces clear as day."

Tom sank onto the old wooden park bench. "I don't know what to do."

Father Paul's gaze reflected Tom's pained expression.

"At first, I thought it must have been someone who saw another boy who had run to me one afternoon from the gym.

He was shirtless and sweating, probably from running, but he was in a panic and ran right into my chest, clinging to me and breathing heavily. I didn't know if anything had happened, but he seemed to just want the security of a hug. He never mentioned it afterward, so I let it go."

"Well, that's very interesting. I guess if someone saw that, it might look suspicious. Some of these kids get no affection or encouragement at home. Nowadays, we have to keep our distance to protect them, but I think it is a loss to the kids who are most in need of it. Like I said to the bishop, I can't think of a single thing or boy that would fit the description of this allegation. I'm so sorry you're going through this, and I'll help in any way I can. I think a lot of you, Tom, and I've only heard glowing things about you as pastor at your church. What's it called?"

"St. Francis. I love that parish and the school. It's like losing everything you care about in a single blow." Tom closed his eyes for several seconds until Father Paul lightly patted his shoulder. Tom gazed at his friend. "Well, thanks for seeing me. I didn't know what to expect, but I appreciate your gentle thoughtfulness. You always had the gift."

"You're too kind."

Tom stood up. "Oh, one more question. Deacon Stodder."

"Alex?"

"Yes. I didn't work with him a ton. I hate to even ask, but could the man be confusing me with Alex? Should I forget even thinking he's a possibility?"

Father Paul sighed. "No. I don't think there is, and, God bless his soul, pancreatic cancer took him five years ago."

"So sorry to hear that, and please accept my apologies for even asking."

"Tom, give me your number. I will think hard on this and let you know if I have any memory breakthroughs. I'll do anything I can to help, and—"

Tom turned.

"And I'll be praying for you."

"Thanks, Father Paul."

"Sorry to say this, but I should probably head back alone. The bishop told me that you aren't supposed to be in the vicinity of any schools or parishes until this gets sorted out. I know that is painful to hear, but I would honor it if you want to resolve this."

On the way back to Boston, Tom felt no further ahead after they visited Salem. "I really don't know what we're going to do here. Father Paul Feeney couldn't think of a single thing to shed some light on this, and neither can I."

Luke said, "And they still can't tell you who the hell is making these allegations against you?"

"Not at this point in the process. They don't want victims to be afraid to come forward and not feel protected. I know it makes sense, but it makes no sense. I have to remember that this person may have been abused and is suffering," Tom replied.

"Why would anyone who was abused blame someone else?" asked Luke.

"Our minds and reclaimed memories are complicated and delicate things, especially when damaged by trauma or abuse. I just can't forget that this real person has been carrying around a lot of hidden pain for a decade and a half."

Luke dropped back in his seat. "Only you, brother. Only you."

Tom pulled over a few hundred feet from the entrance to St. Francis. "Thank you, guys, for being there and going all that way with me. You should probably get out here since I'm not allowed any closer."

"Tommy, why don't I stay with you?"

Tom nodded slightly. "I wish you could. The bed's barely big enough for one, and there's no couch. Stay here and watch out for the place with Angelo. I'll be okay—I hope."

When he returned to the apartment, he opened the drawers to his bedroom bureau, where he found a worn leather-bound Bible. There was also a notebook and pen at the small desk in the sitting room. He held the Bible in one hand and the blank notebook in the other, thinking he probably needed the former right now, but chose the latter as he laid the Bible on the table.

He pulled the remaining Chinese food out of the refrigerator and sat at the table with the notebook. He put two markings on the blank page, a curve and then two smaller curves, both with the open side down. Despite the name of the accuser having been blotted out with a black marker, he was able to catch the tops of the beginning letters of the first and last name because they were capitalized. There was only one possibility for the first letter of the second name. *M.*

The first name was a little bit trickier. The possibilities were *B, C, D, G, O, P, Q,* and *R.*

He racked his brain, trying to think of first and last name combinations to narrow down the possibilities. He was at it for several hours with no luck and finally decided to get some sleep and try again in the morning, but he remained restless all night. His mind raced with the reality that he may never again be a priest. He may never see St. Francis and his parishioners again and might have to go to jail for a long time.

Sleep finally came, but that only brought on the nightmares of being in a rat-infested jail cell and then being crushed by the weight of an angry mob out for vengeance to rid their city of—

He woke suddenly in a cold sweat, the back of this t-shirt soaked, screaming, "I'm innocent!"

Tom peeled off his shirt and stood in front of the small bathroom mirror, staring at himself as he splashed his face with cold water. "Maybe I'm the one with the suppressed memories? Maybe I should be in therapy?"

Chapter 45

Word must have traveled around the town fairly quickly. Maybe he was being paranoid, but the neighbor in the apartment next door gave Tom a wary and angry look. Luke called to see if he had gotten any sleep. He hadn't but was more disheartened to find out from Luke that someone had smashed a section of the large rose window above the church entrance. Being angry at him was one thing, but to blame St. Francis seemed wrong. Then he remembered that people were still angry about being betrayed by Church officials in Boston all those years ago regardless of how much the new leaders worked to never let that happen again. How many victims were out there still in pain, angry enough to break a window and kill five men?

Tom was scheduled to meet one-on-one with Bishop John that day. No Brooks or anyone else this time. Just the two of them for a frank discussion. Tom sat in the office waiting area as his administrative assistant, Emily, quietly typed away, not offering her usual friendly conversation. Tom didn't bother to force her into any talk about the weather or what she was planning for the summer but quietly said his Hail Marys on each bead of the rosary he clutched in his pocket. Finally, the door opened, and Bishop John waved for Tom to enter.

"Tom," said the bishop with a sigh.

"Bishop Connors."

"How are you holding up?"

"I'm not. I've never experienced the range of feelings I'm going through right now."

Bishop John sat. "I guess that would still be only a fraction of what one of these abused kids deals with. That's why we must do our due diligence to protect and find the truth here. You can understand those two main objectives, can't you?"

"Absolutely. The kids' safety is the priority. What I don't know is how we're going to get to the truth. I don't get how this works."

"I'm glad you believe the kids come first. It's not just about sending a message to our kids, parents, parishioners, and the town, but also to the world, that we are taking this as seriously as it deserves to be taken and that no one, and I mean no child, is ever the victim of a priest again. Damn it; one kid is too many! It's the opposite of what we are all about. It's in total conflict with our teachings from Christ. I can't take *any* chances with the protection and safety of one single boy or girl. I can't, and I won't."

Tom felt the same sincerity and passion as Bishop John did, but he knew there was more. Maybe he didn't want to hear anything from Tom in this session.

"When I got this accusation dropped on my desk, I became physically sick. Almost all the cases I see are old ones, but it didn't hurt any less back then, nor do these victims feel nothing now. I was also sick because it was your name on this accusal." Bishop John scratched his head. "I couldn't believe it. I still don't believe it, but I have to—"

Tom sighed. "I know. You have to treat this as a real and credible accusation. You have to take it as seriously as anything you do and follow an objective process versus your personal feelings. Is that close to what you were going to tell me?"

Bishop John opened the tin on his desk, pulled out a mint, and held the tin out for Tom, who waved off the offer. "Yes. I have to treat you like a sexual predator until we prove otherwise. And I can tell you that our energies aren't focused on proving otherwise; it's in believing this person, especially in the face of having a witness who has signed an affidavit." He shook his head. "I honestly don't know what to think."

Tom stared down at the floor.

"Tom. I know you feel like Daniel in the lion's den right now, ready to be devoured, but remember that he was saved by God. God's dominion will never end. 'God will be my judge' is what his name means, and, in the end, God will be your only judge. I hope you find some peace in that, no matter what happens."

Tom left the bishop's office feeling dazed and a bit lost, without a plan of how to impact anything about the outcome. He sat at the dining table back in his apartment, turning the Styrofoam cup of coffee he had picked up on the way back. "Cup of Joe," he mumbled to himself. "I wish I had a Cup-O-Joe," he said with a laugh. He remembered one of the stories about where the nickname "Joe" for coffee came from. In World War I, the Secretary of the Navy, Josephus Daniels, banned alcohol on all U.S. Navy ships, so the strongest drink available was coffee. "I'll have me a cup of Josephus!" said Tom with a hint of sarcasm.

Cup-O-Joe made Tom think about his last encounter with Sam Gately. Would there be any more murders for the Sacraments of Marriage and Holy Orders? Was there still some priest out there that would end up on Sam Gately's wall of organized clippings? The possibility finally hit him that *he* might be that next priest.

He stood up and paced. There was no way out of this apartment if anyone forced their way in. He checked that the front door was locked. Each of the murders seemed to be tied to someone who was known by a member of the Tuesday group. Joey? Cup of Joe. Joey "Donuts." But he only knew Joey from the streets. Joey was never an altar boy or even a Catholic, and he had only been friendly and generous to Joey.

He quickly sat down and pulled the notebook toward him, spilling the coffee in his haste. After cleaning it up and wiping off the brown liquid from the sheet of paper, he stared at the letters again. He thought M was for the last name. *What could be the first letter of the first name? B, C— Wait a minute. Josephus 'Joe' Daniels! D for Daniel. Daniel Murphy was the name of one of the group members, but which one was he? I never met George Stroupe, Terry*

Rivers, or Daniel Murphy, so I don't know which one he was in the gathering across the street from the pizza place.

Tom continued to pace, not sure what to do next. He couldn't go to Brooks because he wasn't supposed to know the name of the accuser. Why did the bishop mention the Bible reference to Daniel? Did Bishop John really believe he was innocent, or was this God trying to help him, judging him as innocent?

He continued to think. *Who is Daniel Murphy? Who knows him? Sam Gately and Len Weitz know him. Joey "Donuts." How about Brian Flaherty? No. He's still the police, and I'm not supposed to know it's Daniel Murphy. Wait a minute!*

Tom dialed 4-1-1.

"City and State, please."

"Salem, Massachusetts."

"Say the name of the business or resident you want."

"Immaculate Conception Church."

"Hello, Immaculate Conception, Father Paul speaking."

Tom hesitated. "Hi, Father Paul, it's Tom Fitzpatrick."

"Tom. I've been thinking of you. Can I help with anything?"

"Maybe. I don't know if this is even right for me to ask you, but can you tell me if a Daniel Murphy was at St. Bridget's?"

There was a momentary pause. "Murphy. Murphy. I think there was someone by that name. I mean, there've been lots of Murphys in parishes I've been at, but that name does sound familiar. Why do you ask?"

Tom asked, "Do you think he was there when I was running the youth programs? The name is not ringing a bell to me, and I knew the kids pretty well. I've just been trying to remember different names."

"Even ones that don't ring a bell? Now that I think about it, there might have been a young man named Murphy, maybe Daniel? I don't know. I think he liked sports and boating and such. Like I said, my memory isn't what it used to be. Tom, can I ask you if you think this is the young man who is accusing you?"

"I don't know, Father Paul. I'm just struggling here to know what's happening. The rug's been pulled out from underneath me, but I don't want to lose sight that there may be someone out there in pain either."

"I understand, Tom," said Father Paul. "I will be praying for you."

"I appreciate that. I think I'm going need all the prayers I can get."

Tom hung up the phone and let out a long and loud groan, feeling completely frustrated with where to go with his emotions and proof of innocence. He picked up a pillow from the bed and held it to his face, screaming into its fibers.

Chapter 46

Angelo and Luke were back in the morning with bags of groceries, books, and encouraging smiles. Without asking, Angelo started cooking an Italian omelet while Luke brewed up some coffee. "What's the game plan today, Tommy?"

Tom was hurting, and he was well aware that Luke knew it, but the upbeat visit from the two closest people in his life opened the door to hope just a crack. "I think I need to pay another visit to Dr. Rose."

Flipping the large omelet, Angelo said, "Why Rose?"

"It's possible that he may know who the accuser is."

Angelo brought over the filled plates. "So, you've been doing some detective work instead of sleeping?"

"Who can sleep?" replied Tom.

Luke glanced at Angelo, and they both replied in unison, "No one here."

As they stood in front of Rose's office, Tom prayed that the doctor might be in and could provide some helpful information. Rose must have heard a noise in the waiting room that he wasn't expecting because he interrupted his counseling session to peek out from his office. When he saw the three sitting on the couch together, he shook his head and closed the door. As the top of the hour approached, a young man furrowed his brow as he entered the waiting room, appearing confused at their unexpected presence.

Finally, the door to Rose's office opened, and a woman exited, followed by Dr. Rose. He turned to the young man. "Edward, why don't you go into my office while I see what these gentlemen need?"

Edward nervously entered Rose's office as Rose closed the door and turned. "I can't imagine why you are here other than harassment. Please tell me I'm wrong."

Tom stood. "Dr. Rose. We're sorry to bother you, and I know you have a client waiting. I only wanted to ask you if you know a Daniel Murphy? I believe he was part of the counseling group that Dr. Silverstein facilitated until two years ago?"

"Daniel Murphy?" Rose paused. "Why are you asking? You know that I can't talk about any of our clients."

Angelo asked, "Could you talk about him if he wasn't a client?"

Rose closed his eyes. "Look. This has to be completely confidential."

Tom nodded.

"And then you have to leave me alone."

Tom nodded again.

"I believe he came to us for some time. He was struggling to process the death of a close friend of his, but, in my assessment, he had other issues from his past that he was avoiding or suppressing. He didn't believe that was the case. Dr. Silverman recommended he join the Tuesday group that met at the library to see if he might open up when he saw other men doing so. I really can't say more than that."

"Thank you, Dr. Rose," said Tom.

"Now, can you leave me alone?" pleaded Rose.

"We promised and will honor that. Do you know where Daniel is today?"

Rose shook his head. "I have no idea. He lives somewhere around here."

"There must be something?"

"I really can't help you. The only thing I remember about Daniel is that he loved the ocean and sailing. It was something about being off the land, where all the hurt was, that he felt safe, so maybe he moved to the Cape or somewhere he could find peace. I have no idea. I've already said too much."

Outside the office, Tom stood on the sidewalk with Angelo and Luke.

Luke said, "So, what's next?"

Before Tom had a chance to answer, a car pulled alongside, and the window rolled down. The driver leaned over as Tom approached the passenger side. "Officer Mullen."

She waved him closer. "Father Tom. I've been looking for you. I wanted to let you know that formal charges may be coming down pretty quickly. They were filed with the Charlestown police, but it's been referred to us since you and the alleged events happened in our district."

"Thanks for the heads up. How is Brooks doing?"

She glanced down. "He's taking things pretty hard. I try to make no judgments, but I know he's pretty disappointed. Oddly, I think that's a reflection of how highly he regarded you."

Tom pursed his lips. "Past tense noted. I do appreciate your stopping."

"I try to stay open-minded, but I don't know how much time you have to find out what you need," said Mullen before rolling up the window and pulling away.

"What did she say?" asked Luke.

Tom replied, "That we've got to think fast. I've got to find this Daniel Murphy, and the only way may be members of the Tuesday group. I could try to catch Brian Flaherty, but I'm concerned about putting him in a compromising position."

"I think we may need to pay a follow-up visit to our friend staying in the North End," said Angelo.

"Sam Gately," said Tom. "I think you're right, but I should go alone."

"Is that a smart idea? With the things they found in his apartment and resentment against some of these murder victims, he's a strong candidate for being the main suspect in these killings—or protecting the killer. He could be dangerous."

Tom paused. "I know, but I think I might have a better chance of getting more out of him if we don't show up with a posse that could put him on the defensive."

Angelo glanced toward Luke, shaking his head.

Tom headed back to the North End waterfront apartments and found Sam Gately on the harbor walkway leaning over the railing and peering down into the deep dark waters. Tom approached and leaned on the railing without greeting him. Instead, he said, "There is something about the sea that draws you in, doesn't it?"

Sam quickly turned, realized who it was, let out a deep, growling sigh. "Why are you here?"

"I wanted to talk."

"I've been talking for twenty-nine years, and it hasn't helped a bit." Sam turned back toward the harbor, and Tom joined him, leaning with both forearms on the railing. "Twenty-nine years. Every time I see this harbor, it just looks so deep and dark. You know what I think of doing every time?"

Tom remained silent.

"I think of jumping in. I mean, can it be any deeper and darker than the black hole that has been my existence? I've just needed it to end one way or the other."

"My heart aches to hear that," said Tom.

"Now I hear you are part of the problem. Part of why someone else can't have a life, can't get close enough to have a relationship, a family, a moment of real joy." Sam turned and glared at Tom, but Tom only returned a look of sincere empathy that held Sam's attention for a moment before he shook it off and blurted, "Ahh. I don't trust anyone."

"Sam, Daniel Murphy is part of your Tuesday group. You know him, right?"

"Why? Are you suddenly feeling guilty?"

"If I wasn't guilty of anything, what would you tell me about him?"

Sam peered into Tom's eyes and laughed. "No one's guilty, are they? No one takes responsibility. 'I only meant to help the boy. To show him the affection he never got at home.' I've heard it all, and I'm sick of it!"

Sam turned and grabbed Tom by the collar of his shirt and lifted him so easily that Tom was sure Sam could force him over the railing and into the harbor water with little effort.

Tom struggled to get out his words. "Harry Simon... should have known...better and treated...you with dignity... and respect, and Jon Alpheus should have protected you."

Sam slowly let go of his forceful grip, squeezing his eyes tight.

"You didn't kill Harry Simon, did you?"

A tear slid down Sam's cheek.

"You were at the scene after the murder, though, weren't you? Mary Quill saw you there and never told anyone because you scared her into keeping her mouth shut. Why were you there?"

Sam rubbed the palm of his hand back and forth across his forehead. "I didn't do it. I got a message saying, *Breathe again as justice has finally been done with the evil drowned in the Brewer Fountain.* I went straight over and spotted the hand and the heart. I don't know why I took the photo, but I didn't believe who it was until the news came out the next day. How did you know? How did you know I didn't do it?"

"Because you're a Yeats guy. Jonas Alpheus didn't kill Harry either, did he?" queried Tom.

Sam shook his head. "I don't believe he did. Who would leave that many clues literally pointing to himself?"

"Why do you think the killer did that—let those clues point to Alpheus?"

Sam didn't respond.

"Because he enabled Monnot? Kept quiet for too long and convinced you to say nothing?" Tom said.

Sam remained quiet as he stared into the sun's reflection on the lapping waves of the dark ocean.

"Did Joel Silverman molest Len Weitz, and was Avil Rose an enabler?"

Still no response.

"Was Rowan Montecchi molested by Peter Boulanger, and was Olivia aware of it?"

Sam finally spoke. "She loved Rowan, and Rowan loved her. Boulanger didn't want Rowan anywhere near his daughter because he didn't think anyone was good enough and because he wanted Rowan for himself and took him. Olivia loved and feared her father and didn't tell what she knew to be true. She wanted to bury it and run off with Rowan. All those years of torment became too much for Rowan, and he needed to take control of his life. Olivia lost all hope when she found out he died, so she found a way to be with him in death." Then he murmured, "They were both braver than me."

"You've been the brave one in more ways than you know." Tom paused. "The same with George Stroupe and Terry Rivers?"

Sam nodded.

"Did Rowan's death push Daniel Murphy over the edge?"

Sam pulled back. "What are you talking about?"

"Rowan's suicide was at the beginning of January, and the murders began only a few weeks later. Tell me about Daniel."

Sam pressed his lips together and paused for a moment. "Murph is a good guy. The best. He came into the group after losing his closest and only real friend about four years ago. He thought that was the only reason he came, but I could tell he'd been hurting for a long, long time. I don't think he recognized or could accept it, but I could tell. He's been close to everyone in the group and is very protective, but I can't believe he could do this. I don't, so don't you assume he is."

"So, you believe he was molested as a child or young adult somewhere along the way?"

Sam's head snapped back. "Shouldn't I be the one asking you?"

Chapter 47

When Tom returned to his apartment, Angelo and Luke were waiting for him. "Thank God you're safe," sighed Luke with relief.

Angelo eyed him. "What is it, Father Tom? I can tell when you've got something percolating."

Tom replied, "I just need time to process things. I made indirect contact with Daniel Murphy."

"What does that mean?" asked Luke.

"After I talked with Sam, I felt more unsettled about things, and I went back to ask him if he would give me Daniel's number to contact him. He refused each time I repeated the request, getting testier each time I pushed."

"And?" asked Luke and Angelo at the same time.

"He finally agreed to send him a text. We waited for a long time, but there was no response. Then he sent a follow-up telling him I would meet him under any conditions he wanted."

"What?" exclaimed Luke.

"I know, but I have to do something to resolve this. Once this goes to court, they'll be no chance to talk to him to find out the truth."

"And where are you going to meet?" inquired Angelo.

"I can't tell you," Tom replied. "I promised."

"Hmmm. That's a bad sign. If this is the killer and you are next on the list, why play into his hands? Why give him complete control of the location, time, and opportunity to achieve his goal?"

"I know. I need time to process this, but I need your trust that higher powers watch out for us," replied Tom, putting his arms around Angelo and Luke.

Luke shook his head. "Was he watching out for the other victims too? Did he watch out for Kathryn?"

Tom paused to gaze into his brother's pained expression. After much pleading, Angelo and Luke reluctantly agreed to go home for the evening as the night sky grew dark. Tom kept his promise and gave them no idea what day or place the meeting with Daniel Murphy would take place.

Despite the starlit sky, the moonless night was dark, and Tom proceeded down the quiet street. Ascending the seven granite steps outside, he pulled open the large wooden door to a place he was now forbidden to enter. His stress was momentarily replaced by a rush of peace as he entered St. Francis Church, and his senses took in the visual beauty, the faint but familiar smell of incense, and the quiet that felt full of the Holy Spirit. This felt like home.

The handful of burning candles offered a glow in the darkness, and Tom genuflected before he began to walk down the center aisle, listening to the sound of his heels against the tiled floor. There was no one else in sight. Maybe the man he was to meet would not show up. Tom entered the front pew and pulled down the kneeler to begin praying. Despite trusting fully in God's plan, he had to admit that he felt an uncomfortable level of nervous anxiety in his chest, listening for any sounds of someone entering the church. He prayed, "I know I shouldn't be here, but it feels like exactly where I should be. Please give me the strength and trust to follow your plan and to be an agent for good and justice and whatev—" Suddenly, he felt intense pain on the back of his skull and then blackness.

***

While most of the sisters at the convent were early to bed, Sister Helen was more of a night owl in comparison. As she sat by a single light, mending the hem of her habit, there was a faint rap on the door, and then another. Because of the recent vandalism at the church, she cautiously opened the door a crack to see who was there. "Father Feeney? Is that you?"

In the dark of the night, he removed his hat. "It's been a long time, Sister."

She opened the door several more inches. "What is it you'd be wantin' this time of night, Father?"

"I think I need to get into St. Francis Church alone, so I thought you might have a key."

"The doors are always open to the church. Father Tom wanted people to be able to visit the Lord when they needed to and never run into locked doors in a time of need. I have to agree with him on that one," responded Sister Helen.

He scratched his head. "Maybe something's changed. I went over to the church, and all the doors were locked tight."

* * *

Dizzy and disoriented, Tom reached for the back of his skull, where he felt a pulsing ache, but his hand couldn't move. He hadn't realized he was flat on his back, and turned his head to see his wrist tied with some type of braided nylon rope. He turned his head before he felt a similar tightness from the other hand and his feet. He stopped trying to twist his body and took a deep breath. A man wearing a black jacket and black ski mask pulled the rope on his feet tighter. "What are you doing?" pleaded Tom.

No response came.

"Can't we just talk this out?" said Tom, realizing the knots tightened the more he pulled against them. His assailant had bound him to the large cross that normally hung over the altar.

The masked man stood, looming over Tom as he stared down at him. Silent. He lifted a piece of wood with writing on it, showing it to Tom before nailing it to the cross just above his head. It read, *Pater Thomas Fitzpatrick, Hostis Innocentes*.

Tom translated the Latin in silence, *Father Thomas Fitzpatrick, Enemy of the Innocents*. He quickly realized he was not there for any kind of conversation, only a horrific execution. He closed his eyes and recited the Our Father.

The masked man stood over Tom and shook his head to signal that his prayers were of no avail.

Tom's heart was pounding in his chest, making it impossible to act calmly in whatever attempt he would have to save himself. He took several deep breaths and let them out slowly. The man stepped aside and started to pick up the large black bag on the floor when Tom asked, "Why are you doing this, Brian?"

His head snapped back toward Tom with a glare in his eyes. "What did you—" He paused and stepped forward. "How did you know?"

"When Sam said your text read, *I will only agree to meet at a safe home for both of us. 9 p.m. at St. Francis Church*, I wondered if it was you because you always say, 'Safe home.' I called Father Feeney back just before I arrived here and told him I was meeting you here tonight. He said that he checked with people who knew Daniel Murphy, and they said they hadn't seen or heard from him in four years—about the time Sam Gately said Daniel had lost a very dear friend to suicide and when you joined the Tuesday group."

"Shut up!" yelled the man as he peeled off his ski mask, leaving no doubt that it was Brian Flaherty.

"Brian, I care about you, and I am so sorry for your loss. I know how painful it is and how it never leaves you."

Flaherty lifted a sharp antique sword from the bag and held it tightly in his hand. "I said to shut up! What do you know about pain other than inflicting it on innocent kids? You who vowed to live up to the *virtute ac persona ipsius Christi*. What do you know about pain? What do you know about a life that has been destroyed before it had a chance to begin? Never to have a moment's peace but instead feeling dirty and defiled! You chose to give up your relationships, but that choice to never have the intimacy of a normal relationship was robbed from us!"

His eyes were full of rage as he continued to glare down at Tom and then quickly turned away. "Every one of those guys is worth ten times what you predators are worth, but they can never feel like that is true. Yes, the Tuesday group. What's the saying, 'Tuesday's child is full of grace'?" He laughed. "That grace was robbed from us. Our lives were robbed from us!"

Tom closed his eyes and prayed for time, for a chance to find a way. "Brian, I have no doubt that you have not been treated with the dignity and love you deserved from the earliest days of your life to whatever happened to you."

"Whatever happened to me?! Whatever happened? You were what happened. You are the face of evil, just the same as Simon, Silverman, Boulanger, Costello, Finkle, and D—" He paused, seemingly catching himself. "Each one of them had someone who enabled them. Each one of them had someone who was charged with protecting these boys, but, instead, with their silence, they allowed these monsters to continue."

"Brian, I can't imagine the pain each of you has had to live with. I want you to know that I did not do anything of the kind to you," said Tom, trying to look Flaherty directly in the eyes.

Flaherty gave a half-smile. "Everyone denies it. They all did. They sounded as sincere as you. Maybe their sick minds convinced them they meant no harm. I mean, here is a lonely and hurt child, starved of affection and love, so they offered that. First, friendship and trust with a boy who begins to believe someone might think they are more than nothing worthy of someone's attention. They play on the ray of hope as they spend more and more time together. Someone cares. Someone puts their arm around me and looks me directly in the eyes. He sees me and wants to be with me."

Flaherty paced, clutching the sword. "But it's all a sick game. A selfish and devastating lie, leaving behind a wake of destroyed lives, depression, anxiety, loneliness, and even—"

Tom said softly, "Pain and disintegration of self to the point of suicide to take control and end it."

Tom's empathetic words stopped Flaherty's pacing as he stared down upon Tom tied to the cross.

Tom said, "I can imagine that when Rowan took his own life, it must have brought back the pain of losing Daniel the same way. Enough to push someone who cares and has a strong protective instinct over the edge. Enough was enough." Tom gave everything he had to sound calm and under control while his whole body trembled with anxiety.

"They weren't the ones who deserved to die," said Flaherty.

"But you can live, Brian."

Flaherty feigned a laugh. "Only if I try harder, huh? I tried to find the beauty in the world, in poetry like Sam, in sailing like Daniel, in God like Lenny, in helping others like—" A tear rolled down Flaherty's cheek. "I admired you. I wanted to be like you. But then I found out the truth." Flaherty pulled out some metal objects from the black bag. It became quickly obvious to Tom what his final fate would be. Flaherty held three large spiked nails and a heavy hammer to drive them into his hands and feet. The sword was to finish Tom off, but probably after a torturous period where his arms would give out, and his ribs would crush into his lungs. "Daniel couldn't breathe in the end, and neither will you."

"Brian. Brian. You said you admired me. Why?"

"No more wasting time. Dr. Franks showed me I suppressed the memory of my assault. That doesn't mean it didn't happen, and the pain wasn't there deep down. It took some work and pushing to reclaim that nightmare and find the truth, and now it's time for justice to be served." Brian crouched down on his knees next to Tom's side. He held the large spike with his left hand and rested it on the palm of Tom's left hand. Then he raised the heavy hammer, ready to come down hard on the head of the spike. "Daniel was molested by a priest, too. He would never say the name, but this is for him."

Suddenly, there was a sound from a small doorway next to the sacristy that looked like it hadn't been opened in decades. Flaherty could see the door slowly being forced open with each pound from the other side. "Stay away!" he screamed.

The heavy door opened enough for someone to poke their head out. "Brian! Brian, please don't do this."

Tom turned and could see the face of an older man. It was Father Paul Feeney.

"Please, Brian. Listen to me!" pleaded Father Feeney.

"It's too late for talking!" With that, Flaherty let go of all his might with a loud crash as the hammer hit the head of the nail and drove it through Tom's hand and into the hardwood of the cross.

Tom let out an ear-piercing scream as the searing pain from the bloodied palm of his hand ran up his arm and through his spine. His instinct was to pull his hand as he heard Father Feeney screaming, "No! No!"

Flaherty jumped up as Father Feeney squeezed through the doorway. Flaherty quickly slammed the door shut, muffling the cries from Sister Helen on the other side. He blocked the hidden entrance and pulled Father Feeney toward the cross on the cold floor. "What are you doing here?"

"Brian, I plead with you not to do this. For God's sake, don't continue."

Brian squinted. "This *is* for God's sake. This *is* because of your God. We are his hands, and there must be justice for what these evil men did. No one is protecting the kids if we don't. Letting this go while victims live in pain and these men go on as if nothing had happened isn't justice. Daniel deserved better. I deserved better. You should understand that."

"Brian, you were a good boy. You should have had a good family."

"Well, that didn't happen. But I didn't deserve this," shouted Brian, beating his chest. "He is only getting what he deserves for desecrating the collar he wore and the children he destroyed!" Brian pushed Father Feeney to the ground and scrambled to retrieve another nail as Tom writhed in pain, trying his best to offer it up to Christ.

As he positioned the second nail on the palm of Tom's right hand, Father Feeney yelled, "There is no guilt in this man!"

Brian stopped short, gripping the hammer in mid-air. He turned to Father Feeney, brow deeply furrowed with confusion. "What? I remember. I remember him holding me naked."

Father Feeney shook his head. "No. Your memory is confused. You ran to him for safety. I am the guilty man. I did not intend to hurt you or Daniel. I was confused and hurting myself. That's not an excuse, but I suffered trauma in my childhood and never felt whole, never in control of anything, never mind my sense of self."

Brian stood, squeezing his eyes tight. "What are you saying?"

"I was broken and needed something or someone. I went into the priesthood to help others, not to hurt them, but I got seriously lost. I didn't realize how much I hurt you two until after many years of group therapy and hearing the pain from victims such as yourself."

Brian stood with anger and confusion in his eyes. "The Church knew this?!"

Father Feeney tightened his brow. "No. I took a personal leave of absence for many years and went into counseling for a long time to figure myself out. It was in that process that I saw what I had done. I tried to find Daniel several years back, but no one knew where he went. I saw how well you seemed to be doing and didn't want to bring up old wounds if you had moved on."

Brian shook his head. "What are you saying? You are the one? *You* did all of this?"

Despite the searing pain from his hand, Tom could see how much Brian was seething at this revelation. "Brian, we can still sort this out."

Brian released the hammer and spike he had gripped so tightly in his hands, and they echoed as they struck the stone floor.

"We can talk this out," Tom implored.

"I cannot tell you how much this has pained me and how incredibly sorry I am for—"

Before Father Feeney could finish his apology, Brian picked up the sharp blade of the sword and lanced Father Feeney's side.

Father Feeney collapsed.

"Brian, no!" screamed Tom.

Loud bangs were coming from the door to the basement, finally pushing it partially back open. Tom could hear the voice of Angelo, Luke, and Sister Helen on the other side.

"Hold on, Tommy," pleaded Luke.

There was no time to reach the door to close it shut again, so Brian fled to the side door, slashing with the sword at the sailing rope that had held the door shut.

With a final push, Luke, Angelo, and Sister Helen emerged through the basement door to the sight of horror. Sister Helen rushed across the room to Father Feeney and, putting her finger on his neck, shook her head. She then dropped to her knees next to Tom as Luke and Angelo bolted toward Flaherty to stop his getaway.

***

Flaherty gave the rope one last slash to open the door just as Luke reached him. Flaherty quickly swung the blunt end of the sword handle and landed a blow to Luke's head, sending him to the floor, motionless. He shoved Angelo to the ground and fled into the darkness of the night.

Chapter 48

After climbing to his feet, Angelo turned back to see if Luke was okay and then moved quickly to assist Sister Helen. While she retrieved a clean cloth from the sacristy, Angelo pried the nail from Tom's hand without aggravating the wound and then cut the rope holding Tom's hands and feet to the cross.

Tom winced with pain and stared at Sister Helen as she began tending to the wound with tears on her cheeks.

She did not turn to acknowledge his gaze as she said, "I'll not be having time for that now, and see what you've done to this beautiful hand."

Despite his pain, it made Tom effort a smile. "All this attention is almost worth it."

She shook her head as he grimaced.

"I did say almost." He turned his head and saw the pool of blood that had formed under Father Feeney's body, and Sister Helen pursed her lips, shaking her head. The deep sword wound was a fatal blow.

Tom squeezed his eyes shut, fighting off the tears that began welling up until he noticed his brother on the floor by the side door. "Is my brother okay? Please tell me he's all right."

Pacing to Tom's side and kneeling, Angelo said, "He's going to be okay. But he'll have a nasty bump later on. Flaherty clipped him good as Luke tried to grab him."

Tom started to get up, but Sister Helen chided, "What do you think you're doing, Father? You need a doctor for that hand of yours."

Tom lifted it, wincing again. "Can you wrap it tight?"

"This is no scratch; I'm sure you'll realize it when the pain fully registers," she replied as she finished with the wrap.

Tom walked over to Father Feeney's lifeless body, knelt before him, made the Sign of the Cross on his forehead, and quietly prayed. Then he stood and turned to Angelo. "We've got to find Brian. I think he's in a dangerous place. I don't know what he's liable to do to himself."

Sister Helen shook her head. "You won't be doing anything but getting yourself to the hospital."

Tom's eyes shifted to Angelo. "Can you drive?"

Angelo smirked. "Let's say I'm a bit rusty, but I can get us there in one piece if you have an idea of where we're going."

Tom twisted as Angelo reached into his pocket to retrieve the keys. They could hear Sister Helen scolding them from behind as Tom turned, "Please take care of Luke."

They made their way to Tom's old car, and Angelo made the Sign of the Cross as he turned the key. The car started on the first turn.

Tom said, "Don't tell me prayers don't work."

"Well, we'll be doing a lot of praying tonight," replied Angelo. "Where are we headed?"

"Head toward the North End and over the North Washington Bridge to the Charlestown Shipyard."

Angelo took off down the darkened streets. "What makes you think he's at the Charlestown Shipyard?"

"I don't. I think he's at the marina just past it. Brian's been staying on a friend's sailboat. I think that friend was Daniel Murphy. He said his friend wanted to call the boat the *Sea Warrior*, but Brian convinced him to call it *Cuan Sábháilte*."

"Let me guess, something in Gaelic?"

"Yup, it means safe harbor. Brian would always say, 'Safe home' after someone said goodbye. It's an Irish wish, and it makes sense. These men all needed a 'safe home' in their lives. It's one of the reasons I thought it was Brian I was meeting and the fact Father Paul told me that no one had seen Daniel Murphy for about four years, the exact time Brian joined the Tuesday group."

Angelo sped down Tremont toward the North End. "Huh. If Flaherty was part of the Tuesday group, why wasn't his name on the list?"

Tom shifted in his seat as he held up his tightly bandaged hand, the blood coming through the white cloth. "I think he fell apart when Daniel committed suicide. I'm guessing they were extremely close friends who shared a love for sailing. Daniel may have ended it by jumping off the boat while they were out. He mentioned to me that Daniel couldn't breathe at the end and neither would I if he succeeded with his chosen execution for me."

Angelo took a sharp left turn onto North Washington and crossed the bridge at the outlet mouth of the Charles River. "How does that answer my question?"

"I think Brian assumed Daniel Murphy's name, boat, apartment, as well as vengeance for his tragic death. When I talked with Sam Gately, he mentioned Daniel Murphy joining the group just after the shock of losing a close friend. He said that Daniel couldn't admit that he was dealing with something deeper in this life, but Sam said he could always tell when someone was a victim of sexual abuse. He described Daniel with a lot of the attributes of Brian and never mentioned Brian's name. To him, Brian was Daniel Murphy."

Speeding down Chelsea Street in Charlestown, they passed the Naval Shipyard. "Huh, so how do you know his boat is at the Charlestown Marina?"

"I'm making a guess. Brian said his friend's 'ketch is parked at the corner of Mystic and Charles.' I think he meant where the Mystic River and Charles River meet. It seems like the most likely place." Tom pointed to the sign. "Here, Angelo, take a right and slow down."

"That part you didn't need to tell me." Angelo turned and slowed as he approached the road to the marina, cutting his lights as they pulled into the dirt parking lot.

On an early-season weeknight, the parking lot was empty and pitch dark. There was an eerie silence in the marina as they stepped out of the car and shut the doors as quietly as possible. Listening for any sound of activity from the sailboats and motorboats that lined the floating wooden docks, they crept toward the moored boats. All they could hear were the sounds of the rhythmic lapping water, the sail ropes periodically clanging against the metal masts with the light breeze, and the docks creaking as they rubbed against each other. Only one dim light and the stars above cast shadows and a reflection on the water.

Tom breathed in the salty air as they stepped down onto the dock.

Angelo whispered, "He may still have the sword as a weapon and is running scared. He may even have a gun on the boat."

Tom nodded as they slowly stepped toward each birth to avoid any sound, peering into each boat and listening carefully as they tread forward. The air was thick with tension and anticipation. Tom could feel his heart pounding, not knowing if someone would lunge out at them as trespassers or if Flaherty were waiting in the blinding dark ahead. The clanging of the ropes on the masts could not cover the sudden *clunk* sound the floating dock sections made when they stepped on the edge of one and the heavy metal hinges struck one another.

Step by step, the darkness seemed to grow as they made their way slowly from one section to the next, only being able to see a boat once they were next to it. A chill crept over them as they stole along the dock, peering into each boat cabin, not knowing if anyone was sleeping aboard. There was a creak and another clunk as Tom stepped to the edge of the next float, but no signs other than the lapping ocean water.

Silently, Angelo pointed to a wooden-handled gaff on a boat and gently grabbed it.

Tom's heart jumped into his throat as the light clang of the line on the mast was interrupted by a loud screech and the sudden flapping of wings from a seagull who must have been sleeping in the stern.

Angelo put his hand up and then proceeded, one berth at a time, until they reached the end of the section of docks. Tom thought he must have guessed wrong as they approached the last sailboat, rocking gently in its berth until he tapped Angelo's arm and pointed to the back that read, *Cuan Sábháilte* for 'Safe Home.' Tom's heart thumped harder, and his mind raced, anxious that this might not have been a good idea. They stood still, listening for any movement from the vessel, but there was only eerie silence.

Angelo held onto the gaff and reached for the rail to pull himself on board. As he stepped aboard, a blow came out from the pitch-black shadows smacking Angelo upside the head. He landed hard onto the wooden dock.

Tom reflexively reached down to check him when a man lunged off the boat and onto Tom, knocking him hard onto the wooden dock. Tom couldn't see who it was but instinctively yelled, "Brian, don't do this!"

The dark shadowy silhouette stood over him, holding the sword visible against the stars. "Why? I'm already going to hell; why add a painful prison sentence to it?" He swung the sword within inches of Tom's outstretched bandaged hand.

"You don't know the future," pleaded Tom.

Flaherty laughed as he reared back for another swing. "I didn't think anything in the future could be worse than my past, but now I know it will be." Before he could strike, there was a sudden gasp of pain as Angelo struck Flaherty's leg with a forceful blow of the metal hook of the gaff. The sword dropped, and Tom grabbed Flaherty's leg to tackle him to the ground.

"I won't go to prison!" screamed Flaherty, grabbing Tom's wounded hand and twisting it to exert maximum pain on Tom's grip. Flaherty released his grip and jumped to his feet, knocking Angelo back while Tom gasped at the pain in his hand and climbed up. He tried to wrap Flaherty in a tight hold with one hand.

"No!" yelled Flaherty, finally tackling Tom and shoving him onto the stern of the boat. Flaherty struck Angelo again, grabbed the sword, and sliced the mooring ropes as he jumped into the stern, holding the weapon to Tom's neck while the boat drifted from the berth.

Tom could see Angelo desperately watching them disappear into the darkness.

Flaherty glared down at Tom with his sword in hand.

"Brian, I can't tell you what it will look like, but never give up hope. There is still hope for you. You are still loved."

"That has been a lie since the day I was born. I don't even love myself," said Flaherty as he held the sword over his head with both hands and thrust the sword downward.

Tom closed his eyes and heard a loud thud. He quickly opened his eyes to see the sword driven into the deck and Flaherty diving into the dark waters to end it. Without hesitation, Tom jumped into the frigid water, searching for him in the blackness of the night. There was no sound of movement in the water outside of his own flailing attempts to find Brian Flaherty before he drowned. After several minutes, while Angelo screamed his name, Tom stopped. There was no sound, so he dove underwater, desperately reaching out to feel something. Nothing. He came back to the surface, frantically looking around, and went back down, trying to make a wider circle until he collided with the body of Brian Flaherty. There was no movement as he grabbed the back of his shirt and struggled to pull him to the surface.

Tears came to his soaking-wet face as he shook. He was too late. *Never give up hope* were the only words that came to him. He held Brian tightly with one arm and swam back to the dock with the other. Angelo pulled Flaherty's lifeless body onto the platform as Tom quickly climbed up. Angelo shook his head, but Tom began pumping Flaherty's chest with the heel of his hands, despite the piercing pain from his wound. He pumped, let it up, pumped, let it up. Angelo raised his hand as Tom continued in vain to pump and then tilted Flaherty's head and lifted his chin to begin mouth-to-mouth resuscitation.

Angelo placed his hand on Tom's shoulder. "It's no use, Father. He's gone."

Tom sat up and sobbed, holding Brian's sea-soaked and lifeless body in his arms. "Please, God, don't let this tortured soul never have a chance to know how much You love him."

Suddenly, Angelo gripped Tom's shoulder tighter as he pointed down at the water spurting from Flaherty's mouth as the man gasped for breath.

Tom continued to cry as he placed the palm of his hand on Flaherty's cheek and gazed into his eyes. Flaherty's eyes squeezed tight as he sat up, pressed his painful chest, buried his face into Tom's chest, and cried. Tom put his arms around him and pulled him in.

Chapter 49

Tom sat up in his hospital bed, smiling as he listened to his brother lecture him about chasing after a sword-wielding killer.

"I knew you were crazy, but not that crazy. So, how's your hand feeling?"

He raised his bandaged hand. "The surgeon thinks I'll have most of the mobility back in a few months. It does hurt, though. And how's your head, little brother?"

"As hard as ever," replied Luke, knocking his knuckles on his skull.

"I think the bump looks good on you."

Luke paused and stared out the window. "I've been thinking a lot about things. Watching Flaherty take justice into his own hands didn't feel right. Maybe those guys deserved what they got, but that wasn't his job to be judge and executioner."

Tom pressed his lips together. He knew that wasn't an easy conclusion for Luke to reach. "I think you're onto something."

"Mind you; I'm still working on the forgiveness part. I think that will be a long journey for me."

"Understood," said Tom, patting his brother on the shoulder.

Luke frowned. "I may have a favor to ask you, though."

Tom gazed into his brother's eyes. "Anything."

"I think I'm going to go back to Peru. No, not for vengeance. The town wants to name the school we were building after Kathryn—the Kathryn M. Fitzpatrick Memorial *Escuela*, and I want to be there to make it successful for the kids."

Tom was proud of his brother regardless of his actions, but the declaration swelled his heart. He was momentarily speechless as his eyes welled up. "That's beautiful and says so much about the two of you. What's the favor?"

"If you are feeling up to it," Luke's eyes teared up as his voice cracked. "I would very much like you to come down for the dedication and bless the school."

"I would be honored. Just let me know when."

Brooks cleared his throat at the door and the moment was broken. He and Detective Mullen entered the room. "I'm glad you're okay," said Brooks with a long pause. "And, uhm, I can't say how sorry I am that I doubted you. Can you forgive me, Father?"

Tom shook his head. "It's not necessary. Your protective instincts did what they should, but—I wouldn't turn down a beer at Dempsey's," he added with a laugh.

"Will you be able to hold a beer with that hand?"

"I have two," replied Tom as he raised his other hand.

"And those are consecrated hands, Detective. They are protected from above," joked Luke, who leaned toward Tom. "I'll leave you guys alone, but I'll catch you before I go."

Tom waved to his brother at the door before turning toward Brooks. "I wish we could have solved this one earlier."

"I know. Sometimes the answer is right in front of you. He'll be going away for a very long time, you know," said Brooks. "He thought his life was torture before. He may have wished he had drowned."

Shaking his head, Tom said, "He did, but I hope that is never the better answer for anyone."

Brooks scratched his scalp. "Hey, can I ask you something? So, Flaherty joins this group to deal with the loss of Daniel Murphy to suicide and assumes his name. And, when Rowan Montecchi ends up taking his life because he can no longer cope, you think it pushed Flaherty over the edge?"

Tom said, "Yeah. Brian had an abusive father who abandoned him emotionally. His mother was very needy, and instead of giving a young boy what he needed, he was put in the inappropriate role of taking care of her needs. I think he developed a protector mentality to cope and buried his own negative experience, including the sexual abuse at the hands of Father Feeney. He probably pushed the memory down deeper and deeper as he tried to live with a fraction of himself exposed to the world and himself."

"Huh. So, the police work, counseling, and protecting this group of guys became his reason for existing, but the pain of his traumas lurked underneath, driving this conviction for justice through vengeance."

"Something like that. Daniel and Rowan couldn't cope to the point of suicide, and those losses and their pain took away pieces of Brian when he had little to give up. We can only bury and avoid dealing with painful experiences for so long before they take away our ability to live."

Mullen asked, "Father Tom, each guy in the group experienced sexual abuse that was never revealed or punished. The abusers got away with it and took no responsibility, so he must have believed justice could only be served by making them pay for the pain they caused—for, essentially, robbing these boys of their lives and relationships."

Tom nodded in agreement.

"So he targeted these abusers but also framed someone with each killing?"

"Right. The enablers who allowed the abuse to happen and go unreported. Each of these people knew what happened and let it happen. They not only didn't protect the innocent, but they also enabled the abusers. I think Brian believed this was as morally and criminally wrong as the abuse itself, if not worse. Brian's mother was an enabler, and Jonas Alpheus knew what Harry Simon did and said nothing. He did finally let Harry go and forced him to change his name, but that didn't help Sam Gately. Dr. Rose was aware of Joel Silverman's abuse of vulnerable boys who came to see him. They even counseled men who lived with this pain but took no responsibility for their own crimes."

Mullen said, "Hmm. So, Len Weitz wanted to join that Tuesday group at the library, not knowing that Silverman was facilitating it. Once Silverman realized it, he panicked and abandoned the group, and Brian, whom everyone thought was Daniel Murphy, offered to be the leader so that the group could continue. That could be why he felt so much responsibility for everyone in the group. I do have one question, though—"

Brooks interrupted, "I think I know what it is. If each abuser had an enabler to be held responsible, who was the enabler when he planned his execution of you, Father Tom?"

"Ah, good question. I think, in Brian's mind, it was God. To him, God let this happen. God didn't protect these children. God's grace wasn't there for them as they are in the sacraments, a visible sign of grace. Whether he knew it or not, he was probably pretty angry at God for not protecting him and the others. Why not make the point or get back at God by turning His sacraments upside down?"

"Well, I hope this is your last case, Father Brown. These are getting too dangerous for you and Salvato. By the way, don't tell him I said that," said Brooks with a smirk.

Mullen stepped forward. "Thanks for all you did and for risking your life to save him."

Tom smiled. "You know it wasn't you who kept him from asking you out."

"I do. And I guess it's good that we'll never know who the intended target was for the final Sacrament of Matrimony."

Chapter 50

Tom never tired of breathing in the air of a pleasant summer night. He spent a few extra moments outside watching people strolling along the sidewalk before he headed into the South End Library. Inside were the guys—the Tuesday Group, as they were now officially named—waiting for him. Sam Gately, Lenny Weitz, George Stroupe, Terry Rivers, and Joey "Donuts" Duggan all beamed as he approached and headed to their reserved meeting room as they did every week.

Sam said, "I know you come every Tuesday—"

"And you say this every Tuesday," said Tom.

"Well, I appreciate you coming. We all do," he replied.

Tom started with a prayer for everyone in the group and special prayers for Daniel Murphy, Rowan Montecchi, and Brian Flaherty. Then he looked around the room and said, "Who are we?"

"We are royal sons of our Father," everyone responded loudly.

"Where does our value come from?"

"Our Father!"

"Why are we special?"

"Because God loves us!" the group shouted in unison.

Tom nodded. "Now we all have to figure out how to believe all that in the depths of our being, in our souls."

"It's hard," said Lenny. "Some days, I get up, and I believe it. When I'm with you guys, I even feel it, but on other days, it's tough. Tough to get up. Tough to like myself. Tough not to keep blaming myself."

Terry turned to Lenny. "And what do you do on those days?"

Lenny smiled. "Call one of you guys to give me a kick in the butt."

"I like it," said Tom. "We are in this together. We believe in each other. And we remind ourselves that we aren't what has happened to us. No matter what, there is a plan for us and this group; this friendship is part of that plan."

Joey leaned forward. "I guess most of you know that I started a job last week. Father Tom spoke to a friend of his who owns the Comghan grocery stores chain, I mean nice ones, and he's giving me a shot."

The guys reached over, shaking Joey's hand and patting him on the back.

"You can do it, man; plus it gives you a place to return all those cans and bottles." George chuckled.

"I figured if I can get all you guys to believe in me, I might as well give it a shot," replied Joey.

Tom said, "Joey, you seem as if you have something more on your mind tonight."

"How do you always know? Well, I was thinking about things a lot. Everyone here was a victim of someone that is now in God's hands to deal with, except me."

"How does that make you feel, Joey?" asked Tom.

Joey sighed. "Like I said, I've been thinking a lot about this. I saw my father touching a friend of mine when I was ten. I couldn't believe it and didn't know how to process it. When I told my mother, she told me to forget what I saw. My friend never came back to the house." Joey cleared his throat. "I've never told anyone this before, so give me a second."

"Take your time, Joey," said Sam.

"Okay." Joey took in a deep breath. "Okay, well, I was the boy he was touching next. Maybe he always was, and I never understood what was right and wrong, but I became the target without my friend coming over. I was frightened, and my mother told me I would be okay if I kept it to myself."

"Oh my God," said Lenny. "What did you do?"

"I left home."

"At ten?"

Joey nodded.

While Tom was not completely surprised by Joey's revelation, a sudden welling of emotion rose within his chest, and tears came to his eyes.

"I ran away and have been on the streets ever since. It felt safer. Even on freezing cold nights, it felt warmer. I wanted to punish them. My parents frantically tried to find me, and everyone eventually gave up and assumed I was dead. I realize it had been my way of hurting them back, making them pay. Funny, they've gone on to give workshops on marriage and parenting. My father even has a book out. I assume Brian would have made them the next target once he found out who abused me."

Tom said, "That was brave of you to share. Why do you think you finally did?"

Joey raised his head to keep the tears back. "Like I said, I've been thinking a lot about what we've been talking about each week. I don't want my father dead. I've been punishing him for so many years, seeking my revenge, and it hasn't helped me a bit. The strange thing is that I still love both of them."

"What do you think you want them to do, and what do you want to do?" asked Tom.

"I'm not all the way there yet, but I think I want to see them. I want him to own up to what he did and get help. I found out that he lost both of his parents in a crash when he was young. The family was split up, and he ended up in an abusive foster home. That's no excuse for anything, but I want him to get help. Who knows what could happen next."

Tom smiled. "I think you're on a good path, Joey."

"We're behind you, man," said Sam.

On Wednesday morning, Tom drove out to the outskirts of the town of Walpole. He sat at a metal table, talking to the corrections officer he had gotten to know as he waited for the inmate to arrive for his weekly visit. Tom glanced over when he finally saw him approach and sit across from him.

"Fancy meeting you here."

"How are they treating you?" asked Tom.

"It's like no resort you've ever stayed. We had 'seafood surprise' last night that would be hard for me to describe," he replied with a half-grin. "I still can't believe you come to see me."

"Me neither," joked Tom. "I'm glad you didn't have to go through a trial."

"Yeah, well, I could be the first murderer whose intended victim shows up at his sentencing hearing to be his character witness. Every night, I think about what you said, but I can't seem to let it in. How can you believe those things about me?"

"Brian, none of us are perfect, but we are all made by the same God with love and mercy. Growing up, you got a raw deal, but I heard true remorse from you at the hearing. No matter what we do or how far we fall, it's never greater than God's mercy and desire for you to find your way back to Him."

Flaherty shook his head. "Even trying to kill a priest in church?"

Tom smiled.

"How can you smile about that?"

"I was thinking about one of your favorite poets. Didn't Eliot write the *Murder in the Cathedral* where Thomas Beckett said—"

Brian interrupted. "You mean, *The last temptation is the greatest treason / To do the right thing for the wrong reason?*"

"I think you actually *believed* you were doing the right thing for the right reason, but—"

"But what I did wasn't right. I can't believe it's forgivable."

"I know you can't, but you're going to have to trust me on that one. You have a loving Father, and you have a friend in me who believes in you and believes there's still a purpose and plan for you," said Tom as he caught Flaherty's eye.

"Yeah, yeah. Well, I guess I have one hundred and twenty years in here to figure that out. Then, again, I guess I've built a prison for myself all my life."

"Haven't we all? You have gifts to share, Brian. The guys from the Tuesday group you worked with are doing well and send their best," said Tom.

"They're good guys, every one of them. I feel like I let them down. I just don't feel worthy of forgiveness for what I've done and because I didn't forgive."

"I know. Guess what? None of us are worthy. None of us deserve it, but that's a good thing about having a Father who loves us that much—unconditionally."

A tear fell from Flaherty's eye and rolled down his cheek. "I, um, I started up a group here in my cellblock." He forced a chuckle. "Two of the guys are ones that I arrested, so we had a few interesting sessions at the start, but there are a lot of hurting men here. Maybe I can do some good."

Tom smiled broadly as he gazed at Flaherty. "I know you can. What was that line near the end of Eliot's *Ash Wednesday*? *Even among these rocks, Our peace in His will.*"

Tom reached over with the hand that had been pierced by the nail and held Flaherty's hand.

With a nod, Brian accepted it.

The End

About the Author

Jim Sano grew up in an Irish/Italian family in Massachusetts. Jim is a husband, father, lifelong Catholic and has worked as a teacher, consultant, and businessman. He has degrees from Boston College and Bentley University and is currently attending Franciscan University for a master's degree in Catechetics and Evangelization. He has also attended certificate programs at The Theological Institute for the New Evangelization at St. John's Seminary and the Apologetics Academy. Jim is a member of the Catholic Writers Guild and has enjoyed growing in his faith and now sharing it through writing novels. *Fallen Graces* is his sixth novel.

Jim resides in Medfield, Massachusetts, with his wife, Joanne, and has two daughters, Emily and Megan.

Published by Full Quiver Publishing
PO Box 244
Pakenham, ON K0A2X0
Canada
www.fullquiverpublishing.com

Made in the USA
Las Vegas, NV
13 October 2023